Tea Tale

Tea Tale

TALES OF TRELVANIA BOOK 2

Kristina W. Kelly

Space Wizard Science Fantasy
Raleigh, NC
www.spacewizardsciencefantasy.com

Cover art by Serene Chia, Lettering by Audrey Logsdon
Editing by Courtney Brooks
Book Layout © 2015 BookDesignTemplates.com

Tea Tale/Kristina W. Kelly.— 1st ed.
ISBN 978-1-960247-53-7

Author's website: https://kristinaseyes.com/

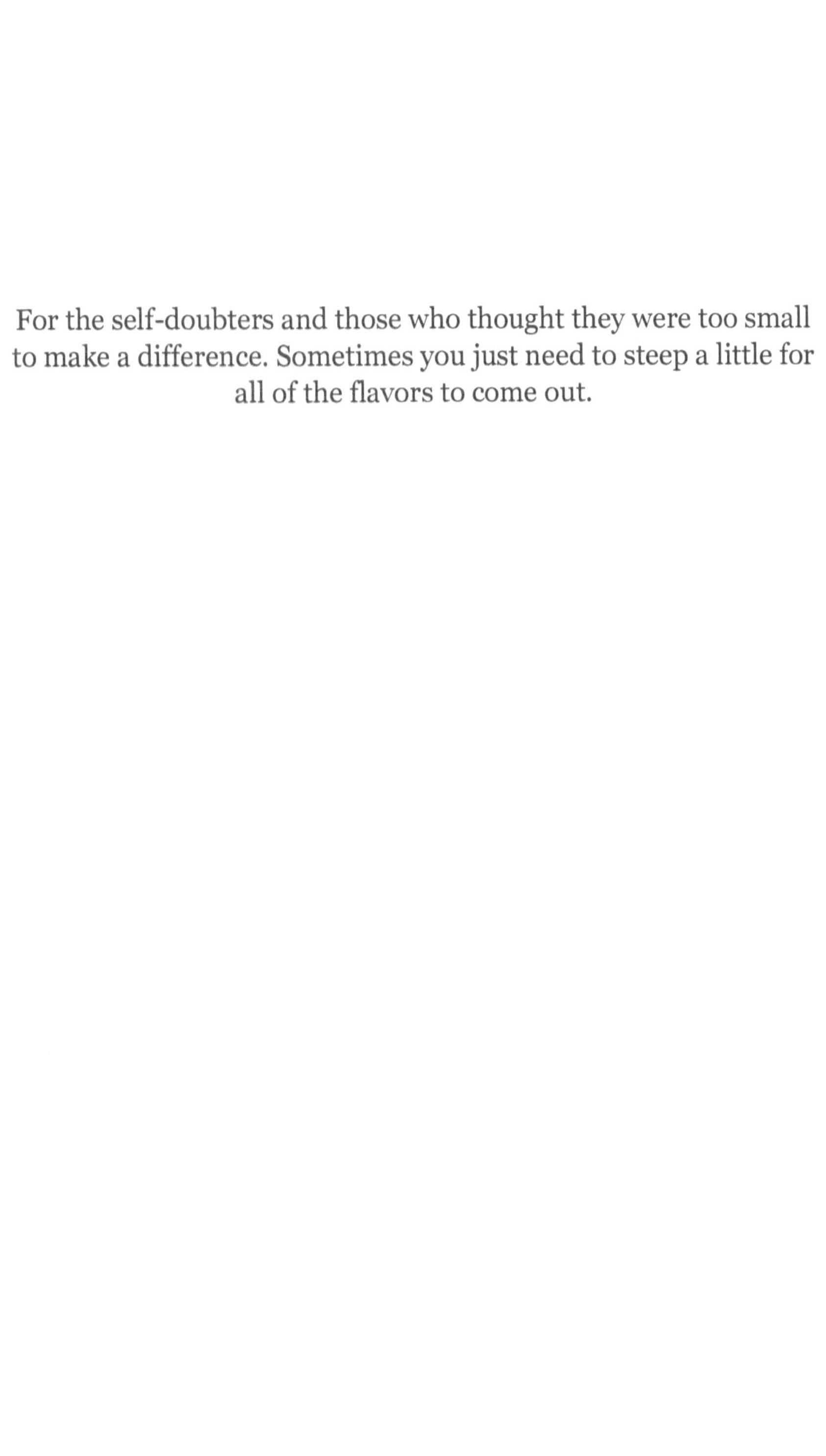

For the self-doubters and those who thought they were too small to make a difference. Sometimes you just need to steep a little for all of the flavors to come out.

CONTENTS

Horns of Trelvania
Soulshroud Ocean
Frostshard Sea
Breakstone Mountains
Frostspire
Icewern Plains
Nelithor
Scrying Tides
Dellvale Dock
Arosia
Borian
Mt. Velken
Weathered Crossroads
Trelvania
Prismatic Grove
Norell
Moon Mire
Oulron
Brag
Iramont
Foleria
Unmar
Syphondor
Desagati Desert
Dragon's Roost Island
Breathward Island
Fariatan
Snake Cove
Tail of Trelvania
Spine of Trelvania
Floating Island of Zenith
Lonely Island
Serpent Sea
Island of Broken Dreams
Glymrskey Ocean
Vax Solhavn
Solhavn
Thorenvessh
Lake of Good Omen
The Bone Shackle
Ripplesmarch
Ser1bing Waste
Alistraysia

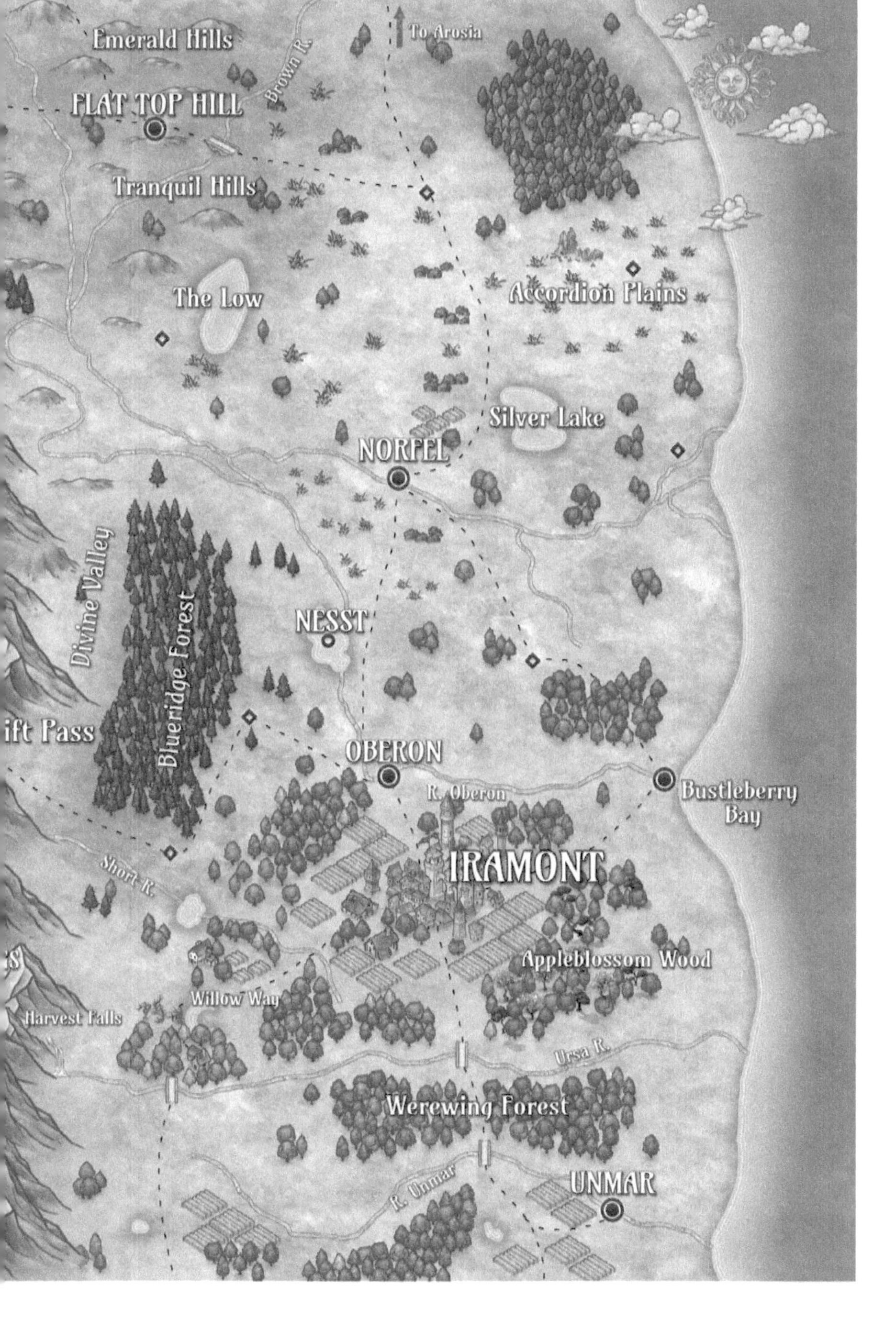

Emerald Hills
FLAT TOP HILL
Brown R.
To Arosia
Tranquil Hills
The Low
Accordion Plains
Silver Lake
NORFEL
Divine Valley
Blueridge Forest
NESST
ift Pass
OBERON
R. Oberon
Bustleberry Bay
Short R.
IRAMONT
Harvest Falls
Appleblossom Wood
Willow Way
Ursa R.
Werewing Forest
R. Unmar
UNMAR

CHAPTER ONE

Steeped in Sapphire

Untethered strings whipped across the alabaster sky like someone had cut threads from marionettes. A sole hooweet flapped its brown and beige wings, airborne though it was a flightless bird. Divine grasped her talisman tightly, pressing the crescent moon and sword of the golden locket's face into her palm as wind thrashed her short hair into her eyes. Perched on the rim of a teacup, a rainbow bird tumbled into an illimitable fall, cackling like a human. Below the deities' floating continent, clouds made steps from Zenith into nothingness. A black and red glove drifted, its gauntlet-like arm guard obscuring the landscape before turning into blackness on the ground. Trelvania should have been there, but instead of a continent, a blackness inked into the oceans like black spots along pumpkin vines. The temples and buildings of Arosia, her home, melted and became a part of the murk. Divine stumbled near the edge of Zenith as a boradain smacked into her back before he plummeted over the edge, the creature's four hairy arms pinwheeling him into a gentle glide. His blue lips moved.

Divine's eyes sprang open as familiar words echoed out of the nighttime image into a dull headache.

"You needed the separation to know how deep you could drink."

Breathing deeply, Divine let her magic well gently wash over her, soothing her trepidation. She rested her hand at her throat, where her Goddess locket and talisman used to be before touching her wrist and the multiple bangles there.

Running a hand over the bed sheets, she found a cold indentation left by Saph. The tavern owner was likely downstairs, preparing for the first ever morning opening. It was a big day. Changes and novelties awaited. The past few weeks had been full of preparation for not only an influx of visitors for the Midwinter Nights Faire, but the tavern's brand-new service. Many failed tea combinations had left bad tastes in their mouths but finally they had the right ones practiced. Divine hoped she could help make the morning's trial succeed for Saph.

She rubbed the sleep out of her eyes and tried to brush the after images of the dream away.

Divine swung her legs over the edge of the bed, thankful for the thick yarn of her pants as her feet hit the cold wood floor. As the temperature continued to drop outside, Divine got closer to asking Saph to use a Passionate's Pyre to warm up the room. The heat provided by the tavern fireplace downstairs never seemed enough, yet Saph's body always seemed warm. A great obsession for Divine to wrap herself around frequently while sheets tangled in moving legs.

Drawing the knitted blanket with axe patterns around her shoulders, Divine pushed off the bed and stood. Light shown in golden rays across the floorboard as the sun rose behind the buildings. Outside, tiny white puffs floated in the air, swaying and swirling with a gentle brush of wind. They filled the air and already a thin layer of white collected on the bare branches of the nearest apple tree, fluffy hats of cold wetness decorated the few fruits still clinging, and the tops of the hanging signs of the Essentials District.

The first good snowfall of the season.

Though Divine disliked the colder weather, there was something enchanting about snow. The way boots crunched prints across unblemished walkways. How the rush of daily to-dos slowed and people transformed into blobs of fur-lined hats over long coats. Until now, the snow had been dustings in comparison.

The lazy drift of snowflakes heralded merriment to come, and Midwinter Nights Faire. The week-long celebration in every city was her second favorite festival next to the autumn festivals. Whether of the God of Day and Deceit's doing, few winter-grey skies ever ruined the joy to carry over into the festivities under the stars. It often took Divine a while to get over a stretch of days where the sun remained blocked by dull clouds. Her connection to the emotions of those around her through her magic well didn't help—everyone radiated a mixture of grumpiness and listlessness at one point or another, leaving Divine always picking up the mood from someone.

Divine blinked. Past Saph's thriving spinetooth pot and the succulent's tangle of narrow triangular leaves, she squinted at a shape through the frosted windowpane.

Someone stood across the street.

Her ex-girlfriend stood under the lamppost. Divine's mouth parted. Madeline's short brown hair stirred around her face like a storm had suddenly blown in, her clipped undercut fully displayed. A dark oval shimmered into view behind her. Divine gasped as the portal sucked Madeline into the void. Just like Divine had plunged her into the in-between six weeks before.

Divine's breath hitched and she took a step back, yelping when she bumped into something.

"Didn't mean to frighten you, darling." Saph's warm lips pressed a gentle kiss against Divine's cheek before she rounded Divine. "Apparently, I have on my stealth shoes. Did you sleep well?"

Divine took in Saph, letting the woman's presence steady her reeling heartbeat. Saph wore one of her favorite under bust corsets, purple to match the eyepatch over her right eye and the bauble in her left nostril. Below the corset she wore a flowing dress of spring green leaves and pastel blossoms with a low heart-shaped front. She had paired the usually thin-strapped garment with a harmonizing long-sleeve that echoed the tan of the branches in the dress's fabric.

Divine flicked her eyes to the window.

"I had...another dream," Divine answered, though now dreams were seeping into her waking hours.

Her heartbeat slammed against her chest. Divine dipped into her well, relaxing with the perfume of rain on rose that enveloped her. Though her talisman was now her rainbow bangles rather than her locket, Divine was thankful her magic carried the same scent. It even retained the hint of lemon from her mother's favorite pink roses.

"Boats, boradains, and betrayers?" Saph asked.

Divine nodded. Close enough. It captured what Divine suspected was the source of her nightmares; the end to the quest in a chest and her autumn adventure with Saph. While the black spot had cleared from the vegetation in the area, Divine's soul had developed its own blemish. There were unanswered questions about what her Goddess, the Goddess of Souls, and the other deities had imprisoned in that upside down boat. And what disturbed Divine most of all was how Madeline had known she needed Divine to unlock the demon from his prison.

"Do you want to talk about it?" Saph tilted her head.

"Thank you, but I'd rather forget it." Divine tugged the blanket tighter.

Saph had been beyond supportive after their return to the city of Iramont and learning of Divine's Goddess's involvement in the creation of the First Soul, the first Elder-turned-demon. She had given Divine space to reconnect with her lost magic and let Divine live in the tavern with Saph rent-free. Saph joked that Divine paid in heated gazes and soft hands, but Divine was tired of letting Saph carry them both. She wanted to leave the fight with the boradain and Madeline in the past and move on. But the past kept having other plans.

"I brought you another blend to try." Saph cradled a brown towel a shade darker than her hand, supporting a mug. Steam rose in elongated swirls from the top and warm-brown liquid filled three-fourths of the clear mug.

A familiar scent of vanilla and something else tickled Divine's nose. She could almost taste it in the inhale.

Saph proffered the mug's handle and Divine took it.

"Careful, the tea is hot." Saph smirked, harkening to the previous week's tea-testing and burnt tongues. "I wish I could figure out how to serve these without scalding everyone in the process. I guess you could heal yourself, though I'd rather you not have any injury to begin with."

Blowing gently across the mug's top, Divine watched Saph over the frothy brim, happy to let her continue talking, distracting her from her vision. At the tilt of Saph's head, the light glinted against the hoop pierced at her helix.

"If you like it, I'll call it...*Divine-i-tea*." Saph fondled the beads of her layered necklace, the teal and blue lines tinkling softly.

Divine smiled at the play on her name as she took a sip. The heat burnt the tip of her tongue but felt like a warm elixir, soothing as it washed down her throat. The vanilla was strong with a gentle earthy bitterness and a hint of something spicy or minty that she couldn't quite define. She took another sip. It was sweet. And she loved it. She groaned.

The eyebrow over Saph's eyepatch raised. "That good, huh?"

"Tarrow root?" Divine guessed.

"Your favorite." Saph beamed. "I figured since it gets brewed for an alcohol-free option in taverns, it was worth a try hot." Crossing her arms under her chest, Saph's breasts lifted even more. Divine couldn't look away, her memories reminding her hands how soft Saph's skin felt.

"What do you think?"

Try them hot? Saph's breasts were always warm. Divine loved the way it made her feel, pressing their chests together, heat igniting between them. To get any hotter, they'd need to go to a bath house. Hot water...

The tea, Divine. Deities above, she's asking about the tea!

"It's fantastic." Divine took another sip to cover what she was sure was her cheeks matching her hair color. "It might be even better than the cold version."

Saph clapped her hands together. "Hot is better! Let's put it on the menu."

The woman stepped closer, placing a hand on each of Divine's hips. Tracing her eyes from Saph's lips to her uncovered green eye, Divine tried not to drop the mug. Saph smirked.

"I see something else I like hot," Saph hummed.

The air tingled between them as Divine sensed delight from Saph with her magic. She held back a giggle. Even after two months, she still wasn't used to the more intense feelings she got with her magic now that she'd recovered her stolen talisman.

Divine held up a finger, then bent to the side and placed the mug next to the spinetooth plant on the ledge, careful not to brush her knuckles against the serrated edges of the long leaves.

She wrapped her arms around Saph's neck as Saph pulled their bodies closer. Their lips touched, soft as they shared kisses that explored the placement of their mouths. Saph drew Divine's bottom lip between her teeth and Divine melted.

Touching Divine's cheek, Saph ended the kiss. "Take your time getting ready, darling. But if I stay here any longer, I won't leave until lunch time."

"You say that like it's a bad thing." Divine's voice came out breathless and she grinned.

"Oh, it's definitely good for me. But we'll never hear the end of it from Sylus if he has to manage both the tea and the tavern business. Besides, the whole Crossroads group will be here soon. Nothing says 'tell everyone about our new venture' like sounds of pleasure from upstairs while they wait." Saph winked. "See you downstairs."

Divine snuck one more kiss before waving Saph away. As the door clicked shut, Saph's axe practice board swung gently, a symbolic focus. Divine vowed to make the day perfect for Saph. Not a spilled drop.

* * *

"What's a *Foggy Iramont*?" Syka asked, staring at the piece of parchment in her hand. "Sounds like my kind of drink."

From where Divine stood with her back to the second-floor stairs, Syka's dark-coated lids cloaked the woman's eyes as she read the menu. One of the skulls on her daggers' hilts poked up from her hip. She sat at the round table adjacent to the fireplace with two others from their usual Crossroads George group; Edward and Sylus.

"It's a bold, black tea that's smooth with a hint of sweet and citrus," Divine quoted. "It smells great. And it's made with milk, so, uh, it's foggy."

Saph sat on the top of a table by one of the far windows, her leg swinging over the edge as she gazed out onto the morning street. She mimicked a silent applause, and a jolt of joy dashed up Divine's spine.

Divine had memorized the tea descriptions so she wouldn't sound like this was the first time she'd ever served tea to guests. Although it was. Regardless, Saph looked pleased, and the emotion Divine perceived from her matched. A strand of lights draped above the window frame for Midwinter Nights dotted Saph's hair and skin with purple and yellow. Saph must have hung the decoration while Divine was sleeping. The glow and the colors made Divine smile and feel warm inside like she'd just stepped closer to the fire.

The lights were one of her favorite traditions of the celebration; miniature versions of the layered strands that were typically hung around the faire. The lengthened spherical shapes were wider in the middle with a pattern that resembled dragon scales, similar to the street lampposts. Though the reed paper that made their tiny lantern shape held a fireworm instead of a Trickster crystal full of sunlight.

Syka bit a black-tinted lip as she studied the choices. Divine had quickly added the new tea option for Saph at the bottom of the menu before handing it to the group of three. Saph's shorthand would only work for behind the bar and for herself—though Divine was learning how to read the code Saph had created at a young age when she struggled holding writing implements. There were few things that the fusing of Saph's long and ring fingers hindered—or that Saph let hinder her.

The tavern's fireplace burned warmly for the mostly empty space, a braided garland of pine boughs and sparkling threads that mimicked the effect of ice hung across the mantle. Beyond the table with the card players, and Saph's table by the window, the rest of the tables had their chairs upturned on their tops from closing the tavern the night before. The stage across the room from the fireplace was empty, giving the gathering an intimate overtone.

"I don't know. What are you trying, Edward?" Syka deflected, strands of pink hair covering her cheek. The rogue had dyed the hair framing her face, but the rest remained her signature black.

"Let me make sure I understand." Edward tapped the menu with his pinky finger. "These are dried leaves and roots mixed with hot water and...milk?"

Edward looked his usual messy-but-flawless self, his tousled hair and thick brows offsetting his boyish nose and cheeks.

Divine leaned over Edward's shoulder and pointed to the menu's options. "*Foggy Iramont* is the only one with milk, but we could probably add milk to any of the others and see how it tastes. Only this one is made with root. Tarrow root, which makes the tarrow-root-beer."

Sylus scratched his chest muscles—his shirt open wide as customary—and stretched. If Divine didn't know him, she would have thought he was trying to impress her. Edward cleared his throat.

"You all have no trouble drinking boiled flowers and old fruit when it numbs your feelings." Sylus put his arms behind his head. "I don't see your problem."

He smiled up at Divine. Hoping to convey her gratitude, she smiled back. Though, it was odd looking down on the taller man who at night moved about the tavern serving others.

"Divin-eye-tee." Syka wrestled the syllables from her mouth. "Oh. Divine-ah-tea. Bleh. *We get it*. You two are *perfect* for each other and *so in love*. Now will you stop shoving it down our throats?"

Syka's tone dripped with her typical sarcasm, all atmosphere and less verity but Divine peered across the room. If the tavern-owner heard the comment, she didn't react as she wiped fog from a windowpane with her sleeve.

Love?

Sure, these past few weeks had outings Saph called dates, as well as intimate moments, but they had also been busy with normal work at the Sultry Sapphire and planning special events for Midwinter Nights Faire. Sometimes Saph went off on her own, Divine didn't ask where. Saph could have another who had captured her interest. She knew Saph's language was flirting and talking to everyone. Divine hadn't asked for exclusivity. Barely three months had passed since they met, and Divine's last love-at-first sight relationship ended in betrayal and her stolen magic. Maybe Divine still had a shield up, in the form of not asking. Then she couldn't know if the answer was Saph only wanted this to be casual and open.

"What's *Snowshroom Spice*? Oh no, please don't tell me it's—"

"Made from snowshrooms from Nelithor," Divine finished for Syka. Then raising her chin to the far window, "I guess we need to put descriptions with the drink names."

Saph swatted the air. "If a patron doesn't know a draft, me or Sylus tells them. That lets us make a recommendation based on their personality. We could just do that with tea."

Divine nodded, turning her attention back to Syka. "There's hints of chocolate and cinnamon, with other spices that's sure to warm you after a cold walk. It's sweetened with honey and almost smells like fresh baked pumpkin pie."

Syka grimaced as she faked a gag. "Blech. You'd need all of that just to cover up the nasty mushroom. I'll try that Foggy Iramont."

Order placed, Syka leaned back in her chair and propped her boots on the table in front of Edward. Never removing his eyes from the menu, Edward grasped one of Syka's boots with green painted nails and pushed her feet toward Sylus.

"I'll go safe." Edward handed Divine his and Syka's menu. "The tarrow root one, please."

"I've smelled them all in the kitchen." Sylus winked. "And that cinnamon has been calling my name. If you would be so kind."

Divine took the last menu. "I'll start your teas. Should be about seven minutes."

"You are amazing not writing any of this down," Syka said as Divine twirled from the table.

Others echoed the praise. The room filled with the sweet aroma of rose blooms and Divine hesitated. Danger? She glanced out of the window near the door, but nothing looked amiss, and the door stayed shut. Instead of worried she felt...happy? While her magic had bloomed after recovering her talisman, Divine hadn't been able to associate which additional floral scents showed up when. She knew it flared wild, accosting her senses, with danger. This, though, was more like the headiness she would often get with Saph.

"And for helping the boss with this new idea," Sylus lowered his voice.

Divine tossed a look over her shoulder. "Of course."

"The tavern she won with luck. This, she grew. Thank you."

A short chortle escaped Divine's mouth, a giddiness tickling her insides. She cleared her throat to cover the sound.

"Saph will bring your mince pies—they're from the Dragon's Egg."

The group began chatting and Divine hurried to the bar. She slipped behind the lacquered length, placed the menus on the surface and gripped the bar. That feeling wasn't danger, it was dizzying bliss. Not as intoxicating as when she first put her stolen talisman back around her neck and regained access to her magic well. But...similar. Her hand strayed to her left wrist, touching one of her four rainbow-hued bangles.

Saph's hip bumped Divine as the other woman slid behind the bar.

"Divinely done. And looking good while doing it." Saph brushed a finger along the band of Divine's brown waistband before spinning to the shelves on the wall.

"This is really a great idea, Saph." Divine gathered three mugs from under the bar to distract herself from the fluttering of her stomach. "I really like that you decided to add the snowshrooms tea. It will be something we can advertise during the faire as on-theme."

Saph slid a Passionate's Plate in front of them and placed a sphere with water on top. It was a fraction of the size of the Passionate's Pyre that heated rooms of well-off homes, and lacked the lazy swirls of flames, but the design from the servants of the Deity of Love and Fire was similar.

"Snow themed seemed like the right direction to go, with the Goddess of Frosted Wilderness part of the double-deity jubilee. By the dragons, she has a long name."

Divine chuckled. "Most deities do."

"Be right back," Saph said, walking away. "The egg pies in the oven are probably heated."

Saph disappeared through the swinging door at the end of the bar that led into the tavern's kitchen and food storage. From under the bright wood of the bar, Divine pulled out small tins that contained the blends Saph had mixed; enough to brew for a day's worth of guests if they had as many patrons as the evening goers. She began measuring the dried pieces for each mug.

The rest of the ingredients were in the kitchen. They bought what they could from the last market exchange in the fall from the north. With the absence of Iramont's red leaf tea and no traders coming in with bulk of Arosia's black tea leaf, they'd had to experiment with brewable ingredients.

They'd gotten lucky when a traveler passed through.

"Syka," Divine called over the empty bar stools and chairs, interrupting a hushed conversation between the friends at the table. "Did you find out why that sailor had that bag of snowshrooms?"

"On his way to Pariatan. Thought he could bribe his way onto a Kellas pirate ship."

"With their favorite snack?"

"Common misconception. At least that's what I told the soon-to-be unemployed sailor. He left the sack, and I took it. Desire, acquired. You're welcome."

Divine shook her head, though a smile spread across her lips.

The aroma of window garden rosemary and sage preceded her as Saph exited the kitchen and delivered the plates of golden-crusted cheesy goodness to the three guests.

Hips swaying, Saph ambled through the empty front of the tavern, and returned to Divine's side. She handed Divine a mince pie from the Dragon's Egg café. People stood in a long line daily to get their hand pies and pastries. Saph was lucky to have arranged a supply for the morning teas.

"Saved you one," Saph said.

"All of my favorites in one morning?"

"Your happiness is a sunrise."

Divine bit into the warm crust, the savory flavor of sausage and egg that felt like clouds filled her mouth. She deposited mesh strainers and the blends into each mug as she devoured the magic that was both flaky and soft.

Water bubbled in the transparent vessel on the Passionate's Plate. Deep blue strands swirled through in the glass of the container and it had a spout, handle and lid. Its function and design gave it its name; boilspout. When they had found it next door in Otto's pawn shop, Otto said the container came from Pariatan and was used by mermaids that lived in the nearby cove to collect the tears of their victims. More likely, a Sandshaper of the Goddess of Stone and Sand had made it; there were plenty of beaches with sand near Pariatan, which was why most glass came from the coasts. Divine had learned early on to ignore most of what Otto passed on as anecdotes. It held hot water and that was what they needed.

"You know, next year I can have more than just egg pies," Saph said, leaning on the bar and cradling her chin in her hand.

"Hmm?" Divine queried, hunting around for the container of sugar cubes they'd procured from one of the general stores in the Essentials District.

"Well, that black spot ruined most of the nearby crops. Since you and I fixed that little problem, there could be strawberry or pumpkin muffins, or...watermelon pie!"

Divine eyed the boilspout, willing it to go faster, and searched below the bar's counter for the sugar. "That's right. You won't have to rely on last year's harvests, or pay those ridiculous prices to transport from Arosia."

"Or through the Spine of Trelvania. And I will never pay a Harvester to magic ingredients straight from a farm. No one would buy tea and food at the price I'd have to charge to make money on that."

Moving a towel aside on a shelf behind her revealed a jar of sugar cubes.

"Found them!" Divine exclaimed.

The water in the boilspout rolled and Divine removed the container from the Passionate's Plate as she continued.

"Listhinci said clay pots could enhance the flavor of some of the tea. Something about heat levels. Does Solhavn grow tea? Anyway, if this goes well, you could look into experimenting with the effects."

"Let's see how things go in a few days with the faire. I have to make back my investment before I expand." She tapped the side of her nose.

Divine poured the water into each mug, filling them halfway as steam rose from the tops. Each tea blend swirled in the water, slowly tinting the contents.

"Oh, Sylus's honey."

Saph patted Divine's shoulder. "I'll get it."

"And the milk, please."

While she waited, Divine gave the Sultry Sapphire's open gathering space a final appraisal. Adding light strands draped from the rafters could give the tavern more of a Midwinter Nights Faire feeling, but then it would be heavy on representing the God of Day and Deceit. The frosted windows naturally manifested winter, but the space needed something extra. She tapped her lips as she pondered the walls and the support posts of the tavern and the stage along the right wall.

Saph returned from the kitchen, setting a beaker of milk next to Divine then spooning a dollop of honey into the closest mug. Rust-red dusted the top of the liquid as Divine tapped a small shaker over the brim.

"I'm actually surprised you celebrate Midwinter Nights." Divine gave the shaker a final rap. "Given your aversion to Gods and Goddesses."

"It's good business, and I like the fun. Poetry every night for a week? Feasting, gift giving? Diversions without needing to worship any of the deities."

Divine lifted the strainer out of the mug in front of her. It dripped with its water-logged ingredients and she sat it on a towel, the brown liquid instantly expanding into the fibers. *Find another way to not make a mess of every towel,* she thought.

"I forgot about poetry. There are so many things to do during Midwinter Nights."

In previous years, Divine had participated in playing music for the event, her accordion an instrument suited for group or solo performances. Though she hadn't had much time with all of her Soulshield healing duties, nor had she been brave enough to volunteer for any of the events that drew a large crowd, like the poetry feasts where audiences became performers.

"Does that mean you'll finally let me hear that one about an axe?" Divine poured the milk as she talked, the white stream diving through the dark liquid like a brown-tailed swiller in pursuit of a minnow, quickly churning the brown into the creamy tan of straw during the fall harvests.

"Maybe." Saph winked. "Here, let me try something."

Brandishing a whisk from somewhere within her outfit, Saph whipped the liquid until bubbles began to form.

"Ah, that's better." Setting down the implement, she walked away with the frothy-topped Foggy Iramont.

An idea forming, Divine plucked a white flower from a vase on the wall display and dropped it into Edward's foaming tarrow root drink. Warm summer evenings and sweetness drifted out of the liquid, adding a floral undertone to the stronger vanilla.

Divine grabbed the two mugs, careful to only hold the handles, and followed Saph. Flecks of cinnamon floated lazily in the medium-brown Snowshroom Spice she placed in front of Sylus. As she sat the caramel-brown Divine-i-tea in front of Edward, the white petals of the snow pinwheel looked like a snowflake. The single vase on the wall shelf wouldn't supply many drinks, but one of the greenhouses might have the summer-to-fall blooming plant.

"Enjoy!" Divine emphasized the blessing by putting her fits on her hips. "Let us know what you think."

Leaning on the wood of the bar, Divine and Saph watched their first customers, although unpaying, taste their drinks. Syka blew on hers before taking a sip, Edward dipped his tongue into the mug like a jungle Iguion, and Sylus tested the temperature with a finger then sucked it slowly. Was he flirting with the tea mug? The emotions in the room felt optimistic and eager.

Nearly in unison the tea-drinkers took a true sip. They whispered amongst themselves, sipping and munching their food.

Saph poured the remaining hot water into a new mug, resteeping the strainer containing the black tea leaf blend used in crafting the Foggy Iramont.

"You know"—Saph leaned closer—"my family has always celebrated Midwinter."

Divine's eyes widened. "Really? Even though they follow the Old Ways?"

Saph snorted. "The deities don't control when the shortest day and longest night occurs. It is the middle of the winter with or without them."

Divine worried her lip, trying to puzzle through the traditions of the festival. "We focus on the God of Day and

Deceit, because of the soon-to-return longer light each day..." She pointed at the string of paper lights.

"We celebrate winter"—Saph tucked a lock of Divine's hair behind her ear—"and how it leads to the returned glow of life. We stay up all night on the last days of your festival to watch the sun rise."

"I guess we include the Goddess of Frosted Wilderness because it just makes sense."

"All that snow and ice." Saph gulped a drink from her mug. "Would be odd to celebrate her in the summer. Want some?" Saph pushed the mug in front of Divine then pivoted to the shelves on the wall.

The cup smelled lovely, the lavender like summer's first bloom, and she took a sip. Richer and more bitter than the tarrow root, the Arosian black leaf filled up her mouth in an enjoyable way. The Foggy Iramont was tasty and Divine found she liked all of their teas, which made talking about them to patrons natural.

From the clinks of plates it sounded like Saph was rearranging their tableware and cutlery on the shelves. Divine let her mind wander as she drank, savoring the sweetness and letting the liquid pool on her tongue until she detected the citrus notes, then swallowing, her body warming pleasantly. Thoughts of hot summer followed as well as Saph's comment on celebrating the Goddess of Frosted Wilderness. Divine wondered if Saph could use the Flurries Freezer to chill brewed tea. The main ability of the Flurries, servants of the Goddess of Frosted Wilderness, harnessed within the device, had become a staple of many affluent households, especially in the summer to keep things cool.

Motion at the only occupied table drew Divine's attention. Syka, Edward, and Sylus turned toward the bar with their mugs raised.

"I can't wait to try that one again!" Edward called.

"So perfectly foggy I almost forgot it was cold outside," Syka added.

Sylus grinned, waving his mug like a flag. "Do I get another one?"

Divine grinned back, her magic drifting the scent of rose around her. A successful morning, indeed.

"I've been contemplating what to call the morning tea business in the tavern. What do you think about the name Steeped in Sapphire?" Saph asked.

Divine twisted to see Saph staring at the multifaceted jewel painted on the wooden sign. It hung on the middle of the wall like the heart of the room over a rectangular planter. The greenery had tiny glitter snowflakes on sticks poking out of the cluster of dark and silky leaves. She slid her arm behind Saph and rested the side of her head against hers.

"I think it's perfect."

CHAPTER TWO

An Inventory of Adornments and Adoration

After the taste-testers had left, Divine and Saph cleaned up the bar, returning the strainers, towels, and ingredient tins to the kitchen for cleaning or storage, ready for the next teatime. Divine's heart raced with the realization that tomorrow would usher patrons to try the tea rather than gentle friends. Divine spun, taking in the room and the golden light that had almost burned away the morning fog in the street. There was still something festive missing from the decorations she couldn't put her finger on.

"I'm going to pick up a few more decorations for opening Stepped in Sapphire," she said, wiping her hands on a towel. Divine also needed to shop for a Midwinter Nights present for Saph without the woman present.

"You think we need more?"

"Maybe? It's missing something. I'll know it when I see it." She hoped she'd know the right gift when she saw it, too. But that was a surprise. "I want people to want to come back even after the faire is over. Need anything while I peruse the districts?"

"Just your smile," Saph replied. "Are you going to the Edge again? You know, they're only paying you for a visit every two weeks. You'll make them feel bad for not paying more."

"But everyone seems sick lately. I can heal them."

"Leaky roofs will do that."

A lot of farmers came to the city seeking aid during the black spot. Iramont had given them temporary housing while they sought work, but conditions at the Edge were passing at best. Saph continued to donate or make bread out of her ingredients that were about to go bad to those in need.

"Their combined coins," Divine continued, "isn't enough to cover the hours I insisted we increase it to in the agreement. I think they know the one-day clinic is a ruse."

"Everyone in the community wants to feel like they're contributing. Self-respect. An ability to take care of their families. Each street collects a friggon, and together the Edge pays for a Soulshield's healing abilities. I'm just saying, undermining that balance might make them feel worse."

Divine frowned. "It's better than dead."

Saph sighed. "And in return they keep quiet about *who* you're healing. Do you want the Agents of Condemnation marching in? I don't."

The human-adjacents that couldn't afford living in the Living District found themselves hovels in the Edge. And Divine's own temple had declared human-adjacents could not be healed. With a mix of humans and human-adjacents visiting the clinic, they had hoped to have plausible deniability should any Agents of the Goddess of Condemnation come enforcing the laws. While Divine still thought it was odd that there was one city in Trelvania where their temple didn't exist, she wished that city were Iramont instead of Arosia.

"You do what you feel. My caution is only that. Just...don't weave so tightly you get caught in your own threads." Saph's tone dipped more serious before her eyes flashed once more. "Speaking of threads, here." Saph tossed a purple pouch that clinked as Divine caught it.

"What's this?" Divine asked, shaking the contents. They elicited the muted tinkle of metal bumping.

"It's about time you got yourself more winter apparel. If we go out during a snow, we can't both wear my boots, and yours will give you icicle toes."

When Divine had left Arosia to chase her talisman and Madeline, she hadn't planned on staying in any location any longer than finding her magic. Since lingering in Iramont, a few items had been added to her wardrobe here and there for layers, but she had been mainly cycling through the same three outfits. The thought of them each taking one boot on their next date was amusing and a smile tugged at the corner of Divine's mouth.

She bounced the soft coin pouch in her hand. "I can't possibly take—"

"Nonsense. Consider it prepayment for working Steeped in Sapphire. Starlights, I'm adoring that name. When Midwinter Nights Faire starts tomorrow, I'll make most of it back anyway."

"From the tavern?"

"Nah, the gambling. There's a game of Crossroads George in almost every building from here to the gates."

"Don't they all know your reputation?" Divine shrugged her arm toward the space of the tavern.

"You think something like winning a tavern from a game of cards stops them? Everyone wants a chance at beating the legend." Saph beamed, thumbing at her chest. "I'll hear nothing more of it. Take the coins. Besides, you'll need the clothes if you stay through the winter."

They hadn't talked about long-term arrangements yet, just going day by day. The most planning either of them had done was how the Sultry Sapphire would transform from a tavern into the Steeped in Sapphire in the mornings. There had been last-minute market shopping before most closed for the season, except for the general stores, hunting for new serving supplies, and scoping out the competition. Sleeping arrangements hadn't been on the list.

"Do you want me to stay the winter?" Divine questioned.

"It's about what *you* want, darling. You focus on what Divine needs."

Saph pushed through the swinging door carrying the mugs on a tray to wash in the back, and Divine felt like her delight was ready to swirl down the drain with the soap. Did Saph not care if Divine chose to go back to Arosia? The door to the tavern swung in before she could ruminate further. Cold air curled around Divine's toes through her boots before the door closed, sealing out the frigid gust.

"Sorry I'm late!" said a man wearing a wide-brimmed hat and matching brown vest. He stomped his boots near the community board and dusted white powder from his shoulders. "Had to help with the delivery of festival decorations. Never seen so many carts for lanterns on strings and ice games. You'd think it was the Bicentennial Faire instead. But my mounts are the best in town to provide swift delivery."

"Viktor! What a surprise." Saph spoke behind Divine as she approached the corner of the bar, with just a hint of annoyance. Or maybe that was the emotion Divine got through her magic.

His frequent know-it-all smirk and flickers of a debaucherous attitude irritated Divine like rolling her face in sand. At least he had been keeping his hands to himself. Mostly.

"Where's the 'hot tea'?" the Palfrey Post owner asked, crossing the small foyer and looking around the empty tavern.

"We just cleaned up. Sorry you missed it." Saph said, without an ounce of sorry included.

"Sounds like I missed some real fun, then! And in daylight. You're wilder than I thought."

Divine and Saph exchanged a puzzled look.

"I wouldn't call it wild," Divine added. "Just brewed water and dried leaves."

Saph put her hands on her hips. "What did you think we were doing, Viktor?"

"I, er, well, I thought it was, uh, *suggestive* in nature."

Divine groaned and jerked her head to the front door. Saph gave an approving nod.

"It's only tea. Which one of them blabbered?" Saph inquired. "It was Edward, wasn't it? Well, we're not open for business until tomorrow morning."

Divine left Saph to handle the former tavern owner and grabbed her coat from a hook near the door. Advertisements for businesses with Midwinter Faire events sparkled with their snow and lantern art tacked around the wrinkled map of Iramont on the community board. The biggest one a notice of something hot coming soon to the tavern. Divine chortled. *Leave it to Viktor.*

"Smack Saph's ass again today," Divine called out, not turning around, "and I'll make sure your ale is made from bean juice. Boundaries, Viktor."

Hood raised, Divine inhaled as if she could create a shield with her lungs then opened the door. Immediately, she regretted it. Her cheeks felt the breath of cold, and she dug her hands deep into the coat pockets to try to hold on to the warmth of the Sultry Sapphire. Her healing and empathetic influence held no sway over winter weather.

The new fallen snow had been squashed into melted slush under the many denizens of the city. Some of the tracks were visitors from their homes in the Iramont province. The excitement of the city vibrated through Divine as she flanked the windows of the tavern. Snow still clung to tree branches and shaded rooftops, but the flurries had lightened. She glanced up the slope of the avenue toward the Living District and wondered which vendors would be set up in the bazaar, braving the cold the following night.

Cattycorner and across the street from the Sultry Sapphire, Viktor's Palfrey Post had most of its barn-like doors closed but the tracks connecting it to the street showed that the travel business still prospered. At least in Arosia, the types of people and shipments varied over the seasons, but the amount of movement over land decreased based on the weather. Especially the trade through the port. Too cold, too snowy, too icy—everything the servants of the Goddess of Frosted Wilderness loved. Sometimes the Goddess Drift Pass through the Spine of Trelvania was impassable for months. But the Serpent Sea, where the sea dragons wintered in the boat channels, shut off travel to and from Solhavn until the spring blossoms began to peek out from the snow.

As Divine walked, keeping the tavern on her right, a bird whistled, triplet notes alternating up and down, and Divine searched to find the source. A tree stood among the nearby garden with pink-red leaves like a five-point star. She hadn't noticed it in the fall with the other nearby flame-tinted trees, but with its neighbors' branches empty, it radiated warmth. A yellow bird with orange wings stood among the top-most branches. The wind gently waved the tree in greeting as the bird sang its morning tune. Divine whistled an echo of the greeting song, and the bird tittered back.

"That bird sings as if there haven't been decimated dreams."

About to wave to the bird, Divine jumped at the voice, lowering her hand. A dark hood covered a woman's face as she leaned against the stone of the nearby wall, strands of pink hair escaping confinement.

Syka pushed off from the wall with her boot, popping her black scarf further up on her neck. "I guess it's up to us to sing the heartache."

"Hey, Syka. Been there long?" Divine asked, scanning the length of the street. Divine must have really been inside her thoughts to not have noticed the woman.

"Just contemplating our existence. Care if I join you?"

Had Syka been waiting for me?

Opening and closing her mouth, Divine found no plausible objections to the brooding card player. It was odd that Divine hadn't had many interactions with Syka beyond the Sultry Sapphire evenings. The other woman always seemed to disappear quickly. It would be good to get to know one of Saph's friends.

"I'm shopping for decorations," Divine answered, pulling on her blue mittens. "Warm clothes and looking for a gift for Saph. You're welcome if that doesn't sound boring."

"Small moments make this short life worthwhile. Lead on."

"Uh, alright. I have to finish all of that by late afternoon so I can help at the tavern this evening, so I'll try to be quick."

"Take your time. Lingering is on my list today."

Not a short accompaniment, then. *How...interesting.* Syka's emotions were hard to read, like something hid beneath her disinterest, but Divine didn't feel anything ominous. Nevertheless, she regarded the woman from the side as they turned the nearest corner.

The Essentials District swam with scents; hot apple pies, cinnamon, and melted sugar. Thankfully, the baked goods were drowning the coughs from the Exotic Meats' chimney; its roasted meat smoke plume seemed to grow worse every day, and Divine found it hard not to gag. Every shop was producing more for the forthcoming event, but Divine had trouble understanding who would want to eat that stench. There was a display of glass bowls she had seen the other day, and—hoping the idea for Saph was in one of the restaurants—she began her hunt with Syka.

"So how long have you known Saph?" Divine asked after a few moments, their boots squeaking on the snow.

"I think I was twenty-two then, so probably five years now. We met just as she was about to quit the mercenary guild and become a tavern owner."

Divine did quick math. She always knew Syka was around the same age and her comments would make her twenty-seven, just two years older, versus Saph who was five years older.

"You and Saph were in the guild?"

"Yeah. I was more of a *repeater*. I'd get the same clients or similar marks. Mostly walking the shadows of dreams and broken promises." Syka snickered, then added as if sensing Divine's confusion, "Stealth jobs. Pick a lock, steal someone's family heirloom. Forge ledgers so the client could tip off the Agents of the Goddess of Condemnation on their rival for some jail time. Stuff like that."

Divine cringed. The Agents of Condemnation loved physical proof like that and would swiftly quote a city-state's applicable law to hand out justice, or punishment, to the offender. Like each Holicratic Council within the hagiocracy, made up of the First Servants of the temples, the Council within Iramont would leave all of the rule-enforcing to the temple of Condemnation. Including their agents' pain-inducing mental abilities and mind-muddling. Divine hoped Syka hadn't caused many people to be wrongly indicted.

"Are you still in the guild?"

"No, I quit a couple years ago. I went exclusive with a client. Well, what ended up being a group of people. Long, arduous story of woe—but I'll skip most of it for you. They were training me to be better at my rogue skills. At least I thought. Turns out they were training me to be an assassin. Which wasn't that bad of an idea. As a kid I was fascinated with necromancers."

"But—"

Syka held up a hand. "I know they're just stories. No deity of zombie-makers has a temple anywhere in Trelvania...that we know of. Anyway. It got real creepy real fast. Serpent steps to your last home, if you know what I mean."

Divine did not but let Syka continue.

"I didn't realize it was that creepy at the time, necrotic fascination and all, until I was trying to explain it all to Saph over a drink. It was a cult. I was in a cult."

Embarrassment radiated off of Syka, and the woman kept her eyes ahead.

Divine touched Syka's arm, pushing a ripple of acceptance with her magic. "It could happen to anyone."

"I know. But it happened to me. If it weren't for Saph, I'd probably be sacrificing wulfs at the full moon. At one point, I stood outside a door where someone on the other side was scratching at it and rasping out odd phrases. 'Darlin', that's not normal.' Saph said, and it wasn't in her flirty voice. I knew I was in trouble if Saph was being serious."

Blood drained from Divine's face. "Have you and Saph ever..."

"Oh yeah. Woman's got a tongue that's—well, you know."

Divine did know. Her stomach fluttered just thinking of Saph's mouth moving over her. She tried to shake off the image of Saph doing that to someone else. While Divine always treated relationships as monogamous, she also had past romantic encounters. It shouldn't have bothered Divine that Saph had past relationships. Still, a twinge of jealousy seeped in.

"Why didn't it last?"

"With Saph, does any relationship last? I don't think that woman can commi—I mean Saph likes things flowing and I...sometimes I just want to weep and not talk about it. Saph likes conversation. We're just not compatible that way."

"It's hard to find the right one," Divine offered, uncertain who she was comforting.

Divine tried to distract her thoughts by taking in the surroundings. Many of the businesses had light strands in their windows or draped from low bushes. People exited stores with bundles wrapped in paper or colorful packaging.

A display of glass caught her attention. They seemed to have a smaller bowl within and pressed between the outer and inner wall were embroidered patches. Some had elements of winter, like snow-covered pine trees, and the others had spring flowers and sun. When Divine craved the taste of the faire long after it was over, her mother had made hot cocoa and served it in a similar glass. It had been a memento from one of the festivals.

"It's them!" Divine said, darting inside the Flutterwing Inn. Syka strode behind her to the entrance of the dining area.

"Excuse me," Divine said as she approached the head waiter behind his podium. "I noticed your bowls in the window. Can they hold hot liquid?"

"Well, yes." The man raised and lowered his bushy eyebrows as if the question both puzzled and delighted him.

"Boiling?"

"I believe so. Our soup is served in them, so the guests can see all of the ingredients in their neighbor's bowl." He leaned forward, a hand over his mouth. "Soup of the day becomes extremely popular when at least one bowl is in the dining room being enjoyed."

"And the sides don't burn them?"

"No, no, of course not."

Divine twisted the moonstone ring wrapped in silver leaves on her index finger, glancing out the window of the display. "Do you know if you purchased them in the city?"

"Oh, I just started working here this autumn. But we aren't busy right now, let me check."

As the waiter disappeared into the kitchen, Syka bumped into Divine.

"The tavern's wooden bowls are without inspired design, I'll give you that. But their darkened depths do give a wonderful view to drop into your despair."

"Huh? Oh, no. I'm not getting bowls. I've seen mugs structured like this. Sandshaper work like our mugs, so they can withstand extreme heat, but the heat stays on the inside layer while the outside remains cool. If Saph could get some for her tea, it would solve the hot sides problem the regular tankards have."

"Your verse sings just for her. You're always thinking of ways to help Saph. She's lucky to have you."

A sensation rose in Divine's legs and she thought she might canter like a horse. Instead, she gripped the waiter's stand.

"No burnt fingers is good for everyone," Divine joked.

The head waiter returned with a smile. "The bowls were purchased from a merchant that was here several years ago for the faire. Our owner believes they have a store now near Pariatan as they were made from the sand there."

Divine's shoulders sagged. "Thank you for your time."

There was no way she could get the mugs in time for the week-long event. And she couldn't give them as a Midwinter Nights gift either. She would have to find something else to gift Saph.

"May blessings of winter and light be upon you."

Divine waved in response to the Midwinter parting from the waiter and exited onto the street. She blew out a breath.

"There goes one idea for Saph off the list."

Syka looked through her bangs. "Let's hear your others."

"A dress or skirt. But I feel like she probably has enough of those. Or a corset?"

"I don't think Saph can ever have enough. Last year Sylus gave her a shawl to match that green shirts she has."

"And what did you give her?"

"A purple belt."

Clothing is becoming not a unique idea. I'll have to find something…bold in the Market District.

Divine turned them around and led Syka back past the Sultry Sapphire. She waved to Otto as they passed, the shop owner rearranging a too-tall stack of crates at the front of his Treasures and Troves of Trelvania and mumbling about running out of space and mockingcrates. They walked up the slope of the street, entering the residential area.

The window boxes of the multilevel habitspaces were mostly dry sprigs and full of snow. Sunbursts or snowflakes made of shimmering materials hung from most of the windows, depending on the deity the residents preferred. Strings of large lanterns drooped out of the now dormant aerial gardens, shared by families in this area of the Living District, connecting the habitspaces or dangled from trees. Like the decorative lights Saph had hung, but these Midwinter Nights Faire lanterns were a hand's span tall, giving more area for the dragon scale pattern to show on the reed shell. The nights would reveal their splendor as the sunlight blocked their brilliance.

Divine remembered Midwinter Nights with her parents from her childhood. Her mother kept her warm with frequent hot chocolate from the vendors in Arosia's faire as they looked at the lights and decorations and played the winter games until Divine, too tired to keep going, had her father carry her home. Beyond enjoying the decorations, and a few favorite foods and activities, she hadn't fully participated in the faire in several years. A week of festivities when there were Soulshield duties still to be done seemed frivolous, though she took time to share music. Music healed the soul a bit like magic.

"Hang on," Syka said, breaking Divine's memory as she darted into an alley.

Slashing across the width of a barrel capped with snow, Skya then pivoted to stab the top of a crate. Both wooden containers splintered with a resounding crash and pieces scattered in the cramped space and slush splattered the narrow walls.

"What are you *doing*?" Divine whisper-shouted.

Syka sheathed her daggers on either hip and squatted, picking up a couple coins and a bundle of herbs from the snow.

"You can't just...just destroy things." Divine waved her hands in front of her. "What if that was someone's?"

Syka snickered. "In this highly sought after damp din of death? If you abandon it in the shadows, it becomes mine. Desire, acquire."

"I don't think that's how this is supposed to work," Divine muttered, fiddling with one of her rose stud earrings and following Syka back out to the street. She made a mental note to never leave anything of hers unattended while Syka was around.

Divine paused. Fear splashed on the surface of her well.

"I think there's..." her voice trailed off as she entered the alley again.

Pushing aside several chunks of debris revealed a white squirrel chewing at its paws.

"Your display of fine daggering trapped this poor critter." Divine shushed at the creature. "There now, it's alright, you're free now."

The squirrel scurried away, its frosty tail disappearing through the far wall.

"How did you know it was there?" Syka asked.

Divine stood, brushing flecks of wood and snow from her knees. "I felt its distress."

Syka entered the main street again and Divine stepped in stride.

"That works for rodents too?" Syka inquired.

"I...I guess so."

She still didn't know what had led Madeline to know that she had a connection to creatures, beyond healing them. Had she actually understood that the orange and red bird earlier was singing about their arrival and hunt for food? Divine touched her wrist, though her bangles were covered by her coat.

She eyed the last line of window boxes with their winter vines draping as the Living District melted into the Market District. An idea formed.

"I think I know what decoration the Sapphire needs. There's a nursery this way, right?"

"Perhaps? Every bud I touch eventually wilts. Liz is good with plants, but their stock is gone except the—ones that aren't. Yes, I think there's a gardening shop around here somewhere."

Divine detected a spike of panic from Syka but it vanished quickly. Maybe she and the shop owner had been girlfriends before. That would explain the strange musing.

Further down the avenue, Divine and Syka's walk curved with its bend. Over the rooftops to the side sprouted the many spires and temple tops from the Holy District, beckoning like an old friend, its triplicate archway hidden but vivid in her mind. Words Madeline said cooed at her over the winter air.

"I can open your eyes to the truth. Help me, and the knowledge is yours." It was just a memory, but she shivered all the same. Divine wanted to know the answers, but would the path lead to more lies? Or could she learn something that would help her understand how she was able to do the things she did? The Goodly One she'd met, Leafy, and Listhinci had all seemed to know something. But Listhinci was back on Solhavn with their Iguion kind. Leafy would know if Madeline had escaped somehow, like her dreams, but he was a two-day journey. But maybe...

"Everything alright?" Syka asked, bending into Divine's line of view, her black bangs falling across her eyes.

"Yes, I just—"

"Saph told us everything. I change which God or Goddess I follow regularly, but I'm not tethered to one by magic. It will take time before you're ready to return to them. Or decide not to return. Either way, it's valid." Syka grasped

Divine's shoulder. "When the musicians play, you decide the music."

Swallowing hard, Divine nodded.

"Are you going to the Deity of Love and Fire again?" Divine asked, the words a frozen channel deflecting the course of the ship.

"Yeah. I raged hard with God of Storms after my breakup with Ash but I'm ready to find another soul to woo."

"I'll keep an eye out for other Foggy Iramont drinkers for you."

"I really like breasts."

Divine couldn't stifle a guffaw.

"I *really* like them. Any size." Syka made squeezing motions with her hands. "They're like daggers to my heart."

Divine giggled merrily and veered down the Market District street that she thought would contain the shop she sought. A sign reading "Flora's Floriculture" rewarded her efforts, and she opened the door to the warmly lit shop. As she lowered her hood, the scent of wet soil and flowers made her think of the conservatory in Arosia she often visited.

Pots with long tendrils hung from the ceiling and she knew the tavern had to have the white and green lengths. Several bouquets contained snow pinwheels and other flowers that looked ready for the festival in shades of yellow and blue.

"It's perfect," she muttered, making her way to the floral counter.

"See something you like?" the florist asked.

"I love your flower arrangements. Do you happen to sell any of the snow pinwheels in pots?"

"We do! But the latest seedlings aren't yet ready. I like to make sure their first stems are strong before selling them to customers. Come back in about three weeks?"

Divine stifled a groan. She could at least get enough bouquets to add an ornamental blossom to the Divine-i-tea during the faire.

"How much for two bundles of cut snow pinwheels and"—she rotated, counting the hanging vines—"four hanging plants?"

"Will you be taking them with you now?"

"Can you deliver them to the Sultry Sapphire?"

The florist nodded and scratched a pencil across a small notebook, then spun it to face Divine. It had a breakdown of the cost of the plants and the additional delivery.

Divine paid, only gritting her teeth at the total once. Her coins from the clinic at the Edge were now completely gone and she'd taken a few from what Saph had given her. But she felt good about the new decorations and stepped back onto the street optimistic.

"Saph's gift acquired." Syka announced. "Shopping for yourself is next?"

"Saph has basically two plants in the whole tavern, and the garland doesn't count as that was my idea. I don't think vegetation is high on her lists. I want to find something that really feels special."

Syka shrugged. "Guess I hadn't noticed."

Divine glanced in windows they passed, hoping something would stand out as the perfect gift for Saph. A berry-red dress with split sides caught her eye in the window of a store.

"Let's try clothing. Maybe I can find myself and Saph something."

Inside, Syka tried to help by holding up shirts and skirts and pants as Divine ran her hand over fabrics, some soft like Saph's skin. Patterns of flowers and swirls, embroidered cuffs and necklines; they all swam around her in a dizzying display. Bold and bright colors seemed like Saph, but Divine couldn't tell if she liked them because of that or if the tavern owner already had similar articles.

In her hesitation, she'd listed toward the dress in the window. One of the shop workers swished close, pulling a shawl tighter around his shoulders.

He waved an end of the shawl at the dress. "That cut is perfect for your height."

"I'm not sure…"

"Pair it with dark legs and those lines would lead right to the corner of your eyes. Drawing the attention of whoever you have your eye on."

He winked and spun away to the sound of someone else calling for assistance. Divine smiled. How would Saph look at her in that dress? She shook her head. She needed sensible warm clothes and that dress was the opposite.

Suddenly she felt like the shop held everything and nothing that she wanted. The joy coming from other shoppers clashed with her own indecisiveness.

She blew out a puff of air when her gaze lingered on a satchel beaded to look like a willow tree, reminding her of Leafy's domain. The talking tree grew his own clothes, in the form of leaves, changing colors with the season. She never thought she'd be jealous of that. *Too bad I can't just think it and change my outfit.*

"I need a break," Divine bemoaned.

"Careful or you might start spouting poetry," Syka said, leaning against the wall near the door.

"Huh?"

"A side effect of us over-thinkers." Syka opened the door and motioned for Divine to go first.

Divine looked longingly at the dress for a moment before drawing her back straight and crossing the threshold.

Passing groups of other shoppers, Divine wondered if she should abandon gift shopping and try instead at the special vendors during the faire. She did have six days before the traditional gift giving night. Unless Iramont celebrated differently than Arosia. She turned toward Syka.

"You know," Syka broke their silence first. "I've been meaning to thank you for what you did for Listhinci. I know that could have gotten you in trouble with your temple, but it was really decent of you. They like to play their injuries down, but I think Liz would have lost use of that hand without your help."

Divine's cheeks heated despite the cold. "It's what anyone would do."

"Yet they don't. That's why—" Syka placed a hand on Divine's elbow, stopping them both. She looked past Divine and over her own shoulder where two Iguions strolled, their tails touching, then lowered her voice. "That's why some of us have to do something."

"But what can we do?"

"Little things. Like what Saph does, taking food to them. And what you're doing with the clinic. Little acts of rebellion make an avalanche. Don't you think?"

"We can all make a difference," Divine agreed. Though she didn't like the comparison to an avalanche. Those caught people in their flow, burying them.

"We'll need to make a big difference soon," Syka added.

Divine studied Syka, unsure if the statement carried more to it than surface value. Divine hoped that she was making a difference. She found that she cared far less now of what her temple thought of her breaking the rules. Or, more precisely, doing what was said to be impossible. Divine's temple had said human-adjacents couldn't be healed by magic and Divine had proved that wrong long ago. She just made it a habit now.

Thoughts of her temple and their rules made her mind transition to Leafy again and his creation. A thing the Iramont First Servant of Souls had said was forbidden. At least she had the decency to admit it was possible as she scribbled her notes to send on to Arosia about Divine. Divine felt terrible knowing that Leafy guarded Willow Way alone for the first time in eons without his brother. She wanted to talk to him even more now, but a several days journey presently was out of the question. *I wonder if a pool would work...*

"A task change might lead to new ideas. For gifts, and helping others. This way. I have a message to send."

CHAPTER THREE

What A Message and A Scry Will Do

Plodding on with purpose, Divine led Syka around and through streets until they made it back to the Essentials District a few blocks from Saph's place. They stopped at a sign that read "Hydro Spondence," hanging off the eaves of a building the size of the Sultry Sapphire. Between the words shimmered a blue pond with rolled up scrolls instead of reeds. It was simple wood without any enhancements to make the water appear to move. Sensible, as the Hydromancers that worked there were servants of the Goddess of Standing Water.

"If you've got messages to send," Syka said, seeming to nod over Divine's head, "I'll head over to the Dark Cottage Apothecary. See you tonight?"

Just when she was getting used to Syka's accompaniment, abruptly it was ending. Divine wasn't sure what to make of it, but at least the rogue didn't vanish on her.

"Of course. You promised to give me more tips for Crossroads."

"Hey, you're getting better."

"If better means losing less quickly." Grinning, Divine gripped the handle but paused as Syka spoke again.

"Hey, Divine?"

Eyebrows raised, Divine swiveled.

Syka rested her palms on the skull hilts of her daggers at her hips. "I know you and Saph handled your own out there. But...next time you go on an adventure, maybe bring me? I can sneak through the shadows pretty good."

Divine tilted her head. "Like that display in the alley?"

Syka lofted her arm and a purple blur arced at Divine. She caught it and her jaw fell open. In her hands rested the coin pouch from Saph.

"I'm nimble when it counts. If Saph is might, and you bring magic, I can be the problem solver. I can scout and pick locks, too. It's dangerous to try to handle everything on your own, yeah?"

Before Divine could reply, Syka rotated in a twirl of her long black coat and jogged into the stream of walkers. The bodies closed around the space, opening again like a wave pulling back from the shore. It would be great to have another friend to hang out with when Saph was busy. *Are we friends now?* But Syka's past with Saph conjured light jealousy, like a bug buzzing in her ear.

Where Syka vanished, Saph emerged. Divine grinned and waved as the woman navigated the street, floral skirt swishing in pastels, over to the Hydro Spondence.

"Busy out here today." Saph motioned with her head. "We might have a decent crowd tomorrow morning."

"I hope so. Got rid of Viktor?"

Saph rolled her eye. "Yes, he didn't stick around too long. I think you were right. He can't let go of the tavern even though he lost it in a fair game of Crossroads. But I got everything washed and ready for making tea again. I recalled a few errands but saw you and thought I could walk with you a bit. Or behind you. So I can stare at your ass."

Divine pushed Saph's shoulder. "It's covered by this coat."

"Not in my mind."

Blushing, Divine approached the door.

"I'm seeing a distinct lack of packages or bags in your hands."

Divine halted mid-reach for the door handle. "I, uh, haven't found anything yet to wear. But there's still time."

"Also, I wanted to ask you," Saph said as Divine gripped the door handle. "If you'd like to have dinner with my parents on one of the last days of the festival?"

A hiccup issued from Divine's throat as she pushed open the door. "Your parents?"

"Yeah. In addition to watching the sunrise, we eat food with the colors. Pink, reds, and oranges. Normally any fruit those colors from the last harvest, but"—she shrugged—"this year we'll have to get creative."

The black spot would continue to have lingering effects, like a long shadow of winter afternoons, until the spring arrived and the farmers could tend to their lands.

"You don't have to answer now," Saph added, closing the door behind her.

"No—I mean of course." Divine tried to contain the sudden racing in her chest. Whispered voices filled the space and she lowered her voice. "That would be lovely."

Five steps down, a long wooden counter divided the entrance from the rest of the business. Being at the top of the steps gave Divine a view over the space.

She lowered the hood of her coat. Marginally warmer than outside, the air smelt musty like a cellar but with the deep scent of moss and a hint of salty ocean. Divine crinkled her nose at the squabbling scents. Along the leftmost wall hung shallow bowls of various designs.

A worker sitting on a stool behind the counter wrote with a large quill in a leather-bound book. She wore a white and blue robe that looked both heavy and warm, while the patterns conjured the image of water. The necklace dangling at her chest had a stone pendant of the Goddess of Standing Water, a yellow-green rectangle with raised imprints of reeds common in wetlands. A handful of similarly dressed workers moved around the space that included a basin of water— almost the same size as the fountain in the Living District, though this one was oval—and a dozen private booths. Some of the workers hung or removed icicle shapes from dangling twine and one scratched with a pencil in a book he held, as he contemplated the pool of water.

The worker at the counter paused writing and gave Divine and Saph a small smile. "Can I help you with sending a message or arranging a pool-to-pool meeting, *inlets*?"

Divine moved down the steps as another possible hydromancer approached the one on the stool. He had been the one scribbling near the water, if Divine was correct.

"Nine non-urgent messages for the hour," he told the woman. "These can be converted to letter only, if you approve."

"Are the recipients within the city, *scryer*?" As the woman turned, a column of hoops flashed a rainbow along the edge of her ear. Divine wondered if any of them was her talisman.

"They are, hydromaster."

"Once they've been written, have them placed in the stack for afternoon delivery." As the other left, the woman at the counter bowed her head before meeting Divine's eyes. "Sorry about that, *inlets*! A busy day. My name is Ayar. Now, how can I help you?"

Is she calling us a...narrow water passage?

Divine cleared her throat. "I would like to do a pool-to-pool meeting, but it's a bit of a strange request."

"You'd be surprised how many of those we get." The woman winked and set down her quill looking at Saph then Divine. "It is likely we can accommodate, *inlets!* Several of our booths are soundproof should you desire words or sounds to go unheard."

Divine held up both of her hands. "No, no. Nothing like that."

Saph leaned on the counter. "Would you say moans and pleasurable shrieks are among the sounds unheard?"

Divine felt her cheeks blush and interjected before the hydromancer could respond. "I have a location that I don't know if anyone here would be aware of."

"Oh, that's not a problem, *inlet!* If you can point to it on a map, we can reach it. I can take some of your details down and provide you a quote for the service, if you like."

Divine nodded.

"Your name and address, *inlet*?"

Divine provided the information, including a request for a pool-to-pool meeting and an estimated length of fifteen minutes. She pointed to a small crescent lake barely visible between forests on the map of Trelvania that was pasted on the counter.

"Your name sounds familiar, *inlet*," the woman said as she finished writing down Divine's answers. "Let me check on something."

She flipped back through the pages of her book before pointing to a spot on a page and tsked. She left the counter mumbling and walked into the hanging icicles.

Saph turned, still leaning an elbow on the counter.

"Think it will work?" Saph nodded toward the map.

"I hope so. I'd like to check in on him."

Saph surveyed the space then pushed off from the counter. "Tell the big tree trunk I send greetings. I'll give you privacy. Oh, I did think of something you could help with if you have time."

"Of course." Though disappointed Saph wouldn't be spending more time with her, helping always boosted Divine's humor.

"Can you pick up our pop-up sign? Now that we have a name for the business, see if Stacked Creations can update our request. Keep the construction like the one the Flutterwing Inn uses on the sidewalk when they have vacancies. Just see if they can add the name."

"Easy."

"Great. I'll see you later." Saph kissed the back of Divine's hand. "Have fun shopping."

Divine watched her leave, noting the purple handle of Saph's axe poking out of the bottom of her short coat.

Odd.

Before Divine had a chance to ponder the revelation, movement from the hydromancer caught her eye.

After touching several icicles, Ayar lowered a trellis-like apparatus that housed a section of the dangling things by turning a wheel on the wall. She untied one of the icicles.

"This was sent for you the other day, *inlet*!"

She handed Divine a shard of ice the length of her hand. It was cold and the end round rather than pointed. A tag dangled from the wider end with the date and Divine's name.

"The sender in Arosia was unable to provide your residence, *inlet,* but suggested we check at the Goddess of Souls temple."

Arosia? Divine's jaw clenched. *The temple? Then Iramont's First Servant of Souls' letter must have arrived.*

She was thankful the temple in Iramont had chosen the less expensive means of communication as it meant news of Divine's encounter with the First Soul remained secret for this long. But if Divine's home temple sent a message through scrying...

"We confirmed this morning you weren't there, but here you are, *inlet.* Destiny! The frozen notelet was already paid for, but I would recommend adding another fifteen minutes to your time with the farsight pond. For thirty minutes, *inlet,* it will be ten friggons."

If she remembered correctly, the sender always paid for the frozen message to be delivered. But since there was no other way to reveal the message, paying for time to watch it seemed a bit exorbitant. Inwardly shrugging as curiosity overshadowed the inconvenience, Divine reached into her coat pocket, squeezing the sack Saph gave her. Opening the bag, Divine withdrew the requested amount and handed it over to Ayar. More funds gone.

"Fourth door, please."

The woman motioned toward the far right where the counter ended and a hallway began. Divine walked into the opening, finding the length lit by blue scones along the wall. Doors led into the main area Divine had espied beyond Ayar and she stopped at the one painted with a yellow four. Ayar smiled through the glass window and opened the door.

"Have you been to one of our locations before, *inlet*?" the Hydromancer asked.

"Yes, though it has been a few years." Divine tried to remember the last time she needed to send a long distance or urgent message. Participating in the inter-temple connection initiative came to mind, relaying weekly messages with a Soulshield from Trag on the west coast. She was a teenager then, and couldn't remember if the workers referred to her as "inlet" as they transcribed the message for in-person delivery.

"I'll give you the shorter version, but let me know if you have any questions." Ayar pointed to parts of the room as she led. "Each door contains private booths accessible only by one of the scryers. This keeps the amount of people in one area limited, *inlet*!"

On either side, booths adjacent to each other created half walls. Some were closed and the open booths allowed a brief view of their shimmering bowls, like the ones on the walls, filled with still water.

"The main farsight pond behind door five is not open to the public." She stopped next to one of the booths. "Too many important messages, *inlet!* Here we are!"

Ayar's enthusiasm for the service was catching and Divine found she was excited to hear the message held in her hand, rather than filled with dread.

"I will connect you to your destination, and then the room is yours. If you need anything, *inlet,* pull this cord"—she motioned to a red knob on the wall near the door's hinges— "and a red ball will raise. That will let me know, *inlet*! I will be maintaining your connection until you pull this cord." She stretched past Divine and tugged a blue knob further in, and immediately a cerulean diamond popped from the booth's transparent top and wiggled on its line.

"Do you know how to activate your frozen notelet?"

Divine had received her one and only frozen message as a child. Her mother sent a message from Solhavn to let Divine and her father know that she had reached the island safely. Divine didn't think of it at the time, but the cost had to have been a burden on Leena. Despite the lofty fee, a mother's love facilitated the quicker message outside of normal letters—so that Divine and her dad didn't worry.

"Place in the center and blow?"

"Almost, *inlet*! Blow first, then place it. The hot air breaks the Flurry's spell and releases the message into our scrying bowl. That's why we do not heat our building. But don't blow too hard or you'll make ripples, and the message will be unpredictable until the water stills."

Divine was intrigued by the operation. Hydromancers ran the business but had incorporated servants from other temples to enhance their offerings over the years. It was nice to see some of the temples working together rather than always vying for new membership. The Flurries among them, capturing the message in their frozen forms.

Ayar entered the room and knelt next to a golden bowl set into a table built to hold the bowl level with the tabletop. She hovered her hands over the surface of the water without touching the liquid. The water transformed into a murky grey before clouds churned beneath the surface, gradually changing shape and colors. Several cream clusters coalesced, then the outline of trees and sky took shape while the rest of the image became defined.

The shore of a lake and beyond, yellow-leafed branches drooped with frost in long strands, like pouring rain frozen in time. A faint path disappeared into the cluster of trees. Willow Way.

"Is this the correct location, *inlet?*"

A mixture of emotions and memories flooded Divine; intimate moments with Saph and fear of losing her to the boradain. But there was also pride. Of finding her new powers.

"Yes," Divine breathed. "Yes, this is the right place."

Stepping into a puddle. Being transported to the bottom of a ship. Another step, a splash to the bottom of a lake. These memories flashed in her mind like the moving images enchanted on the Holy District's arches.

"Very well. I wish you pleasant views and conversations, *inlet.*"

"Ayar," Divine started, her tone hesitant. "Is it possible to travel through the places you scry?"

The hydromancer snorted. "Oh, you're serious. Impossible, *inlet*. Though, could you imagine? Instant travel to anywhere we can see! That Palfrey Post would be out of business."

The woman closed the door behind her. The quiet enveloped Divine. Turning her attention back to the scrying bowl, Divine tried to recall how she had contacted Leafy before. Would it even work through scrying?

Sitting on a chair, Divine scooted closer to the water table, careful not to bump her knees. She didn't have a tree to touch this time to summon him. Instead, Divine dipped into her magic well, picturing the Elder she and Saph had named Leafy, and dove her mind into the depths as if her well and the water in the scrying bowl were the same. She swam deeper, imagining roots that connected to other roots. Before, she had sent a plea for help through the roots of the nearest tree and out into the forest. There were hydrilla plants in the crescent lake. Hydrilla had roots beneath their long, small-leaf stems, didn't they? She sent a thought, a greeting. Of a friend come to visit.

She sat back in the chair. If it worked, it could be a while before the Elder poplar tree came depending on where he was in the forest. *If* it worked. But the breadth of her magic continued to surprise her. She glanced at the frozen drop in her hand before placing it on a side table on top of a notebook. Did her temple know she was healing human-adjacents now at the Edge? Or that her blasphemy in Iramont started with an Iguion with vibrant pink scales and a talisman-severing object?

Divine's thoughts narrowed to the giver of that object, and Divine's visit to them after banishing the boradain in the fall.

With nervous energy and an itching desire to fully heal the Listhinci's arm, Divine had rapped on their door. Yellow eyes over pink scales peeked out as a crack widened and the Iguion led Divine inside. She had found herself in the same room as before, the green-scaled baby Iguion scratching their tiny claws at the hanging bee mobile above their basinet.

"Thank you for letting me see you again," Divine said. "I wanted to try again to heal your hand. I've developed a...well, I'm not sure what it is but my well seems larger,

infinite even. And I can do things that's not part of the abilities of a servant of the Goddess of Souls."

"That is most interesting," Listhinci's voice seemed to hiss on their s's. "How do you mean?"

"It worked. The cutting tool you gave me." Divine pulled the triangular shiny black stone from her pocket. "I made a new talisman."

Listhinci held up their arm, the smaller scales of their forearm bright pink. Not a single black scale. Divine's eyebrows raised.

"It took a few days, but each day the damage improved. I think you underestimated your power before. I thank you again."

A surge of admiration flowed from the Iguion. It made the florals of Divine's magic flare, filling her nose with heady perfume. She felt confident and bold.

"What you said before, about severing the connection improperly. I think that's what happened with this creature I encountered. The area around where he was kept was full of the black spot. Could someone have tried to sever a talisman's connection, and that's the reason for the black spot?"

Listhinci tapped a claw to their thin mouth. "It is possible. I would need a sample of roots from the area, and my tools. I leave for Solhavn and my city Zax Solhavn in three days. Come with me. I feel there is much to learn about, and from, your magic. But these conversations are not for here."

Panic snaked its way into Divine's spine. She meant what she said to Saph—she'd had enough of Goddesses. Her magic well was still a part of that system. Besides, it would be nice to relax in Iramont after hunting Madeline for so long. Things could be...quiet.

Divine shook her head and immediately her magic lessened, as if siphoned away by the breath of Listhinci's baby. "I will come soon, but not now. I need to figure out who I am. I've lost her."

Listhinci's dewlap quivered. "It will be at least a season before you will have another chance." Their disappointment rolled off of them like clouds over the sea. The floral aroma surrounding Divine faded to normal. "But I understand. Iguions believe in being who we are. How can we allow ourselves to follow that course if we do not offer the same to others? I hope you find your path. But remember you can also carve your course, and encourage growth without having all of the answers."

"Rootless one," a familiar voice lined with the rustling of leaves boomed, breaking her reverie.

Divine reflexively straightened in her chair, nearly bumping the table in front of her. The water showed the tall tree, his leaves golden but still clinging to his branches over a white trunk that nearly blended in with the snowscape behind him.

"Leafy! It is good to see you. How are you weathering the winter?"

"Slowly. The forest conserves its energy and I protect. But how is it that you have come to be one with the water?"

"One of the followers of the Goddess of your lake connected me. I wanted to see how you were doing after..." Divine let her voice trail off and instead sent a soothing wave of magic.

"I appreciate your concern. I miss"—his voice became the sound of branches bowing against each other that Divine recognized as the sound he had used for his brother's name—"all the time. But light rises and light falls and what was once soil becomes soil again. Part of him is still inside. Trees, you see, we share our roots, touching and speaking."

"Do you want to tell me about him?"

Leafy's roots seemed to meld with the lake's edge, as if the tree sat down. "When we were seedlings, we grew protected under our mother tree side by side, our roots weaving. We drank the same rain and sometimes I would drink less to make sure he had enough. Then the Goddesses made us Elders. He became my protector, too." Leafy's chuckle sounded like leaves brushing in the wind. "Always investigating any changes around Willow Way. I think the Goddess of Fields gave him a nose for sniffing every drop of sap in the forest and its rightful place."

A comfortable silence stretched, allowing them both to let the memories and sorrow work its way through them like water through stone. The willow trees, blurry behind Leafy, gently swayed on a gust of wind.

"Was there something I could do for you, rootless one?" Leafy asked.

Divine pressed the tips of her thumbs together. "I wanted to ask you if—do you want me to try to create another Elder? To keep you company?"

Leafy's branches creaked. "That is very kind. Perhaps another season but for now, the forest is my evergreen companion."

"I'll check on you again soon, Leafy. I hope to come visit you when spring comes. Or sooner if the winter is mild."

"We are halfway there, as the stars speak their longest now. There were yellow and orange flowers shaped like bells in the grove before the diseased one. I think you would like their scent."

Divine smiled. "I would love to see them. Leafy...before I go, I wanted to ask you a few other things."

"My leaves are turned toward you."

"Have you seen anyone else come looking for the house in the clearing? Or have any of the deities visited?"

"I have seen neither human nor walking soul."

She hesitated, not wanting to voice her worry, then breathed deeply. "Has anything, or anyone, come *out* of the boat house?"

"Nothing that I've seen, nor the forest."

Divine relaxed her shoulders. Madeline and the boradain remained in transdimensional space. Her dreams were only that.

"Get some rest, rootless one. Your foliage appears wilted. The answers you seek will not change whether you find them quickly, or you take the time to be as still as the winter forest.

Perhaps some time with your companion up against my trees again, hmm?"

Divine covered her eyes with a hand, remembering Saph on her knees and her tongue... "I should have known you saw us."

Leafy's laugh was like the rolling of boulders.

"May the winter be mild on your forest, Leafy." Pulling the blue knob on the wall, Divine waited for Leafy and the lake to disappear. When it did, Divine's gaze meandered to the desk. She slouched, staring at the frozen message waiting to be heard on the table.

"Why send a message now?" she wondered. But stones settled in her stomach.

Returning to the Goddess of Souls temple in Iramont as the black spot cleared from the farms had been a mistake. But she had craved answers and turned to those who had given her life its meaning through her young adult life.

To find more lies and lost truths.

Beyond details of Divine sealing the boradain and its soul gem with Madeline in a transdimensional space, and how Divine had remade her talisman, she didn't know what else the First Servant of Souls's letter contained. The temple leader *had* promised to recommend Divine's reinstatement. Even though regular postal delivery was lightning quick compared to Divine's travel by wagon between the two cities, the Iramont First Servant of Soul's message had still likely taken a few weeks to arrive at Arosia. It probably sat unread while local matters had been addressed first. As the Arosian First Servant of the Goddess of Souls, and, being that Arosia contained the Holicratic Ruling Council of Trelvania's provinces, as a councilor of the hagiocracy there was a lot to shift through. And now a message, or chastising summons, eyed her expectantly.

"Like a thorn, I suppose. Better to rip it out before it digs deeper."

She grabbed the notelet and the notepad and returned to her chair. Like breathing on her hands to return warmth to her fingers, Divine exhaled on the icicle and placed it carefully in the middle of the water. Gentle ripples expanded but quickly stilled. An image golden and bronze focused into a figure with a private scryer booth behind her.

"I cannot believe you didn't tell me you were leaving!" the image squealed.

The face was not the First Servant of Souls. It was Meve, another Soulshield Divine had worked with frequently. The image continued, Meve leaning forward.

"Everyone is whispering about you. Well, everyone in leadership and then the servants that pander to them probably told their assistants and—they want to test you to be a Soul Shaper? That's amazing! But, girl, I'm so mad at you. Why'd you keep your talisman being stolen a secret? I thought we were a pair."

Meve pouted.

Divine tilted her head back, focusing through the transparent covering of the booth. Had she misread Meve? All of their encounters were friendly, and Divine enjoyed working with her but she didn't think Meve *cared* about her.

"I know you'd help me find mine if some sleaze-face Condemnation Agent tricked me. And you didn't tell me you had a brother? It's like I don't know you at all. Ok, I gotta be quick but like, some weird shit has been going on while you've been away."

Divine didn't have a brother. She snapped her focus to her notebook as Meve continued to speak, jotting down notes. When Meve's face faded, Divine exited the booth while her stomach felt a little heavier. Her temple was far too interested in her.

She made her way back to the doorway, wondering how many others felt friendship for her like Meve, but Divine had missed it. How many friends did she actually have, or had she been too focused on her guilt over not having the skills to save her mother that she pushed away everyone but Meve? Blinking back a tear, Divine stepped out of the hall to the entrance intent on distracting herself with Saph's sign pick-up.

"Oh, *inlet!* Do you have a moment?" Ayar called as Divine neared the shop's door. "We're short on messengers and I'll make it worth your effort. A refund if you deliver this to Stacked Creations. Your scry for this scry, *inlet?*"

More coins?

"Destiny." Divine smiled, echoing Ayar's words from earlier. "That happens to be my next destination."

CHAPTER FOUR

Creative Requisitions

The Stacked Creations was a feast for the eyes. The store stretched three stories, the width narrow like an accordion folded. Each level had a different style, but the bottom one held her attention—its brick face chalked with a mural of skaters on ice and bundled up sledders. An adornment in honor of the upcoming festival. While Midwinter Nights celebrated two other deities, the Creators from the temple of the Deity of Night and Art were often heavily involved in the finer details.

"Right in the market!" someone exclaimed as Divine closed the door behind her. "He dove straight for my talisman. Like he knew what it was."

The inside was even more spectacular. Fabric draped from the ceiling where colorful mobiles hung near the shop's crowded space. A tiered table displayed various glazed bowls, cups, and plates in unique shapes. Divine's eyes caught on a clay mug with a crescent moon for a handle and she wondered if they had any clay tea pots. Maybe that could be her gift for Saph. Paintings hung along the left wall, some of the scenes moving within their frames by the Creators' magic. The shop smelled like paint and wood and chaos. Divine couldn't figure out where to focus her attention.

"Welcome to Stacked Creations! What can we create for you?" A man with a painter's apron and a long pink jacket with no sleeves popped out from behind a display shelf. "Oh, it's you! We have your sign almost finished."

"That's great!" Divine stepped closer around a rack of glass animal figurines. Over the shoulder of the speaker a tattoo artist sat inking the arm of a Kellas on his cream and grey fur. "Saph decided on a name. Is it too late to add it in?"

"Why don't you take a look and see if we have your design right, and then we should be able to add it."

Devaux, Divine refreshed her memory by peering at his nameplate and preferred pronouns.

"Oh, I almost forgot." Divine handed over the wax-sealed letter from the Hydro Spondence. "A message for someone here."

Devaux took the letter and disappeared through a curtain of hanging beads along the far wall. A tree stump on the right was half carved in the shape of a violin, wood chips littering the floor. A bookshelf held a wooden depiction of the Spine of Trelvania made from several different tones puzzled together.

Another person with a broom backed their way around a display shelf toward Divine.

"I didn't mean to overhear," Divine addressed the sweeper. "But did someone say their talisman was stolen?"

The broom brandisher spun around, flourishing the ends in an arc against the floor. "Oh! Excuse me! I'm practicing my frost-stone chase moves, in case it's a main event this year. My talisman was almost stolen. He grabbed for it, but I whacked him with my canvas!" The young woman, Tania from her nameplate, demonstrated with her broom.

"Did you get to see what he looked like?" Divine asked.

Madeline had worked with at least two others. Presumably one was still alive as he'd run from Leafy when Divine healed the Elder during their boat battles.

"I can't remember anything more than he had off-the-shoulder hair and long gloves. I was doing a painting to capture a beautiful moment during a wedding and to do that, we Creators have to have a singular focus on the design to make the pigments move forever. I couldn't take my eyes off them for more than a second."

"I'm sorry that happened."

Tania nodded sagely, then resumed her sweeping. Divine noted the sweeps were very much like the ice game the Flurries had created. Bumps formed on Divine's arms despite her coat. She tried to remember what the Goodly One had told her about the increase of stolen talismans. The memory was clouded by her failed attempt to convince him to let her use him as a talisman instead of seeking out her own stolen one with Madeline. His clean-shaven face and bright orange robe standing in the district square saying something about humans manipulating talismans, like Kellas could turn them into munitions for their pirate ships.

Deities were gathering power. Or was it reducing the power of other temples?

And Madeline had nearly confirmed it when she explained her talisman-stealing. *"Every magic well is a source of power to a deity it's tied to."*

If it was all truth, the temples were sowing seeds for bitter fruit.

When Devaux returned, he carried an A-frame of wood painted sapphire. He laid it flat on a nearby table, scooting a cup containing murky water and three paintbrushes to the edge to make space. On the sign, in white flowing script had been written:

Special Event!
Midwinter Tea and Breakfast
Warm yourself inside and out
Sunrise to ten o'clock
The week of Midwinter Nights Faire

Snow swirled through the lettering and specks appeared and disappeared all over the sign, like it really snowed within. Divine smiled. The talents of the Creators of the Deity of Night and Art were always worth the cost.

She met Devaux's gaze. "It looks fantastic, really."

"Glad you like it! So, what's the new name?"

"Steeped in Sapphire."

"Oh, I love that. What if we redo the 'Special Event' line and replace it with the name? No!" His wrist flopped at her. "Even better. *'Get Steeped in Sapphire'.*"

Divine grinned. "I think she'd love that."

"Then call it done. That is, as soon as I get it done. We have a few deliveries and then—nope, better idea. If you can help us deliver, I can work on your changes at the same time. Could you?"

Another task? Her short errands were turning into a string of quests. The sooner she finished, the quicker she could get started on the newest decorations and reconnect with Saph. *The clothes!* Divine nearly smacked her forehead. She would need to make time for that. And she still wanted to give shopping another go for a Midwinter Nights gift for Saph.

"Would it be quick?" she asked.

"Oh yes, just near the Living District and the south gate."

Divine hadn't visited the south gate before. Maybe there was something for Saph's axe there. "Alright, why not. We both get what we need."

"Precisely. Let me grab the packages in the back."

While Divine waited for Devaux to return, the door opened and another customer entered, a long tail draped over their arm. Their spikes from head to tail were broken only by the puffy coat they wore. Divine did a double take, but the scales were green and not Listhinci's pink. They moved through the shop and Divine's observation flowed to the tattoo table.

Colorful inkwork wove through the grey and cream fur on the arm of the Kellas under a Creator's hand. His long white whisker's twitched as his upper lip pulled back momentarily over feline teeth. Divine felt a flicker of pain through her magic, but it receded as the Kellas's ears rotated outward on the sides of his head.

Divine stepped closer to the tattoo table, catching the name on the tag. "Excuse me, Ruby. Can I ask you a question?"

The Creator paused her hand, every finger decorated with at least one ring, and looking up, nodded once.

"Have you done a tattoo where the object...comes to life? Say a bird, but it flies off your shoulder."

Ruby exchanged a look with another Creator at the nearest table. The Iguion had paused there and raised and lowered an opaque material akin to paper on an object as if testing it. The Creator near them shrugged.

As if that gave Ruby permission, she started her strokes again. "If the ink is drawn while an Orator reads from it."

"Reads from it?" Divine repeated.

"The tattoo would start as a circle of words before drawing the art within. The Orator would speak the words."

Divine eyes widened. "But the servants of the Goddess of Words take a vow of silence so that..." *So that words won't come to life.*

"I've never done it," Ruby added hastily. "But we've heard of it being done."

"Here are the packages!" Devaux said. He'd appeared next to the Iguion holding one small package wrapped in brown paper and one larger in shimmering gold.

She took the deliveries. Divine still didn't know what it meant to have a living tattoo, but at least she had confirmed her suspicions of how Madeline's rainbow bird might have been created. But learning the silent Orators of the Goddess revered for science, speech, and writing were involved was surprising. She gave herself a wry grin. She wasn't doing very good at avoiding thinking about Gods and Goddesses. The questions stirred her like the drive to heal and solve problems that she'd always had—the drive that fit her role of a protective Soulshield.

The object the nearby Iguion touched caught her eye again and Divine approached. On the table lay a map of Solhavn burnt into a slice of wood. Details like jungle, marshes, and waterfalls without labels filled the island's shape. Closer now, Divine saw that the parchment was thicker than paper with a frosted glass luster. Held above the map it had pale markings on the opaque surface. When the Iguion lowered it onto the wood, the paper became translucent, melding with the wood so that the paper nearly vanished adding symbols and markings to the map.

"You can keep the overlay detached if you like," the Creator explained to the Iguion. "Or we can add a bar here that lets you flip it to the back or bring it over whenever you want."

Divine leaned closer to Devaux, an idea swirling in her mind and making her heart quicken. *This would be perfect.* "How long would an overlay like that take to make, maybe twice that size?"

"With it being Midwinter Nights, everyone is looking for gifts. Custom designs we couldn't guarantee before the end of the festival."

"What if you had more deliveries I could help with?"

Devaux winked. "Be right back."

* * *

The first delivery had been in the Living District—one of the larger habitspaces with its rooftop garden. The door had boughs of an evergreen tree hung from it with a small replica of the sticks used in frost-stone chase. Flurries created all sorts of winter games and many of them were popular during the snowy season. The resident within took the small bundle and Divine was quickly on her way.

The subsequent packages took her near the florist from earlier, and she ducked in after her second delivery, noting the vines were absent. They likely were on their way to the Sapphire, as she should be. She hurried to her next deliveries, trying to ignore the reminder of how light the shop had made her coin pouch in addition to the scrying. But compensation would come if she finished the requisitions.

Snow continued to steadily fall and Divine suspected the Flurries were making sure the Goddess of Frosted Wilderness was well represented for the evening events. Several times the snowflakes caught on her eyelashes before melting in a sparkle like sugar on hot rolls.

The last package was bound for Iramont's south gate. Or near it. A training ground Saph had mentioned a few times as a place she had learned with melee experts.

Down a slope in the Warrior's District, a tall wooden fence grew adjacent to the south gate with its own girded entrance open. Inside, archers practiced aiming at targets in the left quadrant while training mannequins of various shapes and sizes made a semi-circle in the right. Further ahead, wooden steps lead up to a porch surrounding a standard house. A sign hung from a post of crossed flaming axes over a shield and the words Mercenary Guild in simple script. Behind it rose evergreen trees, their branches heavy with snowfall.

Grunts to her right made Divine pivot. A figure disappeared out of the entrance, but Divine thought she saw the tail of a familiar skirt; pastel flowers and green leaves. *Was that an axe...*

The grunts continued and Divine watched as a man hacked at a vaguely ursavara-shaped mannequin with a sword.

A giant mushroom offered encouraging words as the man swiped at the long horns of the mannequin, his feet working the snow into the ground churning it into murk. A Thospor instructor. The nearest village of the human-adjacents, Thosporium, was high in the mountains, though she wasn't sure if there were actually any other villages. She'd certainly never encountered any from one before.

"You're swingin' the sword like you're choppin' wood. That's why you're off balance. Instead, elongate like you're slicing through a sponge cake."

The man swiveled, the sword still gripped in two hands held before him. The rage building within him was as clear to Divine's senses as was his clenched jaw and lowered eyebrows. Sweat beaded on his forehead. Divine glanced at the back of the trainer's cream stemmed body—it was as thick as a willow tree.

"Maybe," the trainee said, advancing, "you don't know what you're talking about because you're a *fungus*."

Divine flinched at the insult. The Thospor scratched the edge of their wide convex cap, the smooth appendage a deep teal, with a staff gripped in a thick arm.

"Now, Thospori may be similar to simple fungi," the Thospor said in a deep voice that had a drawl to it, like western Trelvania. "But edible I am not."

The swordsman's frown deepened. "I didn't say I wanted to eat you like a mushroom. I paid for melee training. Bet your useless stubs of legs have probably never seen a fight."

Divine had only read about and glimpsed a few illustrations of Thospori. So, she was surprised when the stout legs bent and launched the Thospor into the air, the teal cap tucking as the staff holder flipped then landed on tree trunk-like limbs next to the man. The staff swiped under the man's legs and he tumbled into the mud. The Thospor looked down at him with two large black eyes just visible beneath the cap.

The man scrambled backward. "Now you're assaulting me? The city should kick you all out. You're all unpredictable abominations."

Divine's hand tightened on the package as she drew closer. "Is there a problem I can help with?"

Out of reflex, Divine sent a calming wave of energy, focusing on the feeling of being heard—listened to.

"Yes, this *thing* is—"

"I wasn't talking to you," Divine said cooly, turning her attention to the Thospor.

The individual had no clothes on and Divine fought hard to keep her eyes on the Thospor's shiny black orbs. She couldn't see any pupils and the fungi had a brownish ring where the neck might have been, just over their velvety shoulders.

"Are you alright?"

Tilting their teal cap to the side, the Thospor blinked their large eyes and bobbed their head. "Right as shade with mist and woodchips beneath the stalk. I appreciate you askin', strawberry-cap. Your hue is as strong as your kindness."

The praise tickled her spine. Divine tucked the package under arm. "Has he paid you for services?"

"An hour session, though we only just got goin'."

"A few suggestions," she said, pivoting to the man on the ground. She placed her other hand in a fist at her hip. "Let the clearly skilled melee expert train you as you paid them to do—"

"Hmph," the man grumbled. "Melee mushroom."

"Or, I reimburse you and you find a new hobby," Divine offered. "It appears you haven't spent much time on…this. Maybe try archery."

He scrambled to his feet, brushing the seat of his pants and glanced across the training ground. Divine followed his gaze to several archers and her breath hitched. Gloves with gauntlet-like arm guards. *Like my dream.* Long like the talisman-would-be-stealer the Creator had encountered. But the figure rotated, revealing feminine features and blue hair. Divine let out a breath.

"You don't have to do that, lass," the teal cap rumbled, countering Divine's offer.

She waved the Thospor off, focusing instead on another wave of calm with a desire to choose.

The man looked between Divine, the trainer, and the archers before jutting his chin toward the Thospor. "I doubt one of *them* can hold a bow. Seems a human talent. I'll try that."

He held out his hand expectantly and Divine pulled her coin bag out of her coat pocket. Her stomach twisted. The money was supposed to be for more clothes. And maybe that dress she'd eyed that was perfect for the festival. The dress she hoped Saph would like on her as well. But that was things and this was a being.

"How much is a session?" she asked, turning her head to the Thospor.

Their whole stem-like body seemed to sag as they relinquished the information.

Taking the money from Divine, her sack now three-fourths empty, the troublesome human marched across the training ground.

Divine pointed to the ground. "Wasn't even his sword?"

The Thospor bent over and Divine thought the wide cap would topple them, but they successfully retrieved the sword from the muck.

"And blunt." The Thospor held the blade, turning it so that the light hit every angle. "Thankfully. Though it would leave a mighty bruise should he have managed to land a thrust at me. Which I owe you thanks for. He is by far the worst I've encountered."

"Does this happen often?"

"These happenings be more frequent of late. Not always, and the city is big—full of people. But ever since those rules got erected..." The Thospor shrugged.

"You mean, enacted? The banning of human-adjacents from the Holy District?"

"Yeah, that's the one."

"I'm...I'm sorry to hear this."

"Well, sorry don't particularly do much but I appreciate it anyway."

The Thospor headed toward the guild building as Divine thought about what Syka had said. *...make a big difference.*

"Wait!" Divine called, running after them. "What *would* do more?"

The Thorspor *harrumphed* quizzically. "Oh I reckon folks like you saying something to your temples. The temples run the rules, after all."

"The local Holicratic Council decides, but I see your point. With the First Servants representing each temple there, it does feel like the whole temple is responsible. Everyone could do more."

I could do more. Instead of worrying about Madeline's plot, Divine could be working on issues right in front of her. Just because she wasn't a Soulshield at the moment it didn't change that she wanted to look out for all of the souls around her.

"What you got there?"

"Huh?" Divine looked where the Thospor pointed with their staff at the box in her arms. "Oh! I have a delivery for someone. Let me check the label for the name. Myconaris Shroombal."

"That's me." The Thospor tapped where their chest might be with the top of their staff, just below the brown ring. "Though, around here they call me Royal Spore."

"What do you prefer?" Divine asked, handing over the package.

"Can't say I've been asked in that way before. Shroombal pulses well in the gills. It's what my human friends use."

Divine bent her head to the side. Was Shroombal's voice coming from beneath their cap?

"Why do they call you Royal Spore?"

Thick fingers ripped the paper around the package. "I think it's 'cause I'm so old. That is, I come from the oldest line of mycelia. I have memories from my spore progenitors back to the Dragon War and connections across distance."

Dragon War?

"How far back is that?"

Shroombal pulled out several bags from the package that looked to contain chalk sticks and brushes. "Oh, before the temples, I think. Though, hard to say as we didn't come to the cities back then."

Divine had never heard of a Dragon War. As far as she knew, the dragons stayed in certain biomes and never ventured out, like the Dragons Roost Island west of Trelvania. Though the curiosity within her itched to learn more, she knew she had tasks to complete.

"It was nice meeting you, Shroombal. I need to return to Stacked Creations."

"Do you work for them?"

"Just helping out with deliveries while they work on my order."

Shroombal opened the drawstring on one of the bags. "That's very kind of you."

Divine shivered, pulling her hood closer to her ears. "I work over at the Sultry Sapphire. We're serving tea tomorrow if you like that sort of thing."

What did Thospori eat, anyway? Divine inwardly cringed as she remembered one of the teas. Though shrooms were not remotely sentient and Thospori were creatures, it was probably best not to tell Shroombal about the snowshroom tea until they'd read the menu.

"Saph's place? The ingredients could give me a variety in my nutrient intake. Tell her not to throw away the waste and I'll be by to collect."

A slight grimace escaped Divine's control at the thought of eating the left-over tea remnants before her thoughts caught up. "You know Saph?"

"That one's a strong fighter. Good student."

Divine thought of Saph's strong arms and nodded in agreement.

As if reading her mind Shroombal added, "And not just with weapons. You must be Divine she was telling me about. Here, I can't let you walk away payin' my mites." Shroombal handed her a fist of friggons from somewhere within their stem. Divine hoped they came from pockets but suspected not from their slightly tacky texture. "Hope to see you again soon."

As the coins added weight back into her bag, Divine waved and headed out of the training yard entrance, wondering when Saph had told Shroombal about her.

She followed her quest line in reverse. Deveaux had promised to deliver the sign to the sidewalk in front of the tavern before dark. Collecting her rewards from the shops and nearly recovering everything she had spent, she vowed to not offer to be helpful to anyone else before returning to Saph and decorating the Sultry Sapphire with the new plants. They only had this evening before the official start of Steeped in Sapphire.

But as she neared the dress shop, her betraying feet led her inside. The purple coin bag heavy in her pocket and visions of a Midwinter Nights Faire tryst giddying in her core. Just one dress. An early gift for them both.

CHAPTER FIVE

Invite a Decacacti for Drinks

It wasn't just one dress. It was also matching gloves and earmuffs, deep red like they had been dipped in bustleberry wine, two pairs of pants, a set of boots, and several tops. She'd deposited them into the room she shared with Saph, and decorated until the first patrons of the evening crowd wandered in.

Divine fluffed the neck of one of her buys, gathering the plush flannel fabric like a scarf under her neck as she told Syka, Sylus, and Edward about the message from Meve's icicle.

"I have Soulshield status again. And the Arosian Goddess of Souls temple wants me back immediately." Divine placed a card down with an image of a small town. "Apparently."

The smoke coming from cozy little chimneys on the card was tinted purple, giving it a magical feeling. The dealer, Syka, had flipped the center card at the crossroads of the table, revealing the terrain for the game: frozen. As the person left of the dealer, Divine had chosen the alignment of Lightscales, resulting in Syka bemoaning the goodness of the suit.

Divine's card worked well for the card path nearest her, a single tree visible in a dark swirl of fog; shelter for her character. But the dark fog made it more of a Shadowbone type, and she couldn't reap the benefits of a bonus. Her card's top number was the highest on the card, a four after the frozen terrain penalty, and did not win her a card from the deck. The play passed to the next person.

"You got all of that from your friend?" Sylus asked.

Friend. She wasn't used to calling Meve a friend, but looking back Divine realized that's what they were. Friends. And she could have been a better friend to Meve.

"In a way. Meve has a way of rambling, so I've learned to put the puzzle pieces together. A few of the Soulshapers are likely already on the way."

"Why do they want you back now?" Edward asked.

He played a card with a stream of water that looked like it had coins swirling within against a card with a dragon hugging a glowing orb. The numbers on the requisite sides matched; a successful play but didn't win him a new card.

"A lot of reasons."

Sylus studied his cards as Divine continued.

"They'd want to see if I could become a Soulshaper. The First Servant thinks more souls will need Soulshaper guidance in the coming year. That happens sometimes after particularly harsh winters or poor growing seasons. There was the black spot." She shrugged. *Or the boradain's Elder gem I tossed into the transdimensional space. Or how I remade my talisman and my new well.* "There's a lot of stuff."

Divine paused, studying the cards. While she had spoken, Sylus played a card with a silver chalice filled with water. Pink fish with long tails swirled around the cup and Syka had evoked the power of scrying through the Goddess of Standing Water. The table erupted into an argument with some agreeing the cup could be used to gather information and others alleging the use was too loose of an application. Syka had been coaching Divine to be more creative with her plays.

The next card for Divine's character to advance toward the crossroad looked like a girl serving tea in a forest, perhaps to her nighttime snugglies. The corner of Divine's mouth tilted up at the odds of having a tea card, and she played a mermaid holding a bowl beneath a canopy of seaweed. Resource gathered; a much needed drink to continue the journey. The card's edge beat the card on the table and Divine flipped the next card in line to the crossroads over.

Syka tossed Divine a new card for her hand. "What do you think of what your friend said?"

"If Meve isn't exaggerating, I'm pretty much what the temple has been talking about in whispers over the last month. She said the high-ranking servants cautioned everyone to keep their talismans safe. Maybe because I got mine stolen. It's always a risk, but I heard just today while I was shopping someone tried to take a talisman from a Creator. The coincidence is...weird."

Sylus and Syka exchanged a look.

"Like not really a coincidence," Syka surmised.

Divine searched their faces. Could she trust them? An even bigger risk to having a talisman stolen was losing that connection entirely. Divine's mind went to Listhinci and the device that helped her sever the connection to her old talisman. In the wrong hands, it could be used against magic wielders. Could she tell Sylus and the others why her temple would be interested in how she severed the connection to her old talisman? Divine decided she couldn't let anyone know she had the smooth black triangle, lest of all in a crowded tavern.

"I just hope this isn't the new normal." Divine took a drink of her tarrow root beer. "People knowing which accessory to swipe."

"Don't worry, we'll get you more decoys." Sylus elbowed Syka. "Right, thief?"

Syka glowered at the table, her lined eyes unblinking. "She'll be a walking jewelry cabinet."

Edward laugh-coughed into his fist but Sylus rolled his eyes.

The game continued another round. Three of the four road lines had their last cards flipped over. Several were close to reaching the crossroad at the center of the table, including Syka.

"It must be good to know your temple wants you back," Sylus surmised.

"I guess. The under-review status they placed on me is lifted, which means I can go back to Arosia and resume my old life. But..."

Divine couldn't explain it, but she felt like the temple wanted more than simple evaluations. What Meve had said about talismans and their overt interest made Divine hesitant in reuniting with her temple. That aside, did she want to return to her old life?

"You'd rather stay here with us, right?" Syka tried to finish Divine's thought, placing a tree full of ripe red-orange fruit where a card of a wagon had been. Thankfully Divine was on a different card path since she had already used her resource gathering earlier in the game.

A small smile graced Divine's lips at Syka's words. "It has been nice here."

"Better than nice, eh?" Sylus kicked Divine's boot under the table as he played his next card. When she glanced up, Sylus jutted his chin toward the wall across from the fireplace where Saph was helping coordinate the first set of musicians.

"You tell Saph yet?" Edward asked, continuing the round.

Music filled the room. The plink and twang of guitar strings rose and lowered in pitch just slightly to find the perfect alignment. Hand drums thumped a tentative rhythm, mirroring the way her heart did any time she was near Saph.

Divine stared at the card. It had a rider with a staff on what looked like a giant squirrel, looking over a cliff. "I don't think I will. I'm not going."

The music grew louder as a lively song began. Divine recognized it as Boats to Borderlands. She wanted nothing more than to get lost in the music, let the tinkling tones become a language that resonated one thought: joy.

"Good, we like you."

Edward's words warmed Divine.

"Like's a strong word." Syka gathered the fruit of the card by playing a woman holding a basket. So not a sabotage move; she'd set herself up to gather her last needed resource. Clever. "We tolerate."

Syka's gaze followed a woman, plump breasts jostling over the edge of her blouse as she dashed toward the bathroom by the kitchen. Based on the hand over her mouth, the visit was not going to go well.

"Syka's let the cold seep into her bones again," Sylus said, winking. "She's probably half werewing."

Divine knew Syka's jab was only teasing, just as Sylus threw one back at her.

Syka tapped her card as if to emphasize the play's significance. "Werewings are already half human, ale-head."

"But have you ever actually seen one change into a human?" Edward asked, narrowing his eyes.

"Meve say anything else?" Sylus pointedly ignored the squabble.

"She thinks the First Servant of Souls wants to protect me from—how did Meve put it? 'Grave disfigurement.'"

Syka laid her cards face-down and leaned forward on her arms. She peered from beneath pink and dark lengths of hair.

"More details please."

"I should be in jail getting the *best* treatment the agents have. Mind muddling with possibly permanent effects, headaches where bright lights make me vomit, nightmares, hallucinations. I've technically broken several egregious laws." Divine began to tick them off on her fingers. "Abandoned my living space. Healed an Iguion. Basically killed one of the Condemnation Agents."

"No body, no proof," Syka said picking up her cards again.

Divine laughed nervously. "Meve thinks they sent our temple to get me before the agents do. I think I need to focus on our game."

Divine studied the cards on the table, trying to lose herself in the creative processes rather than think about being hunted by multiple temples. *Hallucinations. Nightmares.* Maybe the agents were already here. Maybe they'd always been here. *Madeline's remaining accomplice from the farmhouse.* Didn't the Creator in Stacked Creations describe someone stealing talismans? That person could be one who helped lure Divine to Willow Way. Divine shook her head, as if she could shake the paranoia away. Rumors of talisman stealing didn't mean the man who pretended to assault Madeline all those months ago was still here. Would she recognize him if she saw him? Yes, she decided. She remembered his eyes of grey that seemed to swirl.

She suppressed a shudder, letting her magic wash away thoughts of anything else and soothe her nerves for her turn. The two lines on the card table making the cross had changed significantly since the start of the game. Divine eyed the cards in her spread.

On one card, a ball of cream peeked out from the grass of a sand dune, its green and black quills matching the tufts of grass. Divine glanced at the table and the last played card along her journey line; a dark window. It was a defensive play by Sylus, meant to make other players waste their cards with no chance to progress closer to the center of the crossroad. What could someone do with a window?

As Divine pondered how to navigate her move, she surveyed the tavern. Reflections of the string of lights lit the top of the front windows, making the decoration seem doubled. She imagined the dunaru from her card climbing through one of the panes, scurrying across the floor to nibble food dropped by the patrons; the cute squeaks it would make holding breadcrumbs in its small paws. She looked back at the table, her hand hovering over the card. No one had specified the location of the window on the card. She could use the dunaru to steal into storage of a farm.

Divine snickered. She'd need a lot of dunarus to carry enough supplies for the game. She doubted she could convince her fellow players that one dunaru could do the job. Divine grabbed the card next to it instead, slapping swirling flames on top of the window.

"To stay warm and light the night," Divine declared.

A plate clanked near the table edge. Steam rose from wooden bowls of stew, chunks of dark meat surrounded by a rainbow of root vegetables. The inclusion of meat was a rare occurrence these days due to the dark spot's impact on the food source of farm animals.

"Fuel for the game." Saph lowered herself into the empty chair across from Divine. "Second drink rounds are coming up soon. Are you about out, Sylus?"

"Nearly finished, boss."

The game's participants grabbed bowls, though Divine couldn't bring herself to take one. Her stomach soured at the thought of the creature cared for and fed only to end up in her stomach. Several months ago it didn't bother her as much, but now...

The group argued if Divine's card was in excess. Instead of the bonus of using an outshine to negate the frozen terrain penalty, and winning the play, if it actually burnt down the window's building. Having an eight on the right side versus the table card's seven on the left side wouldn't matter if the play lost the round by vote.

Air vibrated through reeds in melodic chords. Divine snapped her head up, quickly finding the source of the sound. Near the small stage at the far wall, where Divine had decorated, stood several performers warming up their instruments. A Kellas expanded and contracted dark orange bellows on an accordion, the wooden ends painted black and embellished with a strip of stencil work. It was similar to her own accordion, though hers was red like her hair. Longing showed a space inside of her that had gone dry without her instrument.

Divine laid her cards on the table. "I'm out. I'll be back."

The stage was small, only two steps above the main floor, and longer than it was deep. On the wall, Divine had covered the artwork that hung between windows with fabric and tied them each with a bow. She thought the reference to gift-giving went with Midwinter Nights traditions, and the fake gift would please a Trickster of the God of Day and Deceit. She'd attached cords of marbled orange and white beads dangling in loops along the stage's front guardrails, a sprig of green and variegated white foliage at each crest. The small white flowers gave the plant its name, snowstorm.

The musicians stepped on the stage, though the accordion player waited to fasten her straps over her tawny fur. The clawed feline had a diamond patch on her chest and stood a head taller than Divine.

"Excuse me," Divine said, pointing. "I saw your accordion and had to have a closer look. I love the silver swirls. With the anchors there, it reminds me of the water."

"Thank you. I had it painted to look like that. The land of my birth is Reawr, overlooking the rocks and water of Snowshroom Bay. Do you play?" Her whiskers rose on the puffs of her cheeks.

"Yes! Though my instrument is back in Arosia."

"I have an extra one. It is smaller but if you are familiar with how they work, it should be no problem for you."

"What, now?"

Divine threw a panicked look back at her table, as if they could rescue her from the offer. But they seemed to be congratulating Syka for winning the game and its wager.

"Yes, join us." The Kellas bent over, rummaging in a bag. "We're playing familiar tunes. Do you know Darkness to Daylight?"

Divine rolled onto the balls of her feet. "I played it almost every Midwinter."

The Kellas straightened, bringing with her an almost identical accordion. She handed it to Divine. Though the instrument was smaller than the Kellas's own, the one in Divine's hands seemed perfectly human sized.

"You smell familiar." The Kellas sniffed the air.

Divine shrugged. "I've been here for a few months now, though I've never played."

Looping her arms through the straps, Divine positioned the accordion on her chest and let memory move her. Her hands situated on either end she pulled, expanding the lungs of the instrument through a familiar resistance. She touched several buttons in a sequenced pattern, first on the left side then echoing the rhythm on the right. Full airy notes sang and their vibrations tickled Divine's chest.

With a nod, the Kellas stepped onto the stage and Divine followed. The lead musician tapped four beats with his foot on the stage and the music began. A wind instrument that looked like holes had been bored into a clam fluted merrily while spoons clacked together in bright claps and tinks. The crowd applauded, some rising from their seats or exiting the bar to dance to the lively tune. Divine followed along, providing a harmonic line that accented the other accordion's melody.

Soon Divine was grinning, the crowd's enjoyment light and palatable in the air. Bobbing along with the tune, Divine surveyed the crowd. Each time she caught an eye and the patron showed enthusiasm, like a wave or a grin or a thumb raised, Divine gathered more strength and confidence. Then her eyes fell on Saph.

Divine's throat closed and her fingers flubbed a note in an offending dissonance. Saph leaned forward, laughing, as she placed her hand on someone's knee. A new player at the table.

How can she flirt with just anyone?

She pried her eyes away from the card table, seeking anyone who would look her way. A table raised their mugs at the stage as the song ended, and Divine's mood lifted. She played another song with the group, relishing the exhilaration that came with creating music with each pull and push of the bellows.

The second song completed, Divine thanked the Kellas and the other musicians and left the stage lamenting the loss of the instrument. The tavern's applause pressed close to her soul like a blanket.

Divine collapsed into a free chair as Sylus clapped her on the back.

"We didn't know you had even more talents." Sylus raised his flatnut butter sandwich and took a bite, the next words coming out around a mouthful. "I approve."

"Too cheerful," Syka said picking at her nails. "But impressive."

Divine grinned. Gone were the worries of earlier today, replaced with giddiness and delight.

Saph wrapped her hand around Divine's. "When you said you played, I imagined you playing...expressive pieces that

Syka would probably like." Divine snorted but Saph continued. "I see now that I still have a lot to learn about you. And that excites me."

Divine squeezed Saph's hand, the flirting she witnessed nearly vanishing from her memory with Saph's attention.

Saph squeezed back before rising. "I think it's my turn to refill the drinks."

Cold air swirled along the floor and around Divine's ankles, its grip reminding her that everything wasn't twinkling lights and sugared nuts. The flames of the fire bent and the front door shut.

The tavern grew silent. Black cloaks fluttered toward the door as if drawn to the darkness, their leather armor a deep maroon over their chests. Though hidden, Divine knew similar protections covered their arms—one never knew when a citizen would fight against their accusations. Both wore the symbol of their Goddess as a belt buckle; thorns wrapped around a hootweet.

Falling into her well, Divine drew her magic protectively around her. They'd come for her.

"Can I help you fine folks with a beverage?" Saph called to the Agents of Condemnation.

The nearest one handed Saph a rolled up piece of paper. "Consider yourself warned of your violation. Future violations will be fined."

"Violation?" Saph broke the seal and unfolded the message. She scoffed. "Now I can't serve human-adjacents alcohol?"

"It's only temporary," the second agent clarified. "Until the mixtures can be analyzed against their interaction with their mental fortitude."

"Mental fortitude?" an Iguion hissed, their dewlap flaring orange as they stood. The chair creaked ominously.

"Roshk, please," Saph held up a hand. "It'll be alright."

The bar owner caught Divine's eye, touching the side of her nose and nodding toward Roshk. Divine stirred the surface of her well. The agents weren't here for her after all.

She drizzled serenity over the Iguion. The sea lapping against the shore. Finding purpose and community.

Saph made her way around the bar, stopping in front of the two agents.

"It's Midwinter Nights," she said, tugging on the cloak on the nearest agent's shoulder. "Surely we can let them all have a little bit of fun."

"That's not possible," the second agent replied. "The law is specific."

"Yes, yes. That it is." Saph flicked her eyes to Divine, then to the agents.

Divine would need to influence them, it seemed. Reaching deeper in her well, Divine drew a bucket full of magic, trying to convey the impression of a job completed. Law upheld. Order.

"Come, join us for a game of Crossroads George." Saph sauntered back to the card table. "If you win, drinks are free from my bar for the rest of the year. If we win, you look the other way during Midwinter Nights."

The agents exchanged a look, but followed Saph.

Divine watched as Syka and Saph controlled the table, weaving a narrative of cards both complex and entertaining. The whole tavern narrowed in around the table to watch. At the end, Saph played her card in the center of the table. She'd reached the Crossroads, and won.

"Well played," Saph congratulated everyone at the table. "Free drinks all week for you two, my treat."

That seemed to thwart any argument from the agents. Divine relaxed, relinquishing the steady stream of her calming magic that she'd unconsciously been bathing the tavern in. No wonder no one had celebrated too loudly at the win.

As Divine leaned back in her chair her eyes grew heavy. Her body weighed against the chair. She was exhausted.

Yawning into her elbow, Divine watched the final performers, the night fading into a contented blur until the tavern began to empty of its last patrons.

"Good luck tomorrow," Syka said, wrapping her scarf as she reached the door. "Most new businesses fail within the first year. But this tea thing has potential."

"Dull blades, thanks Syka." Saph scraped a chair under a table, Sylus close behind with a mop. "I hope you don't get robbed on the way home."

"Someone rob me? They'd have to see me first."

Saph threw a wet rag. "Get out of here, you thief."

Syka dodged easily. "Thieves are sloppy. I'm a professional."

The door clicked behind Syka.

Shaking her head, Divine gathered the cards into a pile and pushed the mugs together. Saph cleared her throat and Sylus grunted before leaning the mop against the table and grabbing the mugs all at once by their handles.

"I'll go wash these," he said, then nodded to Saph before leaving the room.

"Don't you go anywhere." Saph pointed to a chair. "Close your eyes."

Divine pressed her lips together, but did as Saph asked. Intrigued, she thought about all of the things Saph might turn into a surprise. Showing off a new skirt? Another tea blend? Several moments passed with the warm fire at Divine's back, the gentle cracking of the logs like a winter whisper. Alcohol and stewed vegetables mixed with the woodsy smoke of the fireplace. A trace of damp fur. The people who had enjoyed the evening. And her rose, now calm, an ever-present layer.

Something thunked on the table. Divine felt Saph's excitement in simmering bubbles.

"I know the faire doesn't start until tomorrow, but my family has a tradition for the night before. I hope you like it."

Divine opened her right eye just a squint and looked up at Saph.

"I can open my eyes?"

"Immediately, darling! I've waited all day."

Before her stood a clay pot on the table. From the pot's soil grew a green clump with ten prickly tentacle-like stems.

It wiggled its top three tentacles as if in greeting. The whole thing rose a handspan tall.

"I thought with your affinity for plants, you might like one to care for. The spinetooth on my window isn't much of a garden, and they told me roses don't really grow well indoors. But these are pretty resilient."

Divine beamed. "Where did you get a decacacti?"

She touched the top, the part that most resembled a head, and the decacacti *hmmed*. It bent marginally toward the fire.

"You know how Liz had all of those plants in their house? They have a friend who stays all winter in Iramont and they took Liz's leftovers that couldn't go on the boat. This was with them. Do you like it?"

The Syphondor desert native looked like a plant yet was more of a snake crossed with a sea invertebrate, but Divine didn't want to correct her and dampen Saph's excitement. Despite her jealousy from earlier, Divine's heart filled to bursting over the thought that went into the gift. Saph really saw her—not just empty compliments—she had remembered the details.

Divine rose and kissed Saph. "I love it. It's cute. But not as cute as you."

The decacacti gave a low sound like a mix of a *hmm* and a crackle.

Divine snorted. "I think your gift doesn't like being called cute."

"If you say so."

"What do you think that sound meant?"

"What sound?"

Divine looked from Saph to the decacacti. The latter remained quiet and still, the former inspected Divine with a slight tilt of her head.

"Nothing. I'm tired beyond reason. It's a big day tomorrow." Divine squeezed Saph's hands. "I really love the gift."

"I didn't know you'd buy plants for the Sapphire." She motioned to the nearest support pole and the dangling variegated green. "So this feels less exciting than I imagined."

"No, no. Those are just decorations for us and the space. This is personal. I'm very excited." Divine licked her lips. "You remembered my story of healing the plant at the temple?"

"You made it bloom pink flowers. And then there's your mother's rose garden." Saph's head drifted closer. "You seem to really enjoy plants."

Divine traced the tip of her nose down the side of Saph's, bumping her nose piercing. She lingered her lips over Saph's.

"And I really enjoy you," she whispered, then brushed a kiss to Saph's lips.

The other woman mirrored the soft gesture, the connecting touch swelling Divine's magic, and she smelled a night-blooming garden. Saph's hand touched Divine's left breast, slowly caressing until her hand pressed over Divine's heart. Divine thought Saph could feel it trying to escape in exhilarated beats.

"I enjoy you, too." Saph locked her green eye to Divine. "I know things have been really busy around here and we don't get to do a lot outside of the tavern. To Condemnation, I'm always busy either prepping or wrapping up. I hope the plant gives you moments to pause and reflect on the small things that matter."

Divine drew her hands down Saph's sides. "I feel terrible, I don't have your gift yet."

Saph's hands caressed the small of Divine's back. "You're my gift."

The touch sent shivers down her spine and Saph kissed Divine, squashing any rebuttal behind flicks of her tongue.

Pulling away, Divine didn't try to hide the husky sound of her voice. "I think I'll head upstairs. Will you be coming?"

"Soon." Saph groaned, tugging Divine's waistband. "I picked up a few more decorations while you were out today." She stepped over to a corner and lifted a bag to the nearest table. "I'm going to get this tavern looking like a tea shop and then I'll be upstairs. Won't be long."

Divine pushed in her chair. "Well, then I'll help. It'll get done quicker."

"With you nearby, nothing will get done but me taking your clothes off. Go relax, gorgeous. They had you running all over the city and you've already swathed our stage with your loveliness. Besides, you had to babysit some of my most infuriating patrons. I'll be fine. Put on something comfortable. Or nothing at all." Saph winked. "I don't mind."

Divine's cheeks heated. Lifting the pot in both hands, she ascended the stairs as Saph began to whistle a tune heard earlier from the performers. Divine's body ached for more of Saph's touch, like Saph was made of power that Divine went faint without.

At the top of the stairs, Divine remembered the item she carried.

"I guess I need to name you," she declared, looking down at the pot she cradled in the crook of her arm.

Its stems wiggled, probably adjusting to the change in temperature. The hallway seemed to catch more of the warm air that drifted up. It was almost too warm for Divine, but perfect for a desert succulent.

Inside their room, Divine placed the pot on the table beside the bed and changed into nothing. As she climbed into bed, she hoped Saph would come soon. She pulled the blanket up to her neck to hide the surprise and rolled over.

Resting her head on her upper arm she stared at the plant. "I don't suppose you'd want to be called Prickly?"

Two short crackle-hums vibrated in a low timbre from the pot.

Divine yawned, her mouth stretching wide. "No, I guess that won't do it all. 'Sultry' and 'Sapphire' are just as terrible. Too bad you aren't blue instead of green, I could call you cerulean or something."

The decacacti's bottom stems wobbled, slightly rotating in a so-so gesture.

"Hmm, but you aren't opposed to something that describes your nature."

Divine thought of everything she knew about the species; though they had a desert named after them, they were found all over the east continent of Syphondor wherever arid weather blew, and they grew to be between one and four feet tall depending on the species. Some of them bloomed flowers. Her eyes fluttered shut before she snapped them open again.

"I can't fall asleep before I name you," she mumbled, fighting to push up her heavy eyelids. "And I really want Saph to...you don't need to hear that thought. I know you aren't really talking to me, but it is fun to pretend. What about Grumpy?"

The creature crossed its longest tentacles.

"What? You've been against most of everything I've said this evening." Divine's eyes widened as she realized what she saw but when she blinked, the decacacti was in a normal decacacti position. She released a heavy exhale and burrowed the side of her face into her pillow.

The decacacti slurped then crackled.

"Oh, you aren't grumpy? You're just particular," she mumbled. She yawned, her eyes closing and she spoke slowly. "I've made a note of that."

A few moments passed, then Divine whispered a word, though she couldn't be certain she spoke at all.

"Sagacious."

A higher sound more like a zip issued from the pot. Contentment.

"Good night, Sage."

Images of a table full of cards from the night's Crossroads George games danced in her head. Her final thought was of her turning the dunaru card into a pet.

CHAPTER SIX

Do You Dunaru?

Something tickled Divine's arm and she brushed it away, nuzzling against her pillow.

"Hey beautiful. Wake up," Saph whispered. "There's some noises."

"It's probably Otto," Divine mumbled. "Careening through his inventory at unholy hours again."

"Making scratching sounds downstairs?"

Divine opened her eyes to find Saph sitting on the edge of the bed with her axe resting across her knees. Divine pushed up on an elbow.

"I thought your weapon was at the bar."

"At night I've kept it under the bed ever since..." Saph didn't need to finish the sentence. Divine wasn't the only one finding it difficult to move past the incident at Willow Way. How did she miss the shiny metal being underneath them?

"You had your axe with you at the Hydro Spondence, didn't you?"

"I did."

Something felt...off from Saph's energy.

"Why?" Divine asked.

"I've been training again. I wanted to make sure I wasn't losing my edge."

The skirt at the training ground's gate. Divine *had* seen Saph there. She wished Saph had told her.

Faint scratching reached Divine's ears, and she peered at the door as if staring at it hard enough would reveal the source.

Saph rose. "I'm going to check it out."

She was already dressed in sleep shorts and a tank top. Divine loved the set as the top never quite covered Saph's stomach.

Divine scooted to the edge. "I'm coming with you."

Saph smirked. "I wouldn't have it any other way."

Divine hastily pulled on her thick sleep pants and tugged on her calf-high boots, lamenting that she'd fallen asleep before Saph had come to bed. She threw on a discarded shirt, maybe from the previous night. Remembering her conversation with the decacacti—*Sage*—Divine darted her eyes to the side table as she pulled on her boots. The creature looked like a regular plant. Definitely not something that communicated.

Saph grabbed a lantern hanging by the door and handed it to Divine. Pressing a button, the mechanism sparked and lit the candle within. A crash sounded and Divine grabbed Saph's arm.

Sage issued a high-pitch squelch.

Whipping her head around, Divine narrowed her eyes at the plant. In the faint light of the room, she couldn't tell if Sage trembled or if the swinging lantern in her hand cast odd shadows. Divine drew her face closer to Saph's ear.

"Should we check Sylus's room first?" Divine whispered.

Saph patted Divine's hand. "We've got this. I'll bring the might, remember?"

And I'll bring the delusions. Divine shook her head but let Saph enter the hallway first before whispering over her shoulder at the plant. "We'll be fine. Stay here."

Cautiously they entered the hallway and crept down the stairs. The city was quiet in the pre-dawn. Faint light from the streetlamps cast grey shadows through the windows in the empty tavern, making the chairs look larger and less like chairs. The strand of tiny lanterns at the window undermined the severity of the situation with the twinkling glow.

Divine let Saph lead them from the steps toward the low-burning fire with her axe gripped in one hand. Saph paused and they both swiveled their heads, listening. Several crashes came louder and closer this time.

"It's coming from the kitchen," Saph whispered.

She crept closer to the swinging door and Divine took a calming breath, readying her magic as she kept Saph's body between her and the kitchen. Divine let a cooling breeze brush her mind and her heart slowed to a normal pace. A soft trail of rose tinted the air, no stronger than someone who had dabbed their wrists with rose oil before a date. Divine crinkled her nose. Could she no longer sense danger, or were they safe?

Not willing to draw a card blindly, Divine *reached* into her well and filled an imaginary bucket, holding it just at the rim between *there* and the physical world, that in-between place where her magic existed. Saph raised her axe to grip it in both hands before her chest, then kicked the door in. Divine released her pail of magic into a shield around them.

The door rebounded from the hard swing and yellow eyes shined back.

Divine shrieked, raising the lantern. Light fell across the floor and a cacophony ensued. Divine's free hand shot up and covered one ear. Small bundles of cream and white fur scurried around, knocking tins across the floor like a game of frost-stone chase, banging into other metallic debris as their green and black quills scratched against pots and pans that had fallen to the floor. Several were oblivious, scooping five-toed paws into their mouths with clumps from spilled ingredients.

"They've chewed holes in everything!" Saph's axe dropped to her side. She sighed, her shoulders sagging. Her voice was quieter when she spoke again. "How did dunarus get in here? Don't they live on Solhavn?"

Divine stiffened. This was her fault. It was too specific to be a coincidence.

Saph squatted, poking at the bags that were trickling their contents like an hourglass.

"They got into the snowshrooms. The flour. Shit, and the tea. Everything on the bottom shelf."

She tapped a nearby pokey puff with the butt of her axe, and it moved out of her way. Several trembled in a corner, staring at Divine with their close-set eyes, nibbling on their front paws.

"It's me," Divine whispered.

"Temples be knocked. There goes opening Steeped in Sapphire during the festival."

Divine's eyes burned. "It's my fault."

"What's that?" Saph pushed one of the dunarus toward its companions with the flat of her blades before rising.

Prying her focus from the creatures, Divine forced herself to meet Saph's eye as she blinked back frustrated tears.

"I thought about them earlier and how silly they'd look crawling in the window and, and, and here they are!"

She motioned toward the opened window that led into the alley space between the Sultry Sapphire and Treasures and Troves of Trelvania, Otto's pawn and second-hand shop. Divine sniffled and brushed her nose.

"Oh darling, it's not your fault." Saph pulled Divine close, wrapping her arms around Divine's waist. "Me or Sylus must have just left the window open. Or someone's playing a trick for the season."

"And this very non-Iramont, not even Trelvanian, creature happens to come in?"

"I'll admit that is odd. But isn't there an unusual animals vendor part of the festival? They probably just got loose."

Divine frowned. Saph wasn't listening to her. "And came here? Why not the Dragon's Egg or the Exotic Meats, or or the Flutterwing Inn. Your idea is ruined and it's all my fault."

She blinked and a tear from each eye finally escaped.

"Hey, hey," Saph soothed, brushing Divine's cheeks with the back of her hand. "It's a setback, sure. Look, the tins are unopened. We probably have enough for tomorrow morning and then we see what ingredients we can find in the city."

Divine let Saph pull their bodies together and Divine laid her head on Saph's shoulder.

"There's been a lot going on up here"—Saph kissed the top of Divine's head—"trying to figure out how your magic works now and who you want to be. Don't go carrying the weight of everyone's problems, too. That's the old Soulshield."

"I just wanted to help," Divine said, her lips brushing Saph's neck.

Suddenly, Divine was lifted. She gripped Saph's shoulders tighter, feeling Saph's hands beneath her. Then she was sitting on a counter, Saph narrowing her uncovered eye at her as she leaned close. Her lips brushed Divine's as Saph's hands pressed, stroking the inside of one of Divine's thighs. Her hand moved up then around, gripping Divine's left hip. Air left her lungs like she'd been knocked back and Divine wrapped her legs around Saph, her hands finding the back of Saph's head and running her fingers through her loose hair. Saph pulled Divine's top lip between her teeth and flutterwings took flight from Divine's stomach into her chest, beating their pairs of spear wings. She moaned into Saph's mouth, bucking her hips closer. Saph deepened the kiss before pulling back, out of breath.

"You do help." Saph kissed the tip of Divine's nose. "The tea tasting, decorating the tavern. And you are the best distraction." Teasingly, Saph traced the line where Divine's leg connected to her hip.

The touch was intoxicating, and Divine squeezed her legs tighter around Saph. The bar owner chortled, then lightly unhooked Divine's legs.

"More distractions soon. And this is the kitchen. But first, there's a mess to clean. I'll go get a broom. It's probably out by the bar. Maybe I can push the dunarus out with it..."

Divine bit her lip to hide her disappointment. Twice in a matter of hours Saph had teased her to want her, to crave her, only to put the tavern first. The swinging door sang its whooshing sound as Saph pushed through, and Divine hopped down from the counter.

"You've been very upsetting." Divine huffed at the dunarus. There had to be at least a dozen. She watched the creatures dart across the floor, finding new pots to hide behind or friends to cower beside. Divine softened, her body deflating and she knelt on the floor. "But you're probably scared, huh?"

The nearest dunaru wiggled its nose and crept closer. Divine let herself retreat into her well, drinking of the coolness there, and sent the feeling out into the room. More dunarus padded across the floor, their round middles seeming to sway in dance with their movement. Divine reached out her hand and one of them sniffed her hand.

"What are we going to do with you? I don't suppose you all could climb back out the window and go home?"

Divine blinked. Did the dunaru nod? The creatures curled around and lined up two-by-two and began climbing the shelves. Several joined the cluster from the still dark adjacent storage space.

"Right where I—" Saph's statement cut short and she let out a low whistle. "I was trying to be supportive, but I was being an ass, wasn't I? This is you—your new magic?"

"I don't know." Divine shook her head as the dunarus jumped to higher shelves and over to the window frame, then out into the growing morning. "There's more. I haven't told you everything that's been happening."

"More than inviting balls of fur for a late-night snack? Sorry, ignore that. Humor as a coping strategy only works if the other person is laughing too. Sweetheart"—Saph knelt beside Divine—"what's going on?"

Divine put her head in her hands. "I don't think I'm done with the Goddesses."

CHAPTER SEVEN

Foggy and Flir-tea

"I know I don't feel that way about these other people. Not like I feel about you. It makes me itchy *and* it feels good. Deities, it feels *good*. Like I have more power when they...I don't know, appreciate me?" Divine paced in front of the bar. "And look at her."

She gestured toward the decacacti in her pot on the bar. The dirt within squelched.

"Sorry. Him. Sage, do you want to be warmer?"

The plant creature crackle-hummed, his thorns trembling subtly.

"Did you hear that?" She carried the pot over to the fireplace and sat it down on the nearest table. All ten tentacles twitched as the stem swayed gently.

"No, but I see *that*." Saph pointed.

Divine resumed pacing, chewing the nail of her thumb. "I think...I think I can understand creatures. There was this moment in the alley with a squirrel, and I thought I heard a bird tell me good morning. Sage looks like a plant but he's an animal."

"That's not as surprising as I thought it was going to be." Saph shrugged. "Interesting. But after the dunarus I—"

"The Goodly One said to seek him out if I wanted to know more about talismans or that term 'Old Soul'. But he's only here on Wind's Days. No wait, maybe it's his God that's here on Wind's Days?"

Stopping, Divine looked at the ceiling and the newest decorations; baskets dangled long lengths of glossy variegated green leaves. She'd told Saph everything. The dreams and hallucinating Madeline, the encounters with animals she could remember in her past, and her sleepy conversation with Sage. And how people had been making her feel.

She rubbed the back of her neck, then began pacing once more.

"The Goodly One knew, Saph. He knew what was going to happen. He said this feeling is unique to an Old Soul. Did I see him on a Wind's Day, though?" Divine groaned. "And Listhinci hinted they might know something related to talismans. Is all of this because I remade mine? But I let Listhinci sail off to warm beaches and citrus drinks."

Saph sat on a stool, leaning an arm on the bar. "You're cute when you're flustered. All winded sentences. Come here." She patted the stool next to her.

Divine blew air at her forehead even though red hair hadn't gotten in her eyes.

"What do you want out of all of this?" Saph asked as Divine sat next to her.

"To understand what's happening to me. And what to do about it."

"Now, I might not be able to tell a deity from a sideways sneeze, but it seems like you have two options. Either you ignore what's happening, and hope things start to make sense. Or you seek out answers, and you *make* things make sense."

Divine stared at the charms on her boots, the small creatures and flowers waiting expectantly. *And why. I want to know why Madeline needed me for her scheme.*

"But the Midwinter Nights Faire."

"You'll do your research during daylight, right? We'll still have time to enjoy the festivities. It's a night faire after all."

"I mean Steeped in Sapphire. If I'm hunting for answers, I won't be helping here."

"Without supplies, that's not much of an issue. I'll hunt tea ingredients while you hunt your answers. Unless you want me to come with you, which I'm happy to do."

"No." Divine's voice rose and she flinched. "I mean, you by my side is always welcomed but then I'd be taking time away from your tea venture."

Divine didn't want to cause any more issues for Saph. If that meant she stepped into the city again, alone...again.

Then so be it. This was Divine's fault and if she hadn't stayed in Iramont, Saph would have had her tea shop ready for the festival week.

"Then it's settled." Saph draped her arm over Divine's shoulder. "Let's get a little rest before our first tea adventure in the morning. Everything will work out. The best adventures happen when you least expect them."

* * *

Once the sun began to rise, Divine and Saph prepped the tavern for the morning tea.

Divine kept checking the small tins beneath the bar like they were newborns that could turn over and suffocate at any moment. Containing the last of their tea blends, they were precious. There was maybe enough for five cups of each. The Passionate's Pyre was active on the counter, bringing the first pot of water to boiling in preparation for eager tea drinkers.

Sage's pot sat on the mantle above the fireplace, nestled between longer branches of pine that shot out from the main braided garland. Divine felt like he stared at her. Glancing at the door to confirm no one was about to enter, Divine crossed the tavern to the fireplace.

Based on his middle stem's height of about seven inches, Divine assumed he had only been growing for a season. Which meant while he needed water sparingly, he needed additional nutrients to grow.

Divine tilted Sage's pot, examining the gravely soil.

"We'll need to get Sage some food by the end of the week," Divine called to Saph who reappeared from the kitchen.

"Oven's heating up." Saph called back. "He needs more than water?"

"Insects mostly." Divine patted the side of Sage's pot as if to tell him he would be taken care of.

"I realize this is a bad time to recognize this, but I can't have insects hopping around in my tavern. The Iguions won't mind, but the other patrons…"

Divine stared at Sage who crackled and slurped.

"Oh, he says they don't have to be alive when I feed them to him. I suppose that would mimic what happens naturally."

"Which would be?"

"In the desert, insects would be attracted by the sap inside Sage's stems and fall victim to his thorns. Then the ant or similar creature would decompose in the soil and Sage would absorb it."

Saph clinked glass mugs together as she pulled four from the wall shelf. "What a pleasant thought before breakfast."

"He can't help how his body works." Divine touched a small area on the top of Sage's main stalk and the decacacti hunched faintly. "Thankfully the thorns have no effect on humans, besides hurting."

"Well, as long as you feed him upstairs, I don't think the bugs will be a problem."

"Hear that, Sage?" The pot sizzle-crackled. "He says thanks for letting him live. He used all his sarcasm."

"You know Sage," Saph raised her voice, "you and Syka would get along *real* well."

Divine angled away so Sage couldn't see her grin and joined Saph behind the counter.

She busied herself with gathering the rest of the supplies: stirring spoons, sugar cubes, honey jar, and towels. Her rainbow bangles clinked together, and Divine paused. She adjusted the sleeves on her bustleberry-red shirt to cover her wrists and bracelets beneath the rich woolly fabric. She didn't want too many of her talisman-distractors visible for conversation starters. Better that the patrons focused on the tea. She smoothed the fabric along her waist from her brown belt to her hips.

At eight o'clock, several regulars of the tavern opened the door, the bells Saph had added over the frame tinkling cheerfully. Unsurprisingly, they thought the tavern was open for alcohol. One stayed and the others promptly left. They were followed by a trio of older women, the tallest of them pushing the door shut behind her with her boot.

Saph touched Divine's shoulder. "We'll serve what we have and when we're out we close up."

Then she swooped toward the Steeped in Sapphire guests, her sunset print dress barely off the floor, and directed the patrons to their tables. Saph had decided not to use the longer benches unless a large group came in, so the women were placed around a smaller circular table and the single man at the edge of the fireplace. The flames crackled and popped their log song, filling the tavern with a gentle warmth.

As Divine counted out four of the small menus, the door opened again. A tan-furred Kellas and a human woman shook snow from their coats and stamped their boots and paws as they surveyed the room. Divine added two more menus to her grasp.

"Take your time." Divine delivered the same message at the two tables, handing out the menus. "There's a brew for everyone. Let me know if you have any questions. I'll be back around to take your request or help you decide."

Saph had seated the newest arrivals near a window who were hanging their coats on the back of their chairs. They took their menus from Divine as she repeated the message.

Saph disappeared through the swinging door of the kitchen.

"The decorations are very cozy," the human woman said. The faint crinkles around her eyes and mouth made her appear a bit older than Saph's age. "Not what I'd expect from a tavern."

"That's because we're a tearoom right now." Divine winked. "I hung the plants, and did the bit around the stage. Saph, the owner, did the rest."

The woman tilted her head, eyeing the cascading vegetation on the support beams. "I think it looks lovely. Especially the greenery. Well done."

Divine's stomach flickered with flutterwings. She glanced back where Saph emerged from the kitchen holding the milk jug.

"I've seen you before."

Divine refocused on the Kellas. Scanning her features, her eyes landed on a diamond shape in the fur of the Kellas's chest.

"The accordion! Thanks again for letting me play with you."

"These all sound delicious." The Kellas ran a claw down the list. "How do I decide?"

"Well, if you're feeling homesick," Divine offered, "the Snowshroom Spice might be the dash of nostalgia you need."

"I might try them all."

A large grin spread across Divine's mouth. These people were exactly what they needed. Everything was going splendidly. Promising to return, Divine shuffled over to the man by the fireplace.

"Are you ready to order, or are you waiting for anyone?" Divine asked.

Sharp cheekbones led to sculpted facial hair around his mouth and wavy hair fell to his shoulders. He reminded her of her first boyfriend.

"Oh no, I'm alone. Though relationships can spark at any time." Divine felt caught by his piercing blue eyes and how they lingered on her face. "I am charmed by you ladies."

The emotions in the room grew; excitement and a sort of longing or thirst. Divine tried to push it to the back of her mind but it tickled her insides.

"How do you mean?" Divine asked, feeling her cheeks warm.

"To offer something new in this place, that takes courage. My companions weren't brave enough to stay. But I like trying new things. Get 'steeped in sapphire' by...what's your name?"

"Divine," she answered, touching her labradorite feather clip in her hair and silently cursing and praising the sign out front for catching people's attention.

His eyes widened almost imperceptibly, and a smirk tugged the corner of his mouth.

"I'd like to taste your"—he dropped his gaze to the menu— "Divine-i-tea."

"Well," Divine's voice cracked as she took the menu from him. "I'll get you steeped. I mean your tea. I'll get it steeping."

She cringed and Sage's pot crackled in soil-touched amusement as Divine headed toward the women's table.

Was the fire too hot? She fanned herself with the menu as she smiled at the trio. If he was a regular of the tavern, he was probably used to Saph's flirtation. Nothing else to it.

"Are these hand pies from the Dragon's Egg?" the closest woman asked, pointing to the menu item for the mince and egg pies.

"Yes, but they are made specifically for us. They're smaller, more bite sized. And they have more dried herbs from the Iramont gardens."

"Oh wonderful! I'm always trying new things. I was just telling Kristy, wasn't I dear, that the sign out front was new and we had to see about this tea."

"Yes, very clever." The second woman, Kristy, covered half of her face with the menu as if sharing a secret. "You'll want to set yourselves apart from the competition. No sense having the same stuff."

"The place could use a bit more...sparkle." The third woman's voice dripped with disinterest, but the emotions Divine detected were positive like the others. "But let's judge the taste, shall we? I'll try the Foggy Iramont."

The other two women placed their orders, including an egg pie each, and Divine rejoined Saph at the bar.

"I think it's going well," Divine whispered excitedly to Saph as she measured out tea blends for four guests. Dark leaves, purple lavender buds, brown tarrow root, and bits of chocolate floated in the mugs to create two Foggy Iramonts, a Divine-i-tea, and a Snowshroom Spice.

"The truth will reveal in about five minutes. I'll get their food."

While the tea steeped, Divine refilled the boilspout at the bar and placed it on the Passionate's Pyre to boil then approached the final table. The Kellas ordered a

Snowshroom Spice to start and his friend ordered a Divine-i-tea.

"Does this work like the tavern?" the Kellas asked. "We open a tab and pay after all of our drinks?"

Tucking the menus under her arm, Divine chuckled. "How much tea do you plan to drink?"

The Kellas's whiskers twitched. "All of it."

"Tell you what. If you want to try all of the drinks, I'll give you a buy-one-get-two-free deal for this visit. After that, you'll have to pay for your addiction." Then she whispered, "They're that good."

The Kellas purred. "You are very kind. Claws! I could not remember when I was playing our music. Now I know where I had seen you before that. You're the healer that visits the Edge."

Roses bloomed around her, so sweet and full Divine almost could taste the scent on her tongue. It gave her an idea for another tea but, the Kellas continued, breaking the wisp of a thought.

"Thank you. When others turn away, you see us. I will tell everyone about your place here. We must spend our friggons at businesses that make themselves allies."

Chest full, Divine returned to the bar, passing Saph who carried a tray of miniature pies. She grinned at Saph and barely suppressed her urge to skip.

Swapping the towels out for plates, Divine set the strainers aside to use for the next steeping. They'd found that it took two times before the flavor weakened, more so with the snowshroom than the black tea leaves but it would make it easier to remember if two mugs was the maximum for all of the blends.

Sounds of enjoyment floated from the women as they bit into their breakfast. The milk splashed in a tendrilled cloud through the brown liquid as Divine poured. The air was heavy and sweet. She slid the mugs over to Saph, who had jumped up on the bar and swiveled to the other side.

"Next time we set up at the end near the kitchen so we don't have to keep walking around this thing." Saph tapped her fist on the wood.

Divine nodded at the mugs with milk. "Want to get me frothy?"

"Always."

While Saph whipped the mugs into a frothy foam, Divine added the final ingredients to the other mugs, humming a common Midwinter Night's tune and tapping the mugs with the back of the rings on her middle and index fingers with the rhythm. A sugar cube for the mugs with bronzed liquid that had foamed during the steeping, and a dollop of honey with a sprinkle of cinnamon for the Snowshroom Spice.

Divine transferred the finished teas to a tray to deliver. "Can you start two more mugs, please. You beautiful genius of liquid pleasures. Divine-i-tea and Snowshroom."

Saph chuckled. "You doing alright? It's not too much for you? I know we're both tired."

"Tired?" Divine grabbed the tray. "Never better."

"Two of every brew so far?"

"Sounds like a poem waiting to be written," Divine threw over her shoulder as she approached the trio of women.

The door to the tavern opened as Divine sat the third mug down.

"Be right *steep* you." Divine called, then laughed. "Actually, find any table you like."

Divine glanced at Sage before setting down the Divine-i-tea at the solo man's table then leaned her arm on the mantel near the decacacti.

"I was not. I was humming. It's called music."

"What's that?" the man with the icy blue eyes inquired.

Divine stepped away from the mantel. "Oh, I was just thinking that we needed some music. Something calm and cozy."

"I bet you have a lovely singing voice."

Before she knew what was happening, Divine began to sing the words to the song she'd hummed. Her lungs filled with blossoms of summer, sweet nectar on her tongue and petal-rouge on her cheeks and she felt like she could reach out her well would trickle from her pores. This had to be her magic. In the back of her mind, she heard the warning of dissonant chords, but she tightened her hold on the pleasing melody and let it steer her through waves of delight and admiration.

The next moments were a blur.

She twirled around the tables, picked up the remaining drinks and delivered them to the beat of her song. Her magic filled her nose with the perfume of a full garden as the patrons clapped. She sat at the table with the newest guests and made them laugh, rising to share an amusing story with the rest of the room. At some point she'd refilled the Kellas with her second tea, though she had no memory of it. The tavern vibrated with compliments and joy. Synchronized, her magic well spilled over the brim.

Divine blinked. She gawked at orbs of blue, leaning on her elbows in the tray across from him. *How long have I been staring at him?*

He didn't look like a frightening agent with mind-muddling powers, or a servant like her with empathetic influence, but she couldn't remember sitting down. Then the thought floated away like a flutterwing.

"Do you play cards?" she asked. "My friends could probably stare a place for you."

The man quirked a smile at her slip and leaned closer. "Will you be there?"

A soft touch at her elbow and Divine's focus drifted up the arm to its owner. An eye patch and a green eye watched her curiously.

"Why don't you take a break?" Saph asked. "I've got this."

Divine looked around the tavern. Everyone watched her. She could *feel* their focus and their interest. Was Saph jealous? Jealous that Divine was the center of attention in her bar instead of herself?

"Fine," Divine grumbled, handing the tray to Saph.

People liked her. Why did Saph have to ruin it? Divine retreated upstairs and into the room she shared with Saph. She slammed the door. And immediately regretted it.

"What am I doing?" she bemoaned, plopping down on the axe print blanket. Saph wasn't trying to steal attention. She was trying to help her. Oh Goddess, had she been flirting with everybody?

That isn't me. But I liked it. I loved the feeling. What is happening to me?

She grabbed her coat and raced down the stairs. Calling out that she would be back soon, Divine left the Sultry Sapphire and the Steeped in Sapphire crowd with the sound of Sage's crackling slurp.

* * *

The streets were bustling with people getting ready for the first night of the festival. Divine wove between individuals carrying baskets with decorations, gifts, and dinner ingredients. Her insides still vibrated though with each step, each breath, the feeling lessened.

It's like my magic is everywhere. Like I can use more than just the well joined to my talisman. But that's impossible.

By the time she reached the Market District, its center flowed with people. Some had come to look at the fountain, which still displayed an image of Solhavn in its base layer. The cascading water had frozen, capturing the illusion of movement. Others looked through the windows of the shops and read signs on the doors indicating what their special offering during the Midwinter Nights Faire was going to be. Whether a sale or a limited available item, the shops would close early and not open until the evening in celebration of the first festival night. Then, many of them would hold extended hours to participate. One of the signs in Flitch's Stitches read 'Midwinter Scavengers Piece Three Here' and Divine wondered what event the shop with blankets and scarves hanging in the window would be a part of.

Divine hunted the crowd for a closely cropped head in an autumn-colored robe, expecting him to stand spouting platitudes with his robe's fabric the same as before, draped over one shoulder and the opposite forearm despite the cold. When she found no one dressed like a Goodly One or proclaiming the beliefs of the God of Virtue, she knew she had to go to the one place she last wanted to see.

CHAPTER EIGHT

Searching for a Goodly One

Above Divine loomed the violet arches of the Holy District. The three decorated gateways were imperceptibly different than in the fall—if someone didn't stop to examine.

Divine's chin tilted up as she inspected each feature. The waterfall on the highest corner of the third arch was a frozen curve ending a foot above the ground; vines along the edge of the connecting wall bloomed with orange and yellow trumpet-like flowers, unlike the rest of the dormant vines in the city; a sea dragon made of spinning gears raised and lowered its head behind the nearest arch's mermaid; a sun and a moon clashed on the middle arc, with the moon having the higher space.

Normally, Divine would have appreciated the artistry of the arches that stretched as tall as Leafy, and found solace, if not purpose, through them. Now, the arches symbolized obstacles to certainty and veiled lies. Divine took a deep breath and walked beneath them, her boots quiet on the cobbled street.

She stepped out of the archway, and her attention landed on the highest spires and domed chambers. The biggest, most popular deities' temples were in the distance, her own the largest and not a decoration for the season in sight. Divine snapped her gaze to closer temples, not willing to give the Goddess of Souls her attention. Most of the holy buildings remained as usual, with a few donning strings of lanterns.

To her left stood a modest building behind a plain iron fence. Divine veered toward the square temple, surveying the steeply pitched roof as she drew closer. Alternating panels formed the walls, and they appeared to have once been painted, though only the top halves under the eaves retained weathered orange and red.

Stopping at the door, Divine tugged the sleeves of her coat down over her wrists, then rapped her knuckles on the colorful symbol of the God of Virtue. Interwoven links cradled a rainbow stone ensconced by a kite-like bezel.

A moment passed, then the door groaned inward. Divine's breath caught.

"May His Hand of Virtue treat you fairly," the doorkeeper intoned.

He wore familiar autumn-colored folds and a pendant the same as the symbol on the door. But his head was shaven.

Divine bent forward. "We haven't met before, have we?"

He didn't need to answer as Divine felt his confusion before he spoke.

"No," she added. "Obviously we have not. I am looking for a servant, a Goodly One. He was recruiting in the merchant district in the fall."

The man pressed his hands together. "I do not know who that could be. We usually do not do any outreach."

"Is there a log of activity you could check or someone else we could ask?"

"I suppose First Servant of Virtue, Constance, but he is out. Though, it would be highly irregular if someone was seeking followers. Can you tell me what he looks like?"

Divine gestured with her palm up. "Like you, only he wasn't completely bald? I'm sorry, I only met him once but...I'd like to speak with him again."

"I can take your name and see if anyone remembers talking to you," he offered.

"Thanks, but I never gave him my name." She laughed. "This is starting to sound absurd. Let me start over. I'm Divine. Could I come in?"

"I am Longsuffering. We welcome all souls who seek to bring goodness to the world."

Divine blinked. "Did you say Longsuffering? I know servants choose a name after confirmation that represents a virtue but..."

"We have had to get creative." Longsuffering blushed. "Too many Hopes and Graces of the past. We now must have a unique name while we are in service."

"Well, I hope that your name is not your fortune."

"If it means it is not someone else's, then I accept the exchange." He stepped back. "Do you come to us with charity, understanding, and love?"

Divine nodded, and he motioned for her to enter. As they moved into the space, Longsuffering familiarized Divine with the areas they passed. Divine searched the faces in each for the Goodly One she sought. Everything was connected by open doorways from the main area with its central garden, to areas with sleeping cots, and a small library. By the time they circled back to the entrance, Divine's hope had dropped as heavy stones to her boots. There was no sign of the one she wanted to speak to.

Suddenly, a wooden panel popped open on what had looked like a length of wall.

"Cleanliness!" Longsuffering chastised. "We have a guest."

The one called Cleanliness with cropped brown hair appeared to be mopping a room and, eyes wide, she flung the panel shut behind her, but not before Divine caught sight of several human-adjacents.

Divine addressed Longsuffering. "I won't tell anyone. I actually offer a healing clinic in the Edge...mainly for human-adjacents. Unsanctioned by the Goddess of Souls."

"These are families." Cleanliness nodded. "Though the Edge was to be their home, Agents of Condemnation continue to parole the area, scaring the children with illusions. We offer them respite under our First Servant's request. If only some of the other First Servants would advocate for change, we would not have to sneak these souls into our embrace."

Divine's stomach soured. Arosia, too, had its dark alleys, like the predominant belief that human-adjacents could not be blessed by the deities. But she never heard of agents troubling children. The more she explored Iramont, the further the need for change solidified in her resolve. But how? First, she had to fix whatever was breaking inside her magic.

"I thank you for your time," Divine said, bowing her head. "May His Hand of Virtue treat you fairly."

"And you." Then as she approached the door he added, "Several of our members have traveled to Arosia and Pariatan. Perhaps the person you seek is there. You are welcome to return any time. I wish you the blessings you would see on your neighbors."

Divine parted from the temple door, then paused as a thought struck.

"Does your God visit you on Wind's Days?"

"What do you mean?"

Mostly on Wind's Days, the Goodly One had said. *He likes to check in with the God of Storms.*

"Does he come down from Zenith to visit your temple?"

"The God of Virtue promotes kindness by always being in our hearts."

"That's probably a no," Divine mumbled. "Thanks again."

She watched the door slowly close, her only option seeming to come back another time. She had to find him, she couldn't just give up. Feeling the urgency to find the answers she needed like they were trapped bubbles needing relief, she surveyed the Holy District.

Amongst the undecorated temples, the temples of the sponsors of the Midwinter Nights Faire held nothing back.

Flurries from the Goddess of Frosted Wilderness had frozen spouts of water in different shapes, from flower stems to intricate spirals. Gentle snow floated around the A-shaped construction, staying close as if a shield prevented them from visiting a neighboring temple. Lights glowed from inside, and the glass panels making the front façade seemed to sparkle. Divine spotted several of their Temple's winter inventions displayed in the lot leading to the entrance; teardrop shoes for walking on snow, though the Flurries naturally never sunk into deep snow, and long runners used on sleds.

The Trickers, on the other hand, had lived up to their deity's name. Light seemed to escape from every crack of the temple to make it glow even in daylight. But the walkway leading up to the entrance had strings that served as tripwires to dump boxes on unsuspecting victims—fish, Divine detected in her magic—or spring forth odd mannequins of mythical creatures. There was a sign that read "Happy Birthday, Breston", as if that was the current celebration.

Like a betraying boat, Divine's feet glided her deeper into the Holy District and to the temple of the God of Storms. Clouds swirled in the domed roof, punctuated by sporadic flashes of lightning.

"This is stupid." Shaking her head, she pivoted and barreled into an orange chest, knocking herself back a pace. "Oh, I'm sorry—"

"Hello, Divine. I hope Virtue has guided your actions in generosity since we last met."

She touched her throat. The Goodly One she sought had grey-blue eyes. That was the detail she hadn't remembered. His dark hair was still closely cropped. Had he had that smirk before? Certainly, she would have noticed the skip it caused her stomach to make.

Divine tugged her coat straighter. "I don't recall giving you my name, as neither did you to me."

"Constance. I am your servant." He dipped his head. "And no, your name I discerned through magic."

"That's right. You said you Goodly Ones can feel intent since you're"—Divine struggled to find the words—"connected to all wells."

"Yes, something like that. We are connected to the source of all magic."

Divine placed her right hand on her hip. "Did you *feel* that I was looking for you? Is that why you're here now?"

"Something like that." A playful smile tugged at the corner of his mouth and Divine couldn't help but let her face mirror the expression. "It's like a crest of a wave rising out of your well and I see it. Not that different from how you feel others' emotions, I would guess."

"Wait. If your name is Constance, you're the First Servant?"

"Precisely."

Now it made sense. Why he knew so much about talismans and magic. He was the leader of the temple of the God of Virtue. Judging by the tautness of the skin of his clean-shaven face, he was not much older than Divine. And his eyes captured the sun's rays in bright glistening splashes.

"You're fairly young for that sort of position."

Constance shrugged, shifting the cloth around his shoulders. Instead of the draped sleeve, the cloth had been unfolded and wrapped around his back and arms like a cloak.

"We do things differently in my temple. But tell me, what is a Soulshield doing at the God of Storms' temple?"

"Something you said last time made me think I might find you here."

"Oh?"

"But I don't want to bother you. Maybe you can get one of the other Goodly Ones to answer my questions about talismans and Old Souls."

A flicker of surprise passed on his face before he settled his expression. "I can help, it is no bother. As I said, we do things differently. Walk with me."

Constance escorted her to the back of the temple of the Goddess of Words. Silence pressed on her ears as Constance led them into a hedge maze of round sculpted shrubs. Feeding the bushes with certain mixtures could cause their needles to change colors, and these were a pale lavender. Acutely aware of the swishing of fabric and the sound of her hair brushing her shoulders, Divine tried not to breathe too loudly.

At the center of the maze were several benches and a wooden swing beneath a trellis. Beyond the height of the hedge peered the temples of the Holy District through bare-leaf trees and clumps of evergreens. The place felt removed from Iramont's eye.

Brushing powdered snow from the wood, Constance sat on the swing, and Divine sat next to him.

"This hedge"—Constance pointed to the shrubbery—"creates a bubble that traps sound and diminishes its effect. I find it perfect for self-reflection. Please, tell me what has made you seek my knowledge."

"Oof. Where to begin. Do you remember how I wanted to use you as my talisman? I ended up recovering mine. But then, I severed its connection and made a new one."

Constance's eyebrows raised. "Interesting. Go on."

Divine told Constance about following the map from a chest, how Madeline had lured her to the prison of the First Soul, how Divine had called upon fish in the lake to aid her and how she could summon Leafy, and the way her talisman's scent had been predicting danger.

"And now everything is...weird. I think I might be able to understand animals. And when people praise me, my magic flares." Divine groaned. "I started flirting with a whole group of people because of the way I felt. Tell me you know what's happening to me."

"Talismans are inhibitors." Constance rubbed his chin. "Despite what the temple leaders claim, they are not necessary. Yes, they help you discover your well, focus that connection and therefore control your power, but only for a small classification of magic. When you 'confirm' with a temple, you bind yourself to that deity. This locks your magic to be the same as the deity. And the deity's power gets stronger. With every binding, with every worshipper. And a servant loses the ability to use all other magic."

Madeline and whoever she had been working with were taking talismans to redistribute the power. At least, that's what her ex had said. Divine hadn't wanted to believe her, or think about her since, and had put the thought to the back of her mind. For all of her declarations of having enough of the Goddesses, the topic continued to plague her.

"So without a talisman, I could—we all could use each type of magical skill?"

"It doesn't change that not everyone can access magic, or what their level of ability will be. Magic users have an affinity." Constance gestured with his hands as if he held invisible items in each. "Some magic that they are naturally slightly better at. And typically, someone chooses a temple that aligns with that magic without knowing. But when they create their talisman, that specific connection becomes stronger, and binds itself to the deity. The deity gets to use your well, but you get a boost to your affinity. Specialization while everything else becomes inaccessible."

Constance squished his hands together then wiped the palms of his hands on the fabric at his knees.

"When I remade my talisman, I didn't focus on the Goddess of Souls. I focused on what I wanted to do with my magic."

"Which may be why you are experiencing the ability to use magic outside of your temple's affinity."

Divine scrunched her brow. "But I've always been able to heal more than what my temple says I can." She thought of examples, like the fish in her childhood, and the bird at her single-person habitspace in Arosia.

Constance raised a finger, the movement shifting his arm out of the fabric. Divine expected to see a scrawny arm but found a toned arm much like her own.

"This is where I have a theory," he offered. "You may be an Old Soul. The simplest explanation I can offer is that your...ancestry has led you to not need a talisman to focus your magic. You're accessing it the old way, the natural way. Though I would need to observe you."

Madeline had said something about Divine's family too. *Even if you have the lineage.* Divine had spent time with her grandparents and cousins, mostly on special occasions, but any further back in the family lines she didn't know much. What did her family have to do with this?

"Without a talisman, I would be able to access all magic?"

"I think in theory, yes. There is really only one way to know for sure, but I do not have the tools."

"The First Servant of Souls here said there might be information in Arosia's Souls temple about the creation of that...thing I fought. The First Soul. Could that help? The temple wants me to come back."

"Hmm. It may give you peace of mind to understand more about how you are connected to this plot with the First Soul and why your adversaries sought you specifically. But I give caution—anything your temple wants will not be from an altruistic stance."

Divine already suspected that, but it stung just the same.

Constance leaned forward, his palms pressed together and his fingers angled toward Divine. "Do you want to go back?"

Divine looked at her clasped mittens in her lap. "Madeline said my mother was in the archives. I don't know which archives, but my mother never went outside our home province of Arosia except when she visited Solhavn. I could look in Arosia."

"But do you *want* to go home?"

Divine thought of her accordion in her room. The familiar streets and the carrier vessels coming up the Arosia River with their deliveries. She could advocate for the human-adjacents by appearing before the Holicratic Ruling Council. She'd have access to an assortment of ingredients for Saph's tea to bring back. And answers. But the journey would take months. Saph had her tavern to take care of and didn't like long travel. Would Saph miss her if she left? When she got back to Arosia, would Divine get sucked back into Soulshield work and never come back?

She dropped her chin to her chest and whispered, "I don't know."

"You don't need to make a decision now. Think on it. What brings you the most peace is your choice to make."

"But how do I control whatever it is now? I'm influencing creatures to eat Saph's supplies and who knows what I might accidentally do next."

"I think I could help you."

"And these feelings that make my judgement go sideways? They're acceptable when Saph and I are, uh, well, they're just not great in the middle of serving tea."

Constance bowed his head. "Control and discipline are also things I can help you with. Though, I believe it would benefit us both to confirm or disprove my theories before too long."

"Why? Would that change your answer?"

"It would help me guide you best. Would you be willing to show me your abilities now?"

Divine nodded. Constance rose, lifting his robe into a hood and she followed.

They exited the maze, the sounds of the area returning in the faint murmur of the districts and the wind scratching the nearby trees, and traversed the Holy District toward the exit. They passed other temple-goers dressed in their winter coats and walked beneath the arches.

"If the deities—" she hesitated as Constance motioned for her to keep her voice down. "If they take our power, why were you recruiting new followers when I met you? You're a part of the system."

Constance held out his arms. "Do you see any talismans?"

Come to think of it, he wore no jewelry except his God's pendant. "They could be under your clothes."

He chuckled. "You'll have to take my word for it. There are none wrapped around my other body parts."

"I didn't mean—" Divine coughed, choking on a hasty explanation.

"I like how you say things without dwelling on them beforehand. I noticed that previously. What I wanted to say is that my temple—"

"Does things differently?"

"You're starting to understand."

"Taking a sip of hot tea is different than guzzling it," she muttered.

"When you are like a talisman, people want to use you. The God of Virtue does not wish his servants to be used, not even by him."

Constance led them past the storage buildings and the cemetery and out of the east gate. A garden there bordered a small patch of forest that began the Appleblossom Woods. Posts of field fencing gathered snow at its base where wind had made tiny drifts, and blew through large holes in need of fixing. Several blue and black birds perched on the top but took flight into the trees. Dried shoots from old growth poked out of the snow.

"Though it is winter, there should be plenty of little creatures around here. Birds, rodents, insects. Let me see your depth and reach."

Constance paused near a bench flanked by boxes likely holding community farming tools by the side of the road.

Divine blew out a breath, a visible plume of air wafting away from her mouth. She focused on the ripples in her well, the gentle lapping at the distant edges as she stirred her magical source with a mental finger.

Roses mixed with spiced apples assaulted her senses, and she fought back a sneeze.

Danger. Harm. Hurt.

Divine spun. Constance bent over one of the boxes. Like a pirate's treasure, it tempted with golden edges that weren't there before.

"Don't touch it! It's a mockingcrate."

His hand froze. The lid of the chest opened, revealing rows of teeth.

Divine pushed a wave of her magic, covering Constance with a shield. A tentacle tongue lashed out, hitting the barrier. Constance didn't flinch. Beneath the chest's bottom emerged legs.

"Command it to go," Constance directed. He stood tall, arms at his sides and his face clear of worry. His eyes found hers and she sensed his trust. A heady scent of honeysuckle drifted into the floral bouquet.

Reaching into her well, Divine allowed her magic to move through her like a warm drink.

"Go back to the forest. Please."

The mockingcrate hesitated, then the panels of the treasure chest rearranged. It rolled away looking suspiciously like a fallen statue.

Divine released the shield and walked to Constance.

"You alright?" she asked.

He bent his head. "Thanks to you."

"Did that get you what you wanted?"

"It certainly helped. We should start with the control I mentioned."

His eyebrows arched and he raised his chin indicating over Divine's shoulder. She pivoted and tried to sink further into her coat's hood. Birds and scurrying creatures with bushy tails followed the path of the mockingcrate toward the wood. Acutely aware of how her coat got its warmth, Divine vowed to shop only fake fur in the future.

Inside the city, singing bells clanged and dinged in beautiful harmony.

Divine took a step toward the sound. "The festival begins."

Several hours were left before sunset, but the ringing of the bells signaled the opening of Midwinter Nights Faire. Saph was probably wondering where she was.

"We'll start with targeting your emotions and thoughts. And," he added taking her hand, "think about returning to Arosia. If my theory is correct, you may not believe it, coming from me. The proof you need to believe me may be what your mother found—what your ex knew that your mother found. Though I hope with time you come to trust me."

Divine looked down at their connected hands. Could he sense the conflicting swirls of thoughts she had? Before she could figure out if what she was feeling was because of the changes in her magic, or the storm of her thoughts, he let go.

"I need to get back." Divine rubbed her hands together. "I've got to get ready for tonight."

"Meet me here tomorrow morning."

She nodded and watched him walk toward Iramont. Her mind felt as full as a spring burrow and if she learned one more thing about the pantheon or magic right now, the contents of her stomach would land on her boots. She pushed everything to the back of her mind. A date waited for her at the Sultry Sapphire and a night of surprises. Saph had refused to plan what they would do first, stressing that spontaneous dates were her favorite. Divine couldn't wait to see Iramont lit up at night and explore what the faire had to offer. Divine hoped Saph was just as excited.

CHAPTER NINE

Midwinter Nights

"Damn. Maybe we skip the festival."

Though the tavern was full of the usual merrymaking, Saph's voice was the only thing Divine heard over the beating of her heart.

Divine's hand slid down the banister as she descended, the fur of the cuff of her long cream coat warm against her wrist. She couldn't stop the grin that spread across her face.

With each step she felt the sway of her hips peek through the split fabric of her deep red thigh-length dress. The way Saph watched her warmed Divine's belly. Just like the shop owner said. Divine's legs looked longer to her in her new charcoal leggings, the golden stripe tracing from her boots to her hip. The fur-lined hood heavy at her back seemed to nudge her confidently forward.

When she could finally extract her gaze from Saph's heated stare, Divine's breath caught as she took in Saph. She wore a dress of frosty blue that gathered at her waist to create billowing waves at her shins in the front but hung lower behind. Silver threads sparkled along the edges in patterns of snowflakes. Though the dress enclosed Saph to mid neck, the pattern swelled at her chest from a smaller lavender corset fastened around her waist. Saph wore boots a shade darker than her dress that disappeared beneath the skirt, and she had pinned her hair up on one side, showing her hoop helix piercing.

Saph inched closer and at the last step met Divine at the bottom of the stairs.

"We will be Iramont's finest tonight." Saph traced her fingers along Divine's neckline that v'd over her breasts, brushing her skin. "You're gorgeous, my dear."

Divine stroked the silky fabric of Saph's arm. "So are you."

Like a marionette puppeteer, Saph grasped Divine's roving hand and lifted it to her lips, pressing a gentle kiss to the back of her hand, before pulling Divine deeper into the tavern.

"Sit here," Saph commanded at a table near the fireplace.

The bar owner rounded a table and stepped up onto the small stage across from the fireplace. Divine grabbed Sage from the mantel and sat in a chair, shrugging her coat off as Saph addressed the crowd.

"Keep me company," Divine whispered to the decacacti.

"From us here at the Sultry Sapphire, merry Midwinter Nights!" The tavern goers applauded and whistled. "As tradition, we will host poetry readings and games of Crossroads George every night. Tip the readers, tip the musicians, bet well, and drink lots of alcohol."

Saph raised her hands palms up, and the crowd responded by cheering louder. Divine laughed, clapping along with others nearby. She did a double take when she noticed two familiar figures at a table nearest the stairs; the agents from the night before.

The cheering died down and Saph brought out a piece of paper.

"Now, I didn't get all fancy dressed for you lot." People in the crowd chuckled. "So I'm going to read my poem first and then take this other fine lady out."

Saph pointed at Divine and the patrons pivoted, some whistling loudly. Divine gripped the sides of the pot and tried to hide behind Sage's stems.

"No, I don't like the attention," she muttered into Sage's form, but her pulse quickened in a delightful tickle. "You're right, that is a lie. I don't *want* the attention." One of Sage's stems bent toward her nose as his pot crackled. "Why? Because it's making me do weird things, like talk to you. Yes, I'll try to be more specific next time. Look, Saph is going to read."

"This poem," Saph continued, "is titled, Love is Like an Axe."

"love can cleave joy into agony
just as easily as danger into refuge
harming with one stroke
or cutting wood to boil tea
efficient contact
or wild throws
intimate
or distant

sharp!
its edges draw blood
smooth...
it reflects the moonlight
curves sensuous in focused impact

how we choose to wield it
can show us who we are"

Divine and the patrons clapped, then her eyes flicked to Sage.

"I agree, it was full of depth. No, I don't know if it was about past experiences." Sage's middle stems crossed. "Well, I'm sorry to disappoint."

Saph appeared next to the table. "Ready for our adventure?"

* * *

The lights dazzled, like magic floated everywhere and the sky was just a vase for holding memories. Strings of lanterns as large as Divine's head hung from erected poles, cascading down the length of the street in lavender, blue, and pale yellow. Businesses and shops had smaller elongated spheres hanging from their eaves or tacked to their frames. Snow softly fell, catching on eyelashes and ornamenting hair before it melted in its vanishing act. Boots crunched and laughter chimed all around.

Air tinted with fresh baked goods filled Divine's lungs, lining it with a cleansing frost that energized her as it chilled. The smell of butter and cinnamon made her mouth water.

Divine squeezed Saph's hand as they walked tethered together in the flow of faire goers. Their hands rested in a non-interlaced grip, one they had found more comfortable in longer walks when Saph's unique hand was closest. They headed toward the northern part of the city and let the stream guide them, Divine happy to take in the sights.

"I hope Sage is alright being left behind." Divine adjusted the fluffy puffs of her earmuffs over her ears to sit more comfortably. "I haven't really had a chance to bond with him."

"I'm sure the spiney fellow is warm on the mantel and enjoying poetry."

Did decacacti normally enjoy poetry, or was it just Sage?

"Sage and I liked your poem."

"High compliments from a talking plant."

"And a woman of exceptional taste." Divine bumped into Saph's shoulder. "When did you start composing poems?"

"I'm not sure which year, but it was around when I started smithing. Definitely before I lost the sight in my eye. During one of the Midwinter Nights, I decided I really liked it."

Saph nudged them around the crowd when many figures veered into an alley. Divine caught a glimpse of stalls and dangling lights and she wondered if any of the merchants from the fall would be there.

"Too many going to the bazaar," Saph explained. "Let's come back later."

They crossed the street and veered toward the northwest side of the city, passing through the Living District.

"With poetry," Saph picked up the thread of conversation, "the placement of words and the way rhymes build this feeling of anticipation—like the pause before lips touching where breath catches in the thrill of guessing if the kiss will happen. There were plenty of poems to listen to during the week of the faire and I got ideas."

If Divine recalled correctly, Saph had started smithing around the age of ten.

"You were thinking of kisses back then?"

Saph laughed. "Probably. I was interested in exploring early."

Memories of her own subdued exploration of attraction flitted through Divine's thoughts.

"I didn't mean to interrupt. Please go on."

"Not much more to say. I found it easier to communicate what is often written by trading ink for sound. Letters can contain subtleties that are missing without the author's voice. Listening to the poet, you can hear the words they want to stress. And no one had to see my shorthand. As I read it, I was in control."

When Divine had first seen Saph's shorthand, she had learned Saph had developed it in response to how her fingers had fused at birth. Saph had worn gloves in public that had an appearance of five separate digits; her parents' attempt to make her appear normal. Divine wondered if the shorthand had more to do with writing quickly in the presence of others than difficulty in gripping the writing tools that Saph had alluded to before. If it helped her not feel self-conscious, Divine was glad to help Saph by writing the Steeped in Sapphire menus.

"And then you shared it. That takes a lot of strength to share the way you think. How you...feel. With everyone."

"I didn't start immediately, saving it for those I was closest to. Once I took over and made the Sultry Sapphire, I started poetry nights. My domain. I could kick out anyone being rude. It was safe. And a lot like sex. Sometimes vulnerability, but most of the time a lot of fun."

"What happens if we combine poetry and sex?"

Saph leaned over, nipping at Divine's neck. "Darling, I cannot wait to try your brilliant idea."

Divine's stomach fluttered. She'd found something Saph hadn't tried with anyone yet, which she thought almost impossible. An experience both of them could have for the first time together. Wasn't that what couples thrived on? She wanted Saph to look forward to new adventures with her.

The Entertainment District sparkled. Every venue seemed to have their doors wide open, spilling light into the street. There were a few buildings from other districts, like restaurants and taverns, scattered amongst the buildings with musical instruments and theatres for plays. Snow continued to fall, as if the flakes were trying to always keep the streets looking pristine in that un-walked crispness of a new fallen snow. A trio of musicians stood at the next corner playing a measured fanfare, the trumpet's bell ringing crisply as an egg-shaped flute hooted a melody that Divine couldn't help but fall into step with. Her confidence rose.

"Was your poem about a past relationship?" Divine ventured.

The silence lingered and Divine turned to find Saph gazing at her. She almost repeated the question when Saph's mouth finally opened as she focused on the road ahead.

"When you're younger, you think that love is the simplest thing there could be. After all, your parents have weathered many highs and lows. I thought Elissa and I would be forever. A classic first love mistake. I held nothing back from her. But a smith's apprentice wasn't enough for her."

Divine stiffened. "Did she say that to your face?"

"What she said was even clearer. Our time had been 'fun'." Saph shrugged. "No, I think she said 'entertaining for a bit', but she was bored and her other girlfriend gave her more gifts. And to think I thought about marrying her."

Silence passed and Divine fought every ripple in her well to drape a feeling of comfort over Saph. Now some of their earlier dates became obvious—how Saph spread out revealing things about herself was a cautionary step of self-protection.

Divine squeezed Saph's hand and halted. "I think you are more than just entertaining. You are lively and the center of any gathering, but you are also kind and thoughtful and that really means more."

A shuddering breath escaped Saph and she pulled Divine close before kissing her forehead. She pointed up the street where the main avenue led to the north gate and Divine agreed to the course. She recognized some faces just from being in the city, or visitors to the Sultry Sapphire.

"You know," Saph said after a few steps, "I really like having you there in my bed every night."

Did Saph mean just for intimacy or did the tavern owner value Divine for other things? Ones other than physical attraction, like Divine had said about her?

They had reached the city's entrance area, where buildings were a sprinkling of almost all of the districts to accommodate passers-through and temporary visitors. A hand-pulled cart clattered past, heading toward the heart of the Entertainment District. Feeling as confident as the bouncing materials, Divine cleared her throat.

"It was nice of Sylus to watch the tavern for you."

"He's great to have. I'm lucky I picked him up before the Flutterwing Inn did. He's a good cook. And it shouldn't be too bad. The patrons will be playing cards or heading out to the faire. We usually get some couples wanting to warm up before heading back out to the events. It's the singles who stay the longest—come to swallow lament at being romantically alone for the faire."

Other faire-goers hurried to follow the cart and Divine and Saph decided to as well.

In the center of the Entertainment District, ice blocks the size of the people standing next to them lined the space. An officiant was detailing the rules.

"Only conventional tools may be used, no magic. You have until the final day of the festival to complete your sculpture. The winner will be announced at the close of the final night. Outright destruction of anyone's creation is prohibited but general mischief and pranks in honor of the God of Day and Deceit are encouraged. Good luck."

The speaker raised an arm and white shot out of his palm, exploding high above the city in a shower of snow. The officiant was a Flurry. The contestants began to chip and shave at the ice. One had brought what looked like a palm-sized Passionate's Plate and seemed to be trying to melt the ice.

"Have they done this event before?" Divine asked.

"Not that I remember. But it must take all week. Want to find something else?"

"Sure. We could come back another night and check on their progress."

They passed a row of small stalls selling snacks and drinks. A sign advertised everything as hot. A shiver ran through Divine's arms.

Saph tugged on Divine's coat cuff. "Do you want to get something here? A hot drink might help you forget it's cold."

"A hot apple cider sounds good," Divine said, gesturing at the middle stall. "You want to get something here?"

"That's good with me. I think each district will have similar offerings. They usually do. I want whatever brings you the most happiness tonight."

Divine leaned her head on Saph's as they got in line behind another couple. Soon, Saph and Divine were blowing on their small cups as the contents wafted tiny clouds in front of their noses. Divine breathed in the strong tangy sweetness that hinted at a fermentation not yet arrived, under light cinnamon. Unable to wait, Divine sipped and flinched.

"That's really hot, be careful," Divine warned.

Saph laughed. "Did you burn your tongue again?"

Diving tilted her head at Saph. "It's becoming a habit."

"I have serious concerns you're going to get permanent damage to the tip of your tongue no matter how much you heal it. Did you learn nothing from our tea blending experiments?" Saph teased.

"'The tea is hot,'" they quoted, then burst into a fit of laughter.

"Every time I took a drink," Divine struggled through a laugh, "you'd try to whack my hand without making me spill the tea."

"It was like you couldn't wait to sear yourself again even though I'd *just* reminded you."

"I just wanted to know how they tasted!"

Memories flooded her mind of her and Saph entwined on their bed discussing flavors, trips to the market and general stores, annoying Otto as they dug around in his organized mess of stacks in his pawn shop. Just like the furniture of the tavern, Saph gave a new home to mugs and spoons—and saved money. Savings that would now need to be used.

Her laughter hiccupped to a stop. "Saph...I really am sorry about your pantry. Did you find anything to replace the ingredients?"

"Not yet. It's winter, and the last of the usual tea supplies would have been here in the fall. I'm still hoping someone bought more than they need. I just need to find them. But don't worry about that now. Let's enjoy the festival."

Divine tried to put the issue to the back of her mind but felt her mood sober.

A man walked the street, a small box on the front of his coat held on by shoulder straps.

"City maps!" he called. "Every event noted. Play games, win faire coins! Trade Night Coins for unique items. Only available during the festival! Usable at all Trelvania cities!"

"Should we get a map?" Divine asked.

"Nah. That would make it too easy."

The man continued his advertisement. "Save up all week and get one of the best! Or spend them now. Up to you!"

As they walked on, Saph showed a knack for spying the special items other faire goers had purchased from the stalls or the bazaar, like necklaces with sleds and giant plush white squirrels. They lingered in a bakery as the scent of warm cookies issued a mermaid song. Hot, gooey chocolate pooled in their mouths and Divine nearly melted under Saph's smoldering gaze as Divine licked the bitter sweetness from her lips.

They veered toward the market bazaar, eager to find some of these games that had been promised. The snow had seemed to pick up, turning the world a wash of white.

Different than in the fall, the bazaar had fewer food vendors and no marionette show, but still packed with canopies over merchants—this time with glowing lanterns strung between their tops the same colors as the rest of the city. One merchant had figurines of people carving ice sculptures and snowflakes made of crystals. Another sold bunches of winter berries and strong-smelling pine bough trimmings.

Activity tents were a new addition. Under a purple canopy, people hovered over a table where a Kellas vendor shuffled large shells and individuals tried to guess which held a bean. Judging by the wails of disappointment, guessers lost money.

And at the center stretched a long white pole with a dangling rope. At the apex perched a large brass bell as high as the top of the nearest roofs; one of the bells that started the festival. Divine imagined three people could fit inside.

"Test your strength," called the game's attendant, surveying the crowd for someone's eyes to meet. "Impress your lady, Saph. This bell weighs as much as two harvester wulfs."

"She knows you?" Divine whispered.

"Me and Nable used to cross paths in the guild. They still got you collecting lost parcels from animal dens?"

"Just ring the bell, would ya? Last three couldn't do it. Have your arms gone squishy like rotting apples or do you still got it?"

"Saph's arms are definitely the opposite of squishy," Divine said, crossing her arms.

Whispering that it was fine, Saph squeezed Divine around her waist. She stepped forward, pushing up the sleeves of her coat over her forearms.

"Any rules?" Saph asked.

"The bell must ring, that's it."

Saph took the rope in her hands, flicking the long end against the ground like a broom. Worry flashed in Divine's chest as Saph examined the rope then tilted her chin up. Would she be able to get a good grip in the cold?

Then, like she did it every day, Saph deftly wrapped the rope around her waist and twisted it around her forearm before squatting and stepping backward as both hands gripped the rope. Saph squatted deeper, taking another step backward and the muscles in her forearm tightened. Divine reluctantly tore her eyes away and squinted at the pole's top. The bell tilted, hovering in infinity. Saph grunted. The bell tipped. A beautiful gong sang out again and again as the bell rocked in its yoke.

People cheered and Nable handed Saph her three snowflake embossed coins.

"Would you like to try?" she asked Divine.

Divine snorted. "I think I'd need a harvester wulf to help me. But I do want to feel what *my lady's* challenge was."

Winking at Saph, she grasped the rope and pulled. Nothing happened. She grabbed the rope above her head and jumped, wrapping her legs around the twisted twine, trying to pull down with her body like some sort of insect climbing a thread. The bell didn't even squeak, though Divine thought she heard a distant howl of a wulf. Her arms gave out and she fell, the heels of her boots hitting the ground. She pinwheeled her arms but her body slipped backward. Nable's eyes went wide.

Limbs scooped beneath Divine's arms, stopping her fall.

"Careful, darling." Saph set Divine right and swung her around. "I'd hate to have you miss the rest of the fun."

Feeling her face heat as red as her hair, Divine pulled the hood of her coat up tightening the fur around her face. Saph thanked Nable and they moved on.

"Let's see what's out this way," Saph said, leading her though an alley and into the Artisans subdistrict.

"That was impressive." Divine thumbed back toward the market. "Did you learn how to do that for your mercenary work?"

"I did something similar for training."

"Oh! With Shroombal? I met them yesterday."

"Oh yeah? What did the old puff top have to say about me?"

Divine worried her lip. "Well, not much. But maybe you could tell me more about your training."

"Quiet on the topic, huh? First thing he said to me was my shape reminded him of a young Thospor stalk. It was supposed to be a compliment." Saph winked, running her hands down her hips. "But why was I even there, this beauty who could rock your boat with a twist of my hips? I think I was twenty, haunting the Warrior's District after I'd been let go from smithing. It was a whole thing. Couldn't let it go. I wandered into the training yard with my axe and suddenly I just wanted to hit something. It's like the place is lined with aggression."

"I promise, Soulshields can't make a place carry an emotion."

"Oh, I know. But you saw how the training yard is."

"True. I think it can attract people who are already leaning that way. Appeal to their...passion."

"And not the kind I prefer." Saph bumped her hip into Divine. "Well, several trainers came by to peddle their services for a fee, but when they saw my hand they thought it would impede my proper grip of a weapon."

Divine groaned. "People put up these barriers when they don't even know the outcome. They're so short-sighted because of their opinions. And they're not even good opinions! Tell me they wept when they saw you wield the axe like you do."

"I ranked high in the Mercenary Guild, remember? Plenty of tears were eventually shed. Anyway, if I wanted to take on tasks that required armor, gloves and greaves didn't exist that would fit my hand so at the time I thought I was limited as well. I was not about to ask the smith who fired me to make something. But Shroombal came and you've seen their hands—like pastry puffs."

"Shroombal has some surprising skills. They practically flew in the air to fight this detritus of a human with their staff. They were *nimble*."

"Shroombal taught me without judgement. Strength, defense, attack. They even had me visit their village when they went home in the summer. Too hot out of the mountains." Saph leaned closer, lowering her voice. "Did you know, Thosporium is practically all warriors? If a city ever irritates them enough, they wouldn't stand a chance."

Imagining an army of mushrooms, Divine chuckled. "Shroombal doesn't strike me as a preemptive attacker type."

"Nah. They're a softy from their cap through their stalk."

Nearby, a stall took bets on a sled race next to those selling hot beverages.

Six wooden sleds lined the street in pairs, each with a cushioned seat behind their dark brown front arch piece and another seat behind the first.

Two harvester wulfs were harnessed to each sled reminiscent of the plows they would pull in the spring to till the land for farming. Their normally cinnamon colored fur had lost some of its color, making their coats mimic reeds poking out of snow.

Saph leaned closer. "I bet we could win."

"What?" Divine's brows raised. "Have you driven a sled before?"

One of the harvester wulfs snapped at its tethered companion, revealing its fangs in a low growl before sniffing and recentering its muzzle ahead.

"Nope." Saph crossed her arms over her chest, the gesture exuded confidence. "But it can't be too hard, or they wouldn't let just anyone try."

A man and a woman climbed into a sled laughing, the man sitting in front.

"Come on." Saph took Divine's hand. "Before they're all taken."

The sled Saph approached had an embossed fern on its front, painted with light blue and white, giving it the appearance of frost. Small lights along its frame like the light strands in the Sultry Sapphire gave it a glowing outline. Evergreen branches with cones still attached added to the winter wilderness theme. From somewhere wafted sugar and cinnamon coated nuts, and Divine's stomach rumbled.

The nearest harvester wulf huffed. The canis creatures, though tamed and bred to be workers and guards, were as tall as their wild counterparts reaching half as high as a horse. No doubt they were strong on their large paws, but could they be submissive to the whims of humans? Divine gulped, reaching out a hand for the wulf to sniff. It whined and nuzzled Divine's palm.

"See?" Saph beamed. "Nothing to worry about."

"Go on, climb in," an attendant said eagerly.

"You drive," Saph said, climbing into the back.

Hesitantly, Divine took the reins from the attendant as he launched into an explanation.

"The wulfs know what to do, so don't you worry about making a mess of anything." He wiggled his eyebrows. "One shake and shout 'Let's run!' to get them going. Once the sled in front of you turns the corner, go ahead and give the command. We'll time your sleds separately—we can't fit all six on the streets at the same time." He chuckled. "Not a true race, then. But the fastest sled to visit these districts and return here will be the winner. Try leaning into the turns to go faster."

Divine took a card from him that listed the names of the districts.

A Flurry standing on the sidewalk released two shoots of snow beacons into the sky and the first sled took off. When Divine glanced back to the attendant, he'd already moved on.

"Hey wait! How do we stop it?"

"Maybe like a horse." Saph offered. "We'll be alright. I wonder how fast these can go?"

A thousand thoughts raced through Divine's mind. Did she have time to tell Saph they should find something else to do? But she had fought the giant horned ursavara and discovered her magic was stronger than she thought. She could handle a little sled ride.

The sled in front of her turned the corner and suddenly Divine's mouth felt dry. She squeezed her hands around the leather of the reins, but couldn't make her arms move.

"This'll be fun."

At Saph's declaration near her ear, Divine's arms jerked up.

The harvester wulfs dropped their heads as their paws dug into the snow. The sled slid forward then picked up speed as the wulfs pulled into a run. Saph gave a triumphant laugh and the sled whooshed along the snow-filled street.

Leaving the spectators they rounded a corner. People lined the streets, watching and cheering them on. The attention settled her stomach, but she wished for the event to be over quickly.

Wind blew in her face as they picked up speed, creating tiny pillows of water in the corners of her eyes that trickled out along her temple. She thought she could feel the rivulets turn to ice on her skin. The sled slid toward a streetlamp and Divine closed her eyes, gripping the reigns tighter.

Please don't crash.

"What's your favorite color?" Saph asked.

"Are you really asking me that right now?" Divine called over her shoulder.

"You're right, I should already know that. It's an autumn color. Pink. Or orange?"

Divine opened her eyes. "That's not what I—"

"If you could travel through time, would you go to the past or the future?"

Divine leaned with the sled as they circled the district's square. "I...uh...I've never thought about it."

"I don't think I'd go either way. I'm happy to live in the present."

"Why are you asking these things?"

"I saw this list of questions to ask on dates, so I thought I'd try them out. Keep things new."

Divine sat back in her seat, rotating her shoulders to look at Saph from her side.

She smirked. "Like riding in a sled isn't new enough?"

"I just want you to enjoy your time with me."

Divine's chest warmed. "I am. I do." Then she remembered Saph's first-love story. "I like that you ask questions. But you don't have to try too hard, I'm already smitten."

Shouts and cheers crescendoed and Divine snapped her attention to the street. Onlookers lined another stretch of the city. Someone shouted into a speaking cone.

"—fastest so far!"

"Did you hear that?" Saph asked. "See, you're good at this."

The cheers and Saph's praise combined into a bouquet of heavy rose blooms. Divine wanted to go back to the moment before and dig deeper into Saph's question. Find out what Saph enjoyed about spending time with her. Was it all physical? She wished they were somewhere less crowded; just her and Saph and the scents of frosted wilderness.

The harvester wulfs banked hard, turning down a street. A street off the designed race loop. People jumped and dove out of the way as the sled barreled through other Midwinter Nights Faire activities.

Divine shouted apologies mixed with warnings.

"Did something get in their way?" Saph called.

"No, they just suddenly went this way. I don't know what..."

Her voice trailed off as they approached the south gate. They passed through, leaving the city. The lights of the sled illuminated their carriage but ahead there was nothing but darkness.

Leaning her head back, Divine *hmmed* in contemplation as snowflakes drifted down like the stars had detached themselves from the sky. The sled slowed to a stop and without its whooshing sounds, the world stilled.

A place less crowded.

"Good wulfs," she whispered.

Saph's face appeared above, an eyebrow lifted. "You alright? That was thrilling."

Divine nodded and Saph leaned closer, capturing Divine's lips in an upside down kiss. When they released, Divine faced her.

"I think this was me." She shrugged. "Sorry."

Saph looked from the wulfs to Divine. "You really think so?"

"I thought about wanting a place less crowded. To be with you."

Saph chuckled. "I can think of many places for privacy, but Werewing Forest was not on my list."

Divine raised her gloves in a defeated shrug, slumping against the chair back. Pockets of woodland grew near the city, but the named forest was much further away. But semantics didn't change that they were out of the city in the dark.

Saph hopped down into the snow and offered her hand. Divine took it and joined her in the ankle-high drifts. Like the weather wanted to distract her, the wind picked up and brushed Saph's skirt against Divine's legs.

"I feel silly for wearing this outfit." Divine brushed the sides of her dress.

"But does it make you feel good?"

Divine bit her lip before responding. "Yeah, I think it does."

"Besides, I'll get to see it when we get back to the tavern. I'll stare at you as long as you like. Though, I'll also be thinking about what's underneath."

"There's nothing underneath," Divine teased, walking to the front of the sled.

"Mmm. I'd have you right here if we both weren't going to freeze our skin."

As if they were house pets and not sizable and barely domesticated, Divine removed her gloves and scratched behind the ears of both harvester wulfs.

"Then I guess we'd better get these big bundles of fur back to the city. There's more Night Coins to be won."

Wrapping her arms around Divine, Saph snuggled close, her cold nose pressed against Divine's cheek. Divine rotated, looking through her lashes.

Saph kissed the corner of Divine's mouth. "Coins can be won another night. I want you."

Divine's stomach flipped. And then it growled.

"But first food." Saph chuckled. "You'll need your energy for what I have in mind."

Hooking her pinky with Saph's, Divine sent a thought of returning to the city and began trudging through the snow. The wulfs plodded behind, pulling the sled toward the lights. Divine didn't trust herself to not have another incident if they tried to ride. Besides, she had the star-filled sky, the quiet contentment of nature, and the hand of the woman who filled her heart.

CHAPTER TEN

The Tea is Hot

They stumbled through the door together, laughing as light piles of snow fell from their coats. The fire blazed an inviting orange yellow in the empty tavern. They stomped their boots and hung their coats on the wall.

The curtains on the big windows were drawn and faint light lined the top from the string of lights. Some sort of cushioned lounge had been brought before the fireplace while they were out.

"Sylus?" Divine held her palm toward the bench.

"Otto. He thought it would never sell. I knew exactly what I wanted to do with it."

Divine looked at Saph out of the side of her eye. "And what's that?"

"Let me show you." Saph clasped both of Divine's hands and walked backward, tugging Divine along.

The fire warmed Divine's cheeks and her toes began to burn the way they did when the cold finally was driven out of her body. The crackling was a gentle whisper in the silence of the moment.

"Your hands are so cold." Saph brought Divine's hands close to her mouth and breathed hot air into her palms. Bending Divine's hand back gently, Saph kissed her wrist, then worked slow kisses up Divine's arm. Divine shivered as Saph's icy lips caressed her neck.

"How do you want me to please you tonight, darling?" Saph licked Divine's earlobe, taking the rose stud between her teeth. "I want to feel you tremble."

Divine inhaled sharply. "I want to please you, too. Can we do it together?"

Saph pulled back to stare into Divine's eyes. The woman drew her thumb across Divine's bottom lip while biting her own.

"I'd worship every inch of you," Saph breathed. "If you asked me to."

Heady, sweet florals roared to life in Divine's magic; perfumed roses and delectable flowering vines from summer. Divine growled, working the fabric of Saph's dress up with her hands, her fingers slowly dragged up along Saph's thighs. She wanted skin touching skin.

Saph cupped Divine's ass and pulled her closer, her hip connecting between Divine's legs. Divine pushed her hips closer in search of more contact for her desire.

Saph chuckled into Divine's mouth as her tongue glided against Divine's. She tasted like apple cider and sugar. She loosened Divine's belt and tossed it to the side. Hands stroked Divine's hips and worked their way along the slits of her dress. Then Divine was squirming, wiggling as Saph tugged the cloth higher, then released Divine's mouth to haul the dress over Divine's head. Her breasts sprang free as Saph tossed the muted mauve shirt on top of the belt.

Divine expected her skin to feel the bite of cold, but the fire bathed her skin in heat. Or it was Saph's intense gaze lighting her from within.

"The way the light caresses your curves...you're a vision."

Divine glanced toward the stairs, a moment of panic temporarily dampening her longing. "What about Sylus?"

"We have the tavern all to ourselves."

Divine wanted Saph all to herself. The night had been perfect. Divine felt like she was the center of Saph's affections. Could it last? She didn't want to share Saph's flirty winks and crooked smiles with anyone else. At least in this moment, she was hers.

Saph rested a palm on one of Divine's breasts as she connected their mouths. Lightly, Saph ran her thumb over Divine's nipple and Divine moaned as she guided her own hands to the ties of Saph's corset. Divine could barely focus on untying the strings as Saph trailed kisses along her collarbone, swirling her thumb around Divine's hardening nipple.

"Wait," Divine breathed. "You're supposed to let me do some of this, too."

Saph stepped back, raising her hands as a grin spread across her face. "Of course, darling. You're just so addicting."

Divine flicked her gaze to a bending green plant on the mantel and grumbled.

"Sage, this is private." Divine grasped the pot

"If Sage wants to watch, it's fine with me." Saph smirked.

Divine started walking over to the bar as she called over her shoulder. "Clothes off please. I'll be right back." Through the swinging door the kitchen was cold and Divine shivered, bumps raising on her skin as she set Sage on the counter. She couldn't look at him, fearing she'd read a message in his ten shoots.

"Try to forget you saw anything," she whispered, then exited through the swinging door.

Divine halted, her breath hitching. The light of the fire rippled over Saph's side, making her radiate like a Goddess of Day. Naked, Saph leaned an arm against the mantel while her other propped on the bend of her waist, her erect nipples inviting Divine to resume her exploration. She shivered, but this time from a thirst only Saph could quench.

Divine removed her boots, dropping them on the floor on the way. She halted a step from Saph, left only in her charcoal leggings.

"This"—Saph traced the edge of Divine's waistband—"has to go."

Divine pushed the tight fabric down, squirming her hips to shake them off and Saph responded with a hum of enjoyment. Divine studied Saph from her toes to her breasts, watching her own hands glide up Saph's sides then cup Saph's large breasts, kneading them softly, before prying her eyes away to kiss Saph's parted mouth.

Saph guided them in an unhurried turn so that Divine's back faced the fire and they moved in a gradual shuffling of feet. When Saph bumped into the bench, she reclined, propping her legs so that her knees were raised. Her black hair spilled around her face. Perfection. Divine crawled on top. There was enough space on the bench for one body to lay with a bit of space around. Her thigh pressed intimately against Saph while Saph's thigh did the same. Divine gasped, feeling Saph's unmistakable desire coat her leg.

"This good?" Divine whispered.

"More than good, darling."

Divine lowered herself so that their breasts touched as she found Saph's velvety tongue. Saph rocked her hips in a swirling motion, and Divine's arms nearly gave out from the sensation as she let out a yearning growl, sucking on Saph's tongue.

She broke away to trail open-mouthed kisses down Saph's neck and between her breasts, stroking her thigh against Saph in a long deliberate movement. Her stomach clinched agreeably at Saph's purr of approval. Divine hovered over one dark nipple and breathed hot air across it. Saph arched her back, gently grasping Divine's hair.

Divine swirled her tongue around Saph's dark areola, eliciting bumps along her skin. At the same time, she mimicked Saph, swirling her hips and gliding their skin against each other. Saph gasped as Divine took the nipple into her mouth, dragging her hands up and down Divine's back.

"More," Saph panted.

Divine complied, gently sucking on the nipple as she traced her fingertips over Saph's other breast. Saph's pleased response to her touch made Divine's head seem to float. Divine squeezed the breast beneath her hand.

A throaty groan accompanied Saph's fingers moving between Divine's legs and Divine cried out, her body trembling as she let go of Saph's nipple. She was so close.

"Faster," Divine exhaled, urging Saph.

She wanted to show Saph how the woman made her feel; let the people on the streets hear her scream.

Breathing heavy, Divine bent her chin to her chest as she found a rhythm with Saph, each of them rocking and swirling their hips. Divine raked her eyes over Saph's form, sweat beading between her breasts and on her stomach. This woman. This beautiful woman. Who ran her own business, who was strong enough to wield an axe, was strong enough to bare her soul in poetry. Who stayed with Divine through her doubts. She made Divine feel brave. Made her feel like she could do anything she wanted in life.

Right now, she wanted to make Saph explode in release.

Divine pressed her palm to Saph's lower belly, her thumb finding Saph's pleasure point. Saph reached up with one hand to squeeze Divine's breast.

Urgent need wrecked through Divine's body, and she grabbed the hand on her breast, moving Saph's palm over Divine's racing heart.

"Can you feel what you do to me?"

The woman rubbed Divine firmer in response. *Goddess.*

This woman who could have anyone had chosen Divine tonight. Divine would make sure Saph reached Zenith.

"Are you close?" Divine asked, her voice low as she elongated a stroke of her thigh against Saph.

"Divine...I...ugh. So. Good." Saph's back arched again and her hungry growl made Divine gasp for breath. Pressure built inside her to a breaking point.

Divine wanted this moment to last, where it seemed like there was nothing else in the world but the two of them. A perfect night ending in the need to make each other feel marvelous.

Her vision blurred. Panting breaths filled her ears until they faded into thudding heartbeats. Throwing her head back, Divine lost herself in the pleasure, rocking faster as her finger swirled Saph's clit. She pulled her hand back as Saph did the same. They rocked harder into each other, moaning loudly, Saph digging her fingers into Divine's ass as if they could get their bodies any closer.

Saph shrieked as Divine's mouth fell open. Saph trembled under her and Divine cried out, her body spasming as if a million flutterwings burst forth. The ecstasy made her body go taut and she laughed. She thrust her hips slower and fell on her hands on either side of Saph, grinning wildly.

"Wow," Saph breathed.

Still pulsing between her legs, Divine slowed to a stop, giggling. She brushed a strand of dark hair off of Saph's forehead thinking how beautiful this woman looked. She kissed along her jawline before finally finding her lips. Collapsing on top of Saph, she breathed deeply to catch her breath, relishing in the feeling of bliss and their perspiring bodies blending into one.

After a moment, Saph began to chuckle. "Look up."

Pursing her lips, Divine angled her head to the side, nuzzling Saph's neck in the process, and her eye caught movement above. Near the ceiling flutterwings of every color flew, their glassy pairs of double wing spears catching the fire's light in a translucent shimmer. Another manifestation of her magic.

Saph brushed Divine's cheek. "We should do that again."

CHAPTER ELEVEN

Botanical Conversations

The warmth of Saph's body against her back made Divine want to never move. She pulled the blankets over her arms and chest to keep the rest of her body warm.

Could she stay like this forever?

Saph squeezed Divine where her arm draped around her waist.

A knock at the door roused Divine in a heartbeat and she shot up. The blanket was not a blanket, it was Saph's dress from the night before. They'd lay on their sides to both fit on the lounge and had watched the fire burn low as they fell asleep.

The knock hammered again.

Saph groaned. "I forgot to bring in the sign. People probably think we're still serving tea."

"And we're naked." Divine glanced out of the door's small window. It was still dark at least and the curtains of the main windows were drawn, but she threw her dress over her head.

"Is that a problem?" Saph asked groggily, sitting up.

Divine nearly dove after her leggings, then tugged them on. She shook her head in exasperation. "Put your dress on and I'll get the door."

As she stepped over her boots, forgotten in the middle of the floor, her feet registered the cold wood.

"Sage! He's probably freezing."

"I'll go change upstairs," Saph said, gathering her things into her arms unceremoniously. "Tell them we're sorry and to come back tomorrow. Maybe I can find something for tea by then."

Reminded of the destroyed ingredients, Divine's heart sank. Once Saph's naked form disappeared from sight, Divine unlocked the door and pulled it open.

On the threshold stood a figure in a long orange coat.

"Constance? What are you doing here?"

"You did not arrive as we had planned."

The garden. The training.

"Oh no, I'm so sorry I made you wait. I guess I assumed you meant after sunrise. Please, come in."

Divine led Constance to a long table, her eyes betraying her by glancing at the lounge by the fire. She smoothed both sides of her hair with her palms, hoping the waves were not too disheveled. Constance lowered his hood and sat on the bench across from her. He wore his usual orange robe beneath an open coat. Divine rested her hand on the table, immediately recoiling at the stickiness.

I guess Sylus was in a hurry to make the place available for us.

"Can I get you anything? Tea? We have just enough to make a couple cups."

"I must admit I am intrigued by this new hot beverage your establishment is offering. An alternative to intellectual regression. But do not trouble yourself too much. I am here for you, after all."

Divine gulped. She wasn't sure that she wanted to dive into the discussions from the day prior, even if Constance wanted to help. Letting it all slip to the back of her mind had let her feel comfortably nonchalant.

A pink flutterwing landed on her shoulder.

"Interesting choice of decoration." Constance flicked his wrist and Divine squeezed her eyes shut before looking above. Flutterwings perched in the rafters, their glassy spear wings opening and closing. Some balanced along the cascading greenery that dangled from the support beams.

"Yes, well, it is the faire." Divine laughed nervously. She hurried over to the fire, tossing a log and stoking the flames. "Actually, it was me. Again."

"Hm. Have you given Arosia any more thought?"

Divine moved toward the bar and the swinging door to the kitchen and storage. Arosia had been far from her mind. All her thoughts had been on Saph.

"Not yet. Busy night." She entered the kitchen and picked up Sage by his cool pot. Maybe she imagined it, but he looked a little wilty. She whispered an apology and promised to be a better decacacti caregiver.

Back in the main room, Divine hurriedly placed Sage above the mantel as the flutterwing from her shoulder landed on one of Sage's tentacles. Mentally conveying she'd return, Divine got water from the kitchen and prepared tea behind the bar as she continued her conversation with Constance.

"Why do you think I won't believe this...theory you have about what's happening to me?"

Constance steepled his fingers. "I believe you are an Old Soul, which traces its roots to a time before the temples."

Divine nearly dropped the boilspout. "There is—was—a time before the deities? Saph's belief system, the Old Ways, implies that there must have been, for magic to have just existed without the deities. But I guess I couldn't really imagine how that could be."

"It is hard when your entire life has been under the shadow of the pantheon."

Divine poured steaming water into two mugs. "You say that like your entire life hasn't been that way."

She eyed the man. He neither blinked nor opened his mouth to agree. It probably meant nothing. She needed that tea to warm up her thoughts as well as her insides. Popping the tins open, she looked between them and their sparse ingredients. Struggling with the lack of volume in each, Divine made a quick decision and poured them all together. Tea was tea, right?

Constance folded his arms on the table. "You should head to the city soon."

"Which city?" Saph asked, reaching the bottom of the stairs. "And who are you?"

Saph shifted toward the bar, angling for the beam that held her axe like a warning to patrons to behave. A terrible thought crossed Divine's mind of what could happen, and she waved Saph off.

"This is the Goodly One I told you about. Constance. Constance, this is Saph, the owner of the Sultry Sapphire." Divine could have called him the First Servant of Virtue, but Goodly One felt more familiar. She could have called Saph something else, too, but didn't know how to define what they were. Every time she thought about asking, something got in the way.

"May your virtue bring neighbors and not isolation to the table."

Saph cocked an eyebrow at Divine before joining Constance at the bench.

"I hadn't had a chance to tell you yet, but Constance thinks answers for me might be in Arosia."

The particles floated in their strainers. A mix of chocolate, vanilla and spices drifted from the cups like a pie topped with cream, the plate garnished with herbs and flowers. Divine hoped it would taste like it smelled.

"I could look for tea for you from somewhere far away while I'm there. And more tea ware. Maybe I could talk to the Holicratic Ruling Council about how human-adjacents are being treated in Iramont. But...I'm not sure I'm going."

"Why not?" Saph asked.

After removing the strainers, Divine added sugar cubes and carried the hot mugs to the table.

"Well, there's the winter travel. And I'd have to leave...the tavern." She took a sip from her mug and immediately regretted her latest burn. "Who's going to help out?"

Why didn't she say what she meant to say? *I'd have to leave...you.*

"Darling. We'll be fine. Sylus and I managed this place before. And if you come back, you'll know right where to find us."

Divine thought she would vomit the tea back out. How easily Saph dismissed her. *If I come back. Not when. If. Does it not matter?*

"Have you been to Arosia before?" Constance asked. He eyed the mug before picking it up in both hands.

"Nah. It's a long journey and I'm not one for long journeys. Oh, Divine! You could reunite with your instrument. You so enjoyed playing the other night."

"I'll think about it." Divine sipped her tea morosely, the snowshrooms suddenly clashing with the tropical citrus notes. She thought it tasted of disappointment. Another brew for Syka.

Divine lowered her cup. "Do you think Syka would make the journey?"

"You know how she feels about the cold." Saph pointed to the frosted windows. "But, Arosia would be a new challenge for her skills."

Divine nodded. Maybe she didn't have to travel alone. Though she would rather her travel companion be Saph, the tavern owner made it clear she wasn't traveling.

The Goodly One pushed his mug forward. "I thank you for the warm drink. Are you ready to progress in your magic?"

"Let me put on a change of clothes and then I'll be ready."

"Meet me at the spot."

Divine took a final sip of her drink, then scurried to check on Sage. The decacacti's stems looked fuller.

"Do you want to come, too?" she asked. "Come on, let's talk."

Divine took the pot with her upstairs, conversing with Sage as she got dressed. By the time she returned downstairs, Sage had agreed to wear a hat and see how he felt. He wanted to see more than the insides of buildings.

Glad she had bought herself a pair of gloves, Divine stretched a blue mitten carefully over the highest stems and Sage's topmost tentacle arms gathered closer to help as his pot crunched.

She pulled her lips into her mouth. "No, I think you look adorable."

On the street, curiosity from those few strolling bubbled as Divine walked east carrying her hatted-plant. The scarce residents were a reflection of late into the night faire-goers. Divine wondered where Sylus had gone to give Saph and her privacy. And how quickly the atmosphere had cooled from contentment to disinterest.

She pondered what Saph's reaction meant and if she should go to Arosia, then before she realized it, she had reached the east gate and the dormant garden.

A crinkle of fabric and a familiar voice broke her thoughts as Constance folded his arms into the sleeves of his garments. "You seem...contemplative. I would of course accompany you to Arosia. I can provide training and guidance there and as we travel."

Divine's spirits lifted, though marginally. "I would appreciate the help. Travelling that far, who knows what mayhem I could unleash along the way."

"My first lesson is to believe in yourself. When others believe in you, you experience a state where you feel stronger magic. Imagine how your magic would be if you also recognized your abilities. And I don't just mean your magical abilities. Confidence in all that you do."

"I know you're right. When I fought Madeline and the boradain—I just did the things, no doubts, I made them happen. It's just—it's hard to even know what to do when I don't know what my magic is."

"Did you know how to mend bone before?"

"Well, no."

"Hmm."

Divine glanced at Sage, who issued a similar hum. "How do you know he has a point?" Then after a pause filled with squelchy hums, "No, I don't think learning how to suck nutrients from the ground the first time is similar." Sage sizzle-cracked. "You're allowed to disagree."

"While in the city, I suggest avoiding your botanical conversations. Some of the deities are watching the cities and have their servants reporting oddities."

"Are you calling me or Sage an oddity?"

Constance flicked his eyes her way before looking ahead. "Possibly both."

Divine's half grin mirrored his.

She patted Sage's hat. "You're unique, which isn't the same as odd."

The sun rose slowly and beams of light thrust themselves down the road, lighting the way to the east gate.

"I want you to practice positive thoughts. Now and throughout each day. When something doesn't go the way you wanted it to, it's not a failure—it's a learning opportunity. A step closer to your goal. Turn your 'I can't' and your 'I don't know how' into 'I will' and 'I'll learn.' Can you do that?"

"I'll try."

The corner of Constance's mouth twitched up. "Trying is a step forward. Now, for your magic. Tomorrow, about the time I got you today, I want you to meet me in the little copse of trees by the north gate. There should be some carts arriving with visitors. Find a way to help, anything that could make them feel appreciation for you. But don't use your magic."

Cold seeped into her chest and she lowered her voice. "What if it happens when I don't mean to?"

"Trust in yourself, Divine. While you help, I want you to focus on the emotions around you. Try to isolate yours from the adoration of others. I know that it can easily blend into your own, clouding it so the emotions feel like yours."

Divine nodded, thinking of times like serving the day before where the elation took over. And she let it, as if it was her own.

Constance continued. "Work on noticing which thoughts, which feelings belong to whom—or to what. We need to uncover how you perceive creatures and how that is different than humans. Whether you hear them, or feel them, or your magic's scent changes. Note any detail."

Visions of Divine unleashing flutterwings into everyone's faces as they thanked her for helping made her swallow hard. But she was determined to do what Constance said. He was the only one who could help her start making sense of her magic.

Eventually she was left to practice her magic on the nearby fauna and the challenge to stay positive. She'd spend some time at the Edge and find ways to help around the tavern. After sunset the first thing she'd get would be hot cocoa. She was positively craving it.

* * *

The next morning, Constance hid somewhere in the trees, observing, Sage hopefully still tucked warmly in Constance's oversized coat pocket where Divine had left him. The Goodly One didn't want to be seen and so she was on her own.

She had a feeling he was the cause of the current ruckus. Rabbits and raccoons had dashed across the road, some darting back and forth as if they couldn't decide if crossing or retreating was best.

Divine moved to calm them but pushed her magic back into her well as she remembered Constance's instruction. She tried to let the well just exist, and the emotions around her ripple in its surface.

One raccoon snatched a sausage at the end of a string of others that dangled from a side window on the wagon. Divine suspected it popped out to serve as a counter for customers. A rabbit gnawed on a length of carrot.

Hunger and excitement. Urgency. Divine tried to focus. Was there a scent, too? Or just a thought? Was it words or a feeling?

"I knew we packed too much," a woman argued with her husband. She stood on lowered stairs and Divine glimpsed pots and pans hanging behind her. And maybe a cauldron?

"We left too late," her husband countered.

Divine handed the man a sack of potatoes—one of many things that had tumbled from the roof of the wagon as its front wheel hit a hole and splintered.

"Counting tonight," Divine offered, "you still have five nights of the faire. Seems right on time."

The woman huffed. "Our wagon is broken and all of the good spots are probably taken. We came all the way from

Norfel thinking we'd be sought after with our northern food. No black spot there."

"I bet we can get you righted and ready to go before the evening." Divine smiled. "And every spot in Iramont is a good spot. Let me talk to the gate attendants while you...rescue your stuff from the local wildlife. I even know a guy that specializes in transportation." *Though I don't really* want *to talk to Viktor...*

"Thank you, miss." The man touched her upper arm. "My wife and I appreciate it."

A tickle in her chest. A brush of floral beneath her nose.

There it was. But which was her appreciation that the travelers wanted her help, and which was their esteem of her?

As she walked the short distance to the gate, Divine tried to separate her emotions from the rest. Maybe she imagined a strand of warmth within the feeling.

At the gate, Divine asked for the help the travelling eatery needed, then rejoined the married pair.

"There's lots of travelers here for the faire and our front district has everything to get you all fixed up. You should be taken care of within the half hour."

"Thank you, dear. And sorry for my grumpy demeanor earlier." The woman closed up the window and stepped out of the wagon. "We managed to save most of our fixings. Here, as a thank you."

Munching a salted soft pretzel the woman had given her, Divine circled back to the east gate through pockets of trees. Soon Constance joined her and handed her Sage.

"He tried to poke me," Constance said. "In my armpit."

"He says you caused chaos."

"I did nothing to their wagon."

Divine took the last bite of her pretzel. "Yet, somehow you knew this would happen."

Salt clung to Divine's upper lip and she licked it. She turned to find Constance staring at her, lips slightly parted.

"What?" she asked.

He drew in his bottom lip before releasing it. "It is nothing. I did not know it would happen. The morning after the first night of the faire always has consequences. Too relaxed, too tired, too much of a headache—mistakes would happen. More people coming in and out of the city, it was inevitable."

"You really didn't know? I could have stood there for hours waiting for something?"

"Not hours. I would have directed some animals toward the gates. Perhaps unhitched some horses."

Divine's mouth fell open. "You wouldn't. That doesn't seem virtuous."

"Light mischief is part of the season, is it not?" The Goodly One raised his chin though he looked out of the corner of his eye at her. "Besides, a little trouble for a little good evens out. Tell me, what did you notice?"

"I'm not sure." Divine hugged Sage to her stomach. "The animals were almost clearer, like there were words though I'm not sure if I actually heard words. With humans, I get the general emotions. Fear, anger. But not the cause. With the animals there was extra information. I don't know, this doesn't make any sense."

"Confidence, remember?" Constance encouraged. "This is a good first step. You are beginning to recognize the thoughts and feelings that your magic is capable of touching. What about when you helped the man and the woman?"

"That was harder. I know I was happy that I was helping them, but I think it could have been the man's emotions."

"Did you feel stronger, like your well had more power?"

"Oh. I didn't focus on that. But I don't think there was enough to notice. It was more of a tickle than something like what happened yesterday during teatime."

"Starting small, though, is how we control the outcome. And learn to harness the power the way you want to."

They reached the garden again and Divine adjusted Sage's blue mitten on his stems.

"Staying warm, Sage?" His pot slurped and Divine looked above to the long pillows of clouds. "I guess the sun is warm, when you can ignore the gusts."

Setting Sage on the nearby bench, she considered the Goodly One again. "Why are you doing this? Helping me?"

"Would I embody the paramounts of the God of Virtue if I did not?"

"That's not really an answer. What do you get out of it?"

"I assume what you get out of healing people. You do it because it is the right thing to do and to not…"

"Would haunt me," Divine finished. "If I can help, I should."

"It is a good virtue to have." Constance winked. "And by the end, maybe I gain an ally or a friend."

Her chin quivered. Friendship. Meve's message had opened a whole avenue of possibilities; that friendships were candles all around her just waiting to be lit.

Divine tucked her hair behind her ear. "I think that would be nice."

"When you can identify your own emotions, you can use it as a sort of anchor or grounding, translating and segmenting what you feel into shelves."

Divine scrunched her nose. *Shelves?*

"This one contains others' emotions, this contains creatures. And this one contains yours. Then you have the option to take it down and use it, or not."

It made a sort of sense and she nodded. If she could do that, then travelling might not be as worrisome.

"While we're in Arosia—that is, if I go—do you think you can speak to the Holicratic Ruling Council?"

"About what?"

"How human-adjacents are being treated here in Iramont."

"I'm afraid you'll find it's a growing change in all of the provinces."

Divine clenched her hands into fists. "So what, you'll just do nothing?"

"Those are not the words I said. Assumptions are shortcuts to ruin."

Divine averted her contemplation to the bench and Sage. Though his words were kind, she wished she could redo the conversation. She would just need to avoid conclusions before asking the right questions. She sat on the bench next to Sage and Constance continued as if the conversation had been natural.

"We will need to be stealthy in Arosia. If they notice what we are looking for, they may try to take you."

Divine straightened. "Why would they take me?"

"For questioning? For testing? To convert you to their side? All of it, likely. We'll need to lay low and work quietly."

"This sounds like a perfect job for Syka."

"If you have a friend who can help, bring them. Do you have any friends in Arosia who would keep your presence secret?"

"I have a few possibilities."

Constance nodded. "Then we will seek them out directly when we arrive. Things are changing. They have been for some time. And I feel secrecy is needed, especially since I have not been to Arosia for a full changing of the seasons."

Divine thought of the last conference of First Servants the spring before, the temple leaders gathering from each province to discuss methodologies. As just a Soulshield, she had only seen some of the gatherings at a distance. Had something happened then that the First Servants acted on to change policies?

"Why would the treatment of human-adjacents be declining everywhere?" Divine asked.

"Human-adjacents have no talismans and deities can't get boosts from them."

"Then they are useless in the deities' eyes," Divine concluded.

"They fear them, I suspect."

Listhinci had confirmed that the Iguions at least had healing magic, it was possible they had more. If the deities weren't aware of the powers they had, did they suspect? She wanted to ask Constance more, but she didn't know how much he knew of the scaly inhabitants of Solhavn. It was not her secret to share. Instead, she blew out a breath.

"I would still like to find a way to bring awareness. Arosia keeps records of everything, and a complaint could get noticed and end up on community boards where more people would read. I must hope that the majority would not tolerate what's happening here."

Caring for souls had always been Divine's path. Even if her temple withheld truths, her drive to help didn't change. Especially since her temple was not helping human-adjacents. *And if no one is being a voice, then I should. Someone must do something.*

"Your stealthy friend could assist with passing out information as well." Constance pulled a length of his robe out from beneath his coat and into a hood. "Connect with whoever you wish to bring. I'm going to get the weather prediction from the God of Storms. See you in the morning."

"So you do go visit the temple."

"Just on Wind's Days." He winked.

Divine draped her arm around Sage's pot, watching Constance walk away. "Do you get the feeling we missed something?"

One of Sage's thorned appendages rested on the bend in Divine's elbow, a soft scrape of thorns issuing against her coat.

CHAPTER TWELVE

Shortcuts to Ruin

The next day, Divine was coaxing a black-tailed swiller out of a nearby evergreen while Sage watched from a sunny spot on the ground when she heard boots crunching on snow. She whistled what she hoped was an equivalent of 'talk to you later' and pivoted to face Constance.

Her smile fell as she caught sight of his seriously knit features.

"We should leave immediately." Constance folded his hands into his sleeves. "I thought we would..." he trailed off, shaking his head.

"Why the hurry? Don't we need to work on my control first?"

Divine's stomach tightened imagining inadvertently summoning ursavara to one of their camp sites, the bear-sized creature with boar-like horns ripping through the Goodly One with its claws. Without his own magic, he would need her protection.

"Servants from your temple are on the way and while I don't have a reliable source on precisely who or when they left, it's best to move quickly." Constance looked at his feet. "We'll take the coastal route. If they are close to Iramont, we'll miss them entirely and have a few days head start before they find out where you've gone."

Divine's head spun. This was moving quicker than she expected. Her mind moved into a list of things that needed to be done. She had to talk to Saph.

To tell her...to tell her what? "I hope you don't find someone before I get back"?

She swallowed a lump in her throat.

"I need to start packing my things and teach someone what I do for the tea while I'm gone. I should probably let the Edge know I won't be back at the clinic." Divine rubbed her forehead. "When should I tell Syka we plan to leave? I talked to her briefly last night and she was interested in coming."

Constance held her stare with his grey-blue eyes. "Tell her today. Within the next hour."

"Oh wow." Would Saph still be at the tavern so she could say goodbye as she grabbed her things? The lump in her throat descended to her ribs. She'd made a decision without realizing it. She was leaving Iramont.

"Gather your things swiftly and meet me at the Palfrey Post."

Constance retreated up the road to the gate, presumably to gather what he needed for travel from his temple. Divine let him move through the city to keep their distance, though her insides rattled like a bird in a cage waiting to fly. She found it curious that Constance could leave his First Servant duties so easily, but he had said that his temple was different. She made a note to ask him more about what the servants did daily.

Sage crackled from the ground, snapping her out of her musings. Divine scooped him up.

"I do feel conflicted," she replied to his inquiry. "Why? Well, I need answers and I think Arosia is the only place I'm going to get them. But I also like it here in Iramont. I like Saph. And I like Sylus and Edward and I guess Syka isn't too bad. But then again, if I leave, they'll forget me."

Sage's pot issued a sigh and a pop.

"Thank you, Sage. You're unforgettable too."

Though the sun was high, the cold seeped through her coat and into her skin as she hurried back to the Sultry Sapphire.

Using her key, she pushed the door open. It was lunchtime and the tavern sat empty.

"Saph?" she called.

The tavern was quiet but for the faint sounds of the city whispering their way through the walls and the crackle of the fire. She climbed up the stairs and just as she reached the top, Sylus's door opened. He stepped out, shirtless, and a towel around his shoulders.

"If you're looking for Saph, she left shortly after you did. Tea shopping, I believe."

"Here." Divine thrust the clay pot into Sylus's hands. "Put Sage on the bedroom windowsill, please."

Divine spun, ignoring Sage's squelch and Sylus's befuddled brows, and raced down the stairs and out into the street. She jogged, searching in the windows of restaurants before turning toward familiar sundry stores and specialty dealers. Time was an ocean rising behind her eyes and she felt like urgency sat just beneath her skull, ready to crest and crash into a spray of white. She couldn't find Saph and she didn't have much time before Constance would expect her to leave the city.

Oh Goddess, if Constance thinks we should run from my temple then...then something bad is coming.

Placing a hand on her stomach, Divine leaned against the nearest wall. Her breath came out in short puffs of frosted air, and she focused on covering herself with a wave of calm from her well. Panic would not help her. Breathing more regularly, she wrapped her arms around herself like a repentant hug and returned to the Sultry Sapphire.

Divine tried to hold back her tears, but she swiped her shoulder at her eyes and sniffled, launching herself up the stairs. Distracting herself as she worked, finding her disused travel pack from the journey chasing Madeline, Divine spoke to Sage sitting on the windowsill—either visiting with the spinetooth plant or watching city life.

"Do you want to come with me, Sagacious? It'll be months. In winter. I can do my best to keep you warm. Wrap you in a blanket?"

Sage's soil squelched.

"You're right, you probably won't see much." Divine's hand froze over her bag. "Where...do you...see from? Nevermind, it doesn't matter. I don't know if we're taking a wagon but that could be warmer."

The top stems on Sage wiggled as his pot creaked.

"Well, by blankets and soapstone. They're heated in fire and last most of the day. And if someone shares the wagon who brought a Passionate's Pyre then that would be ideal. Though I guess it could topple over and burn someone or the wagon…no I don't guess they would bring one."

Sage's middle stems wriggled so the thorns turned up then down.

"Even if they did, Constance wants to keep things hidden so I guess we won't share a wagon with others." Divine's fingers hovered over a dry sprig of yellow on the windowsill. A flower Saph had bought at the fall market and put behind her ear. It would get crumbled to dust in her bag. Her chest tightened as she listened to Sage's question. "There's probably warm places to rest. On my way down, I stopped at towns and villages that all had a place to sleep. But now we're going along the coast, and I only know what I've seen on maps."

The pot gave a combination of crackles and sucking sounds.

"I do think Sylus and Saph will let you stay on the mantel. And I'll make sure to remind them to feed you tasty bugs in my note."

A mournful hum whispered from the pot.

"I…don't know if I'll be back. Right now, I want to. But I don't know what I'm going to find in Arosia. It's no wonder Saph wouldn't want to come. I've messed up her Steeped in Sapphire. I'm flirting with people like she does. She liked me when I was confident. I'm…I'm not anymore. I need to fix my magic. Find out who I am. And not get Saph messed up in all of my floundering."

And she was rambling. Just like Saph said Divine did when she was flustered.

Divine listened to Sage's sounds, questions in sizzles and cracks and quivering stems. "Constance has been very mysterious about this. Whatever is in Arosia must be really radical since he doesn't think I'll believe him without it."

Divine tossed her last warm clothes and after a brief hesitation, threw all of her clothes in including her new winter dress and topped the pile with her coin bag.

"What if I'm actually a Kellas? Magically altered so I don't look like one? They can convert talisman energy from the attached wells into something new. That's basically what I'm doing, right?"

Sage crackled and popped.

"Now that you put it that way, it does sound preposterous."

Divine flung her bag over her shoulder. "Oh Sage, I'm going to miss your pessimism."

Should she knock on Sylus's door to say goodbye? She shook her head. He'd wrap her in a tight hug and make her cry. Ask why. Divine scooped up the decacacti, tucking him protectively against her chest, his thorns snagging on the fabric, and descended the stairs. Though, she found her feet moved slowly.

Rummaging around under the bar, Divine placed a sheet of paper on the surface next to Sage and his hat and stared, as if the words she needed to say would manifest themselves. Each time she thought of a sentence she blinked away tears.

"I just have to do it," she whispered and began scratching pencil against the paper.

Saph, I have to leave today. I can't be who I want to be without answers. And I wouldn't expect you to leave your tavern. But if you want, send me a message in Arosia.

Thank you. For everything.

Sage wants to stay warm. I think he'd like to relocate permanently to the fireplace. Please take care of him. His food is in the chest that once held a quest.

Divine

She sat Sage on the corner of the message, her vision blurry. Sniffing, she tapped the thornless crown of Sage's main stem. Maybe he would sprout a flower there one day.

"I hope this isn't goodbye forever," she whispered.

She quickened her feet and slammed the door shut behind her harder than she meant to. No going back now. Divine angled her feet in the direction of Syka's favorite apothecary where this time of day on a Soul's Day she would be watching them craft potions out of dead things. Divine needed a thief.

* * *

"I hope it's not too last minute," Divine added to her request. "It was sudden for me, too. I'll understand if you can't leave at the first crash of thunder."

"I'm always ready." Syka said, stepping next to Divine. "Pack light. Walk light. It's the way of the rogue."

"Light?" Divine eyed Syka's small bag slung over her shoulder. "Aren't you always picking up treasures? 'Desire, acquire', right?"

Divine knew there were pockets on Syka's belt as well, but between the coat pockets and the bag, Syka couldn't have more than an extra shirt, a few potions, and some soap with her.

Syka tutted. "Of course. But bringing my treasure on a mission would be a novice move. Get knocked out and someone takes all of your good stuff. My best items are safe."

"Well, I'm glad you can come."

"What kind of apothecaries do you have in Arosia? Take that black bottle in the Dark Cottage Apothecary, did you know that if you combine..."

But Syka's words tumbled into a murmur as Divine's thoughts pushed out everything else. Syka wasn't Saph. There would be no forays in the forest this time, Maybe she could convince Constance that she didn't need to leave right away, and that would give her more time to talk to Saph. Maybe collect the courage to ask Saph what the tavern-and-tea owner really felt for her.

Eventually, Syka and Divine rounded the corner of the Palfrey Post to find someone already waiting in front of the large doors. A moment of panic coursed through Divine in icy cold before she recognized the taller figure. He'd changed into brown pants and a knee-length brown coat, and the ear flaps on his hat accented the Goodly One's cheekbones.

But it was the purple and blue skirt, the blocks of colors like cards, racing across the street that demanded her attention.

"Saph! What are you doing here?"

"He was squeaking." Saph looked down at Sage, a small strip of blue and orange fabric wrapped like a scarf around his middle and a bundle pooling in his pot in addition to his going-out hat. "I didn't know plants could do that."

Divine took the pot from Saph. Emotions threatened to tumble from her eyes. Saph must have torn one of her dresses to help Sage stay warm. If she looked at Saph, she might burst into tears.

"You must have been really upset, Sage, for even Saph to hear you talk. I thought you didn't want to be cold?" Divine paused, listening to Sage's crackles. "Well, I'm glad you trust me to care for you."

Saph thumbed at Constance. "I didn't know he was coming."

"I am a guide for Divine to find her resolve."

"I don't want you to go," Saph blurted.

Divine's heart skipped a beat. "You don't?"

"And when someone aches for you"—Syka tilted her head back, reciting to the sky, arms wide—"the weather becomes sunshine."

"I didn't get to say goodbye," Saph continued. "And I didn't want you leaving thinking I didn't want you to come back. You'll come back, won't you?"

"If you want me to. If you don't mind me showing up months later."

"I'd keep you here if I could. But I know you need to do this. Your magic, the temples, it's all been weighing on you. If I was in the guild still I'd...but there's the tavern..."

Divine took one of Saph's hands in hers. "It's your livelihood. You can't leave it for months."

"I wish it were different—"

"You could be back in a week," Constance interjected. "If that helps."

Divine spun. "How?"

"I know someone."

"I won't ask." Divine then centered on Saph. "But this is great. At least I'll be back quickly."

"If it's just a week, maybe I could get Edward to help Sylus run the Sapphire while I'm away. He does still owe me for a couple of games of Crossroads."

"Sylus would appreciate that," Syka added. "The tavern was a little much for him to manage alone on your last adventure. Service was slow."

"Can you wait a few minutes while I track him down?" Saph asked.

Constance glanced up the street. "Meet us at the Hydro Spondence in thirty minutes and I'll explain more about our plans."

Bouncing forward, Saph kissed Divine on the cheek. "Be right there."

As if the action tethered them together for the separation, Saph locked her gaze on Divine then she winked and bolted across the street.

Divine addressed Constance. "Why the Hydro Spondence?"

"Seems like the man has a message to send," Syka supplied, eyeing the Goodly One from under her black bangs.

"There is someone I must contact before we can travel," he said, stepping into the street.

More mystery. Divine was beginning to think that the God of Virtue's virtues did not include being forthright. Or at least this servant lacked the trait.

"Can we walk there together now you've changed?" Divine motioned toward him. "Your appearance, I mean."

Constance nodded. "Few should recognize me as a Goodly One now."

At the sign of the pond with scroll reeds, the group veered into the building.

"We would like to contact the hydromancers at the Weathered Crossroads. Can you connect us?"

"Certainly, *inlet*." Ayar surveyed their group. "All of you?"

"Yes, please. If you have a room that can accommodate us. We are expecting one more."

"I have a perfect room. How long will the connection need to last?"

"Oh, only a few minutes on your side. The hydromancer there will contact us back so as to not tie up your valuable resources. It will be a substantial conversation, likely lasting through the night. I know you receive far more messages than Weathered Crossroads and each of you need your rest."

"That is kind of you, inlet." She dipped her head. "Shall I charge you a day's rate and we see if you need more time as of the morning?"

"That would be appreciated." Constance placed a tall stack of coins on the counter. "And a soundproof room if possible."

"Of course. Let me get your room reserved, *inlet*, and I'll be right back."

As Ayar left, Syka leaned on the counter, eyeing Constance from boots to hat.

"You've got an awful lot of friggons for a Goodly One." She poked the front of his coat. "How much more you got in there?"

He flattened the front layer with his hands. "As much as might be needed."

Syka leaned in, lowering her voice. "Where'd you get it? Donations?"

Constance frowned. "If you are implying that I have taken from the funds intended to help those in need—"

Syka held up her hands, leaning back on the counter. "I'm just saying it's interesting. You be the version of yourself you want to be. We have such little time to be anything else."

Divine raised an eyebrow. "Are you judging him? I seem to recall you offering me your services of stealing." Divine lowered her voice. "Which is why you're here."

"Let's call it balancing. Redistribution. Stealing doesn't paint the right light on the situation."

Divine chuckled. "No, I guess it doesn't."

Ayar returned before the conversation could go any further. She escorted them as she had with Divine earlier in the week, delivering them to a booth twice the size of what Divine had used. The farsight pond was about the same, but the area around it was more spacious and there were six chairs.

"I hope this gives you room to move around and relax during your conversations, inlet. There're snacks on the far table. Send any one of you out if you need anything—water, hot chocolate, the washroom. What's the name of your last participant and I'll make sure to deliver them."

"Her name is Saph," Divine supplied. "Thank you, Ayar."

Ayar pressed her hands together, then moved into the room. As before, she held her hands over the water, almost touching the surface. The water tinted brown and shapes began to form. A room like the Iramont Hydro Spondence became visible, frozen notelets hanging from the ceiling like someone had painted the moment rain fell from the sky.

A woman's freckled face appeared, smiling.

"Merry Midwinter, Ayar. Do you have a message to send to us for in-person delivery?"

"Not this time. I'm connecting these customers for their conversation. May blessings of winter and light be upon you."

Without another word, Ayar exited and closed the door.

Constance stepped closer to the pool. "Is Ada there? We would like to speak with her."

"Oh yes, I'll go get her."

Several moments passed before a woman's smooth face slid into view, her brown eyes focused off to the side as if she didn't look at the pool at all. Her thick, dark curls gathered on top of her head beneath a green band of cloth typical of Nelithorians. Light caught the golden-brown tones of her cheeks, giving her a warm glow as she chewed the end of a candy bubble. She lowered her chin into her hand with a sigh and pulled the sugary stick from her wide lips with a pop.

"Whatdya need?" she asked, her voice dropping low with disinterest.

Though Divine couldn't detect her emotions through the scrying, it was clear this person did not want to be there.

"Good to see you, Ada."

The woman sat taller, her focus finally connecting to her audience. "Constance. What are you doing out of your self-righteous punishment hole?"

Syka choked on a laugh and Constance cleared his throat.

"Could we establish a connection from your end? I would like to discuss travel plans."

"I suppose." Ada stood, bending closer to the water. She tapped her candy on her lips. "Your new friends have me intrigued. Give me five minutes."

The water clouded as Ada and the building disappeared. The door behind Divine opened and Saph entered. Her axe peeked over her shoulder, and she had a bag slung on her arm.

Divine smiled. "Edward will help out?"

"I'm all set. What did I miss?" Saph asked, dropping into a seat next to Divine.

"Not much. Constance is contacting someone at Weathered Crossroads."

"The Crossroads, huh? I haven't been there, though I've heard some fun stories. When you've got roads from every direction converging there, you're bound to cross paths with interesting people. Did you travel there?"

"I stayed the night, but that was it. I didn't explore."

"The world is so large," Saph mused. "And we see such a tiny part of it our whole lives."

Divine shifted Sage to balance on her thigh. "I think I'd like to see more. I've never left the Arosia province. Well, before chasing my talisman. But I didn't really get to see any of the places between here and there. Did you know there's a crystal forest on the west coast?"

Saph grinned. "Prismatic Grove. You mean you've never seen the Dalga Hot Springs or the Moonmire?"

Divine shook her head so hard her red waves bounced across her face. "And I want to see them. And Shroombal's village. All of it. You probably don't have any desire for that."

"I think if I knew I could always come home to Iramont with you, there'd be some desire."

Always. Divine's stomach fluttered. She should ask. Make sure she wasn't imagining things from the way her magic made her feel.

She twisted her emerald ring. "Saph, are we—"

"Alright, Constance," the pool verbalized Ada's voice. "We are alone. But if the others find out we were talking, there will be questions."

The Goodly One held up both of his hands. "I have been careful."

Ada's crossed arms and stern expression showed how she felt about the situation, even though Divine didn't understand why.

"What do you need?" Ada asked.

"We must travel to Arosia. I believe the balance is shifting and though you refuse to pick a side—"

"Constance." Ada's narrowed brow and tone gave warning.

"I must choose an action. I will take these three with me. I believe the others may be sending their underlings to investigate Divine. If we wait, the opportunity to avoid them will be missed. And Divine may be taken into the hands of the Goddess of Souls or whoever wants to use her."

"Do you trust them?" Ada asked, lowering her chin.

"With your secret?"

"With yours."

Divine glanced at Saph who raised her eyebrow in return.

"I have given them very little and they have trusted my guidance. Divine is *becoming*, and needs answers to the changes in her magic."

Ada's mouth formed an O shape, her resistance seeming to deflate from her body.

"I can get you here, then after a rest, to inside the edge of Arosia."

"My gratitude runs deep. I know how demanding it will be with four of us."

"The water can transport us?" Divine asked, unable to keep the excited edge from her voice. "I knew it. Those puddles in the boradain's prison house had to be hydromancer magic. But...no one knows of this ability. I asked."

"It is a lost art," Ada replied. "Very few have the talent."

The water undulated, seeming to thicken as it dyed a liquid silver. Rectangle shapes began to form. A lighted square for a window slowly focused. A habitspace.

"What she means is she doesn't teach anyone." Constance nodded at the water. "Step in and you'll appear next to Ada."

"Fangs and forests!" Syka exclaimed.

"I don't know if I want to step through puddles again." Saph leaned over the edge of the pool. "You know what happened last time?"

"That's why I'm here, right?" Syka asked. "I mean, I've been following Divine like you—"

"You've been *following* me? Why?" Divine's mind raced as she looked from Syka to Saph. "It was more than you training with Shroombal again. You thought I needed protection?"

"This whole Madeline thing, luring you to the demon—it was unusual. What if it wasn't over? I couldn't always go with you through the city."

"You thought I couldn't protect myself, so Syka shadowed me? Why couldn't you talk to me about it?"

"Ladies!" Syka shouted. "Can we figure out this miscommunication later?"

Then Syka jumped, splashing droplets over the edge, and vanished. As the water stilled, her body appeared in the mirror-like surface near Ada.

"I'm in the Goddess-scorching Weathered Crossroads. George's statue is out the window!"

"We should go." Constance confirmed. "Maintaining the connection drains Ada's energy."

Divine huffed, turning from Saph. She'd thought with the story of Saph's first love that the tavern owner had been open with everything. She'd thought wrong.

Divine stepped over the edge of the pool. Like being at the center of a lake, water pressing into every pour. As if carried on bubbles she heard similar words that continued to haunt her. *You know how deep you can drink. But lack of confidence can be your undoing.*

She blinked and another room materialized. Holding out her foot to shake it, Divine noted her boot and leg were already dry. Not a drop gathered on her lace charms, or anywhere on her.

Saph and Constance followed, stepping out of Ada's pool.

Ada's eyes held Divine's before she sunk into a chair, slumping her forehead into her hand. The images of the Hydro Spondence room faded from the water. Out the window behind Ada, wagons and carts traversed wide streets bordered by multilevel inns and tightly packed businesses advertising food and lodging in Trickster-enhanced glowing signs. Whatever snow remained was dirty splashes against the base of poles supporting awnings and lampposts. At the center of an intersection, where roads from all over Trelvania finally converged, stood the statue of the card game's namesake; George.

Inside the room was cozy. A traditional fireplace and a few chairs with blankets. Shelves on the walls held books and glass jars of dried herbs. Art of the mountains of Nelithor was mounted on one wall.

A potted plant hung in the corner of the room in a braided sling.

"Do you have any rope?" Divine asked Ada, still gazing at the sling.

"Huh? Probably in a drawer over there."

Divine rummaged where Ada pointed and found a ball of twine. As the others conversed, she snipped a length and began tying and looping the rope around Sage's pot.

"Will you come with us?" Constance asked Ada. "We will need a way to swiftly return to Iramont."

"I'll think about it. But I need an hour or two before I can send you to Arosia, regardless."

"Rest. We'll get a cluster of people to think highly of you. You'll recover quickly."

Saph kicked her hip out, placing her fist on the bump. "I don't know much about temple worship, but I thought Divine's Goddess was the one with the healing powers."

Past conversations swirled like pebbles in a bottle. Divine knitted her brows. "Their...appreciation makes your magic stronger. Like what's happening to me?"

Ada reclined in the chair with a sigh as she rubbed her temples.

"You can tell them," Ada said weakly.

Constance lowered his head. "We'll be back soon. Are nuts still your favorite?"

"Only if you're going to roast them."

Chuckling, Constance motioned for the three women to follow him out of Ada's house.

Divine slung the rope cross-body with Sage dangling at her hip, his tiny scarf and bundle of fabric at the base of his main stem still in place.

When the door clicked behind them, Saph posed a question.

"What did Ada want you to tell us?"

Constance didn't reply at first, and Divine moved to close her fist around her thoughts.

"She's what Constance thinks I am. An Old Soul. She has power that the temples say isn't possible."

It wasn't a question. And as the truth of her words sunk in, Divine felt the last thread tethering her to the belief in her Goddess snap. She would uncover the truth behind the pantheon, even if she had to dig under every temple.

CHAPTER THIRTEEN

Wagon Rides to Flatnuts

Instead, she dug for flatnuts.

Warmth heated her body with the effort; poke, step, push, lift. The ground crunched and held on with frozen clutches, not allowing itself to easily be shifted. Each spade lifted minimal dirt and rock, but the displacement would help reveal roots if they had survived the first frosts beneath the soil, as their species waited for spring before sending out new green shoots to gather the sun's energy. Unlike the scents of oiled wheels and every food all at once on the streets of Weathered Crossroads, here everything smelled...crisp. Fresh.

"How many do we need?" Divine asked Constance, as he moved to a new spot between large stone formations covered in snow.

"Enough for at least a bowl full. More if you want to take some home with you for your teas."

Divine thought of the sugar and cinnamon roasted flatnuts she loved from the fall. Yes, that flavor would be lovely if they could figure out how to add it to the tea mixtures.

"That's a great idea. Thanks, Constance."

He hummed in reply and continued his search.

Divine stepped over her digging spot and started anew. Poke, step, push, lift. These plants knew—when things became rough, it was best to hide. No one had to tell them. To survive they knew they needed to lay low until conditions were better. Just like Constance advised Divine to hide, keeping her presence unknown to the capital when they entered the city. Used to fading into the background at her temple, the attention she'd been receiving in Iramont was the vibration of an accordion's full bellows singing loudly.

Could she go back to the quieter being she was before meeting Saph?

Divine straightened, the stiffness in her lower back slowing her ascent, and watched the others at their task. Saph and Constance similarly dug, their coats making them look like black bears as they hunched over promising spots beneath boulders. Divine debated approaching Saph, but her boots were rooted in a quagmire of vexation.

The sun painted strips of pink, reflected on the snow-covered hills that rolled like whales. They breached until they reached the horizon where the Spine of Trelvania was barely visible as its northern tip ended. Weathered Crossroads was an hour the way of the setting sun. No spiraling Holy District existed in the city, but the rest of the staples of any town were there. Syka had walked the streets nearest taverns and restaurants praising the Hydro Spondence services she'd received, in hopes to rally positive sentiment.

According to Constance, Ada would not be ready to send them on to Arosia until into the night.

"But the more who release their admiration, their thanks and belief in her, the quicker she will recover her spent energy," Constance had explained as their small wagon pulled out of the crossroad city. Divine knew the effects of that admiration. "Meanwhile, we will thank her with her favorite treat."

"Because it hastens the recovery?" Syka guessed.

Wheels slushed through brown muck traversed from every compass point as the wulfs pulled them through the eastern exit and into the Emerald Hills, though the snow hid the verdant sheaths that gave them their name.

"Because it is the right thing to do." He smirked. "And it will give us something other than inquiries to focus on. You have questions, and they will be answered when it is productive."

Saph had grumbled something about not fairly trading information and Divine had settled into the bench between them both, her back pressed against the seat and her arms touching her companions. Their bodies blocked some of the cold wind, but the silence between them was just as chilly. The blankets piled on their laps as Divine hugged Sage close. The decacacti vibrated in his pot and she knew he offered comfort rather than shivering. She couldn't help glancing out of the corner of her eye at Saph, but couldn't find the words. A thread of trust had been snipped between them.

A metal-on-metal clang broke Divine's thoughts. Sage squelched from his pot on the ground nearby. Crouching, Divine brushed debris away from her shallow hole.

"Whatever it is," she mumbled to Sage. "It doesn't look like a root or a rock. I'm going to try to clear some more."

Back on her feet, Divine dug around the spot, trying to loosen the top layer of soil and pry it back. When she had stabbed and scraped at an area roughly the size of a chest she crouched again. The low light of the falling sun cast muted colors, but the rectangular shapes were rough to the touch, almost like...

"Bricks?" she voiced her thoughts. "Or a type of road stone."

Sage hummed in a contemplative manner.

"Why would they be out here?"

Divine stood, studying the landscape. Syka lounged against a fallen tree, black scarf pulled up to her nose, her hunt abandoned. Taller trees poked beyond the edge of the wood's canopy nearby. Despite their loss of leaves for the winter, their branches knitted tightly, preventing deeper viewing. Divine could see several trees were draped in vines, like nature had stretched a shawl around them. They had followed a path Constance knew, as there had been no road or markers pointing the way.

"Did you find some?" Saph asked, appearing next to Divine.

Gripping the shovel firmer, Divine focused on the ground. "Surprised I could do it on my own?"

Saph exhaled and Divine thought she would leave but after a few heartbeats Saph spoke low and gentle.

"You are capable of everything you want to do."

Divine spun, and she imagined her brown eyes flashed like dragon's flame. "Then why did you have me trailed like some—some lost cat?"

"I also know that people are capable of horrendous things." A small smile tugged at the corner of Saph's lips. "And I'd rather you make it home safe so I can make you purr."

"Ugh, it's always about sex with you." Divine tossed her shovel and snatched Sage from the ground. "Either it's the tavern or it's sex. I feel like those are the only things that matter to you."

Feeling her head about to explode, Divine stomped toward the tree line. If she could grow wings she could fly above these feelings. Her magic felt hot, magma beneath the surface and hungry to lash out.

"Divine!" Saph called.

Sage crinkled and gave a shiver.

"No," Divine dropped her head to look at the decacacti. "I'm not turning around."

Suddenly, a hand engulfed hers in a warm hold.

"Divine, darling, please stop."

She halted, looking at her boots as Saph's pleading tone filled her with shame. *What am I doing*? Her own frustration mixed with Saph's confusion in a sour scent of berries left squashed in the sun. But Divine didn't seek her well to smooth the emotions. Saph had asked very early in their relationship for Divine to not use her well to influence her, and Divine would respect that. Even if it meant Divine lost her calmly crafted countenance.

"Is that what you think?" Saph reached into Divine's hood, brushing her cheek. Her hand lingered on the side of Divine's face. "That I don't care for you?"

"I..." Divine thought of the Midwinter Nights Faire and the weeks leading up to it. The nights sharing a bed. Saph saying, *"I don't want you to leave."*

In the space of hesitation, Saph spoke again. "I use my body to connect to you. To give you pleasure. I want you to always feel good when we are together. That connection is better than any poetry. At least I thought it was. Do you not enjoy being with me?"

"Oh I do." Divine laughed nervously. "You make me feel *really* good. But sometimes I feel like...well, you flirt with everyone. I just happen to be the lucky one who's landing in your bed for now. Where is this"—Divine motioned between them—"us going?"

Saph pulled her hand back, apprehension adding to the emotional layers seeping into Divine.

"Where do you want it to go?" Saph asked.

Divine's heart raced. "I want to know if you see us long term. If I...if I'm your girlfriend. Or are you keeping your options open?"

A smile crept on Saph's face. "Darling, I named a tea after you."

"Yes, but—"

"That's made from your favorite flavor."

Divine's cheeks burned. "That was really sweet, actually."

"See?" Saph cupped Divine's face with both hands. "I'm all about actions."

"But I need the words." Divine shook her head, the doubts stretching inside her like leathery wings. "And you didn't talk to me. You've been going off training with Shroombal and I thought you were probably seeing other people. And must not think I'm strong since I've been a healer this whole time, or my magic changing was scaring you since you're having me guarded when I could very easily—"

Saph's lips pressed against Divine's and despite her clenched hands, Divine melted into Saph like ice against flame.

"You ramble when you're worried and I love it." Saph said pulling back. "There's only been you since you arrived. I assumed...Shit. I could have communicated this better. I didn't know you thought I was sharing my regard. When I'm dating someone, it's just that person. You and I haven't just been hooking up. We've been dating, learning about each other."

Saph paused, taking Divine's free hand to her lips and placing a kiss on her knuckles. "Can you promise to tell me what is bothering you *before* we're silently freezing on a wagon ride to flatnuts?"

The scent in the air changed into apple blossoms of summer and something within her stopped coiling and expanded. Sage pawed an appendage against her side.

Divine nodded.

Constance had warned her and she hadn't paid attention. *Shortcuts to ruin.* Relying on reading the emotions of a person did not guarantee she understood their motivations. She would do better.

"By the way, I don't think you're incapable of taking care of yourself." Saph shrugged, the axe over her shoulder bobbing. "I was worried. If I wasn't strong enough, what if someone worse than *Madeloser* came and hurt you? We're a team, and I couldn't let you down. You shouldn't have to face the next bad thing alone. So, I started training again. And when I couldn't be there, I asked Syka to watch out for anything strange. You're right, I should have talked to you about this. It's not that I was scared of your magic or that I didn't think you were strong. I don't trust these temples. And I didn't want to lose you."

The temples. Divine's mood darkened. The temples were lying to their followers. Had her own First Servant known why Madeline had lured Divine? Secrets and half-truths. Half-truths became the wheels that spun reality in the way those in authority wanted it to be shaped. And omissions became a tool to manipulate others. To manipulate Divine.

"I understand why you did it." Divine often stood up for others and having Saph want to protect her instead cooled her aggravation. "But I thought you knew how I felt about not being open. And while you never lied, it still feels like it. Because you hid it."

"And I'm so sorry. You're right. I can commit to communicating with words more. Yes, the tavern is important, yes, I absolutely love tangling our bodies. But I want all of you, even the things I can't touch."

Divine's stomach fluttered in all the right ways and she leaned in, kissing Saph slow and soft.

When they separated their lips, Saph placed their foreheads together. "Divine, will you be my girlfriend, my only girlfriend, for sex and everything not sex?"

Divine grinned. "Absolutely yes. This is exactly what I needed."

Sage nearly tumbled as Divine reached her free arm around Saph's back, pressing their bodies together as best as they could in their coats. She balanced Sage against her side as her magic well swirled like a vortex, releasing the fragrance of a rose garden, and Sage sizzle-crackled. Divine sought Saph's mouth eagerly, tilting her head to deepen the kiss. In the twilit darkness of the newly formed night, Divine could imagine it was just the two of them and their frost-touched lips.

"Hey friends?" Syka's worried voice cut into the moment. "What's that sound?"

Divine and Saph pulled away, sharing a confused expression before turning to Syka, who stood staring into the woods. Clutching Saph's hand, Divine tugged and they walked to the edge. Shadows clung to everything as the echo of the sun's final rays dimmed on the horizon, the trees' branches reaching with extended fingers.

Whispers of rhythmic rushing of air gradually crescendoed as a waft fanned the scent of pine. An occasional distant screech punctuated the sound that seemed to press against Divine's ears. Wings that longed to break free.

Sage rustled and squeaked, his thorns scratching against Divine's coat.

"I think I called them." Divine's hand tightened around Saph's arm. "I don't know what's coming but my frustration...it can't be good."

"Hey, whatever it is"— Saph shifted out of Divine's grip, withdrawing her axe from her back—"we can face it. Together."

Balancing the double-headed axe on her shoulder, Saph motioned Syka closer. "We might need to make a quick retreat. Check on the wagon?"

As Syka jogged away, Divine put her head through Sage's rope and shifted his dangling to her back. She was not going to stand there with her hands full while Saph fought.

"Goodly One. You should get to the wagon," Syka instructed. "I doubt virtues will be of use."

Dark figures burst from the treetops. Three of them, beating long leathery wings. They angled up before banking to circle back toward Saph and Divine, the largest one flanked by the others. Like dragons, they had membranous wings with elongated bones though their bodies were only the size of a wulf.

"Werewings," Saph grumbled. "There must be a nest nearby."

Divine mentally flipped through the bestiary she had nearly memorized from her younger days in her temple. But as one of the creatures landed before them, pluming snow like a stone dropped into a bowl of flour, the knowledge wafted away as well.

Identical *thwumps* sounded behind them, signaling the werewings had them surrounded. Divine sensed an unnatural hunger and mentally dove into her well, siphoning and transforming the magical waters into a protective dome around Saph and herself; a hazy waterfall.

No assault of scents? No sneezing?

She glanced over her shoulder. Both smaller werewings approached on their four legs, wings folded—hunters on the prowl—toward Syka and Constance, who stood back-to-back. Their expressions were as unreadable as ink drawings in the limited light of the just-rising moon. They had horned heads and erect ears like a bat. They sniffed the air with their flat noses.

"Have you fought these before?" Divine asked, patting Sage's pot to reassure the trembling decacacti at her back.

Saph shifted her sapphire-blue wrapped grip into a two-handed grasp. "Never. Everyone in the mercenary guild knows to stay away. Someone accepted a mark once and never came back. Werewings are fiercely protective."

"Did the guild person...turn?" The words of the morality lesson in the book came back to her. *When you pretend to be something you are not, it is hard to find the something that you are.*

"Only her bag was found. Do you think the myths are true?"

A cloud shifted and moonlight brightened the snow. Before them, the werewing seemed to crumple in on itself, its parts twisting in unnatural ways. Hollow cheeks on a too thin skull emerged from the blob that was a werewing. It's sunken, glowing red eyes fixed on Divine.

"Let's not find out. I don't want any of us hurt or to turn into werewings. Maybe if we retreat, they'll leave us alone."

"What does your magical scent say?"

"Nothing. I think it's broken. It's certainly unreliable." Divine pointed at the werewing, which straightened, revealing a bipedal form. Sticks and moss poked out of its skin stretched tight on bone, its shape mostly human, except for its long-clawed fingers and toes.

This was her fault. She had to get them out. She stepped back, testing her domed shield to move with her. It did.

"Maybe we can get back to the others, and I can shield them as well."

"So...no fighting?" Saph wiggled her axe.

"We're in werewing territory. Of course they want to defend their home." Sage's pot made a crinkle sound. "And babies."

"Uck, I don't want to see what those look like as infants."

Divine touched Saph's elbow. "Let's try not to injure them if we can."

"I don't know that we'll have much choice. But I support you."

"I knew it," shouted Syka from somewhere behind them. "Undead are real!"

Saph rolled her eyes and muttered, "They're grotesque but that doesn't mean they were once dead."

"Try to send them away!" Constance shouted, his tone commanding. "Like the mockingcrate."

"You fell for a mockingcrate?" Saph chortled.

"Not me. Constance. Let me focus."

Divine knitted her brow.

"It's not *I can't*," she whispered. "It's *I'll learn*."

The werewing-now-humanoid raced forward. Divine's magic was there, she could feel it, but it wasn't doing anything. She groaned and the layer around them flickered. The werewing dove for them but collided with the shield, spinning to the side. Saph kicked out with her boot, passing through the barrier, and caught the creature in its rear. It passed into the shadow of a tall rock formation and shifted into its winged form. It staggered, then beat its wings, rising, and threw a look down at them, peeling its lips back around carnivorous teeth. Then it flew across the field of snow, staying to the places where night's shadows stretched from trees and rocks. Right toward Constance and Syka.

Saph bolted through the protective layer, pumping her arms and the axe clutched in one hand.

"Saph, no!" Divine called, the haze of her shield dissipating as she ran after her.

Divine saw how Constance stood in the wagon, attempting to soothe the bucking wulfs. One moment Syka was there too and the next...gone.

"Where's Syka?" Divine darted her eyes across the area.

Saph grunted, swinging her blade wide as the large werewing dove. It screeched away.

"Probably used one of her disappearing potions." Saph swung again, creating a gap between them and the werewing, and the creature banked for a nearby clump of trees.

"Disappearing? Nevermind, I'll ask later."

They ran again, closing the distance to Constance. Sage bounced at her back and Divine steadied his pot with a hand pressed against it. The decacacti's soil crackled like pebbles dropped on a table.

"I'm not *trying* to make you sick. This is just how I run."

Divine ignored his advice on stride length.

"Look!" Divine pointed at a werewing as it snapped its claws empty over Constance's ducking form.

The snow had darkened as a cloud had edged over the moon, casting the wagon in the grey of nighttime. The werewing had changed.

Syka reappeared and slashed at its back, twin daggers drawing green blood before she sprinted away. The werewing screeched and lifted higher, out of reach, followed by its twin companion. They hovered over the humans.

Saph angled toward them. "Come on."

"Please go away, please go away," Divine tried sending the thought, hoping it would cause them to flee. But nothing happened. "Why isn't it working?"

Divine and Saph reached the wagon as the second smaller werewing dove in front of Constance.

Where's the bigger one?

Divine didn't have time to check as the Goodly One somersaulted off the wagon to land behind the nearest werewing, a short staff in each hand. Divine wondered where the weapons had come from as Constance lashed out at the werewing's thighs, then pushed both of his hands into the creature's legs, sending it flipping. The werewing careened, smacked the snow, then steadied itself as it rose to join the other injured one above them. Droplets marred the snow.

Divine stepped next to Constance, pulling from her well, and in a waterfall, lowered a barrier around them and the wulfs. She touched the wet nose of one then the other, sending tranquil ripples of energy through her fingertips. The wulfs slowed their movements. Divine sighed, glad her magic had worked.

"Nice moves, 'Stance." Saph touched the blade of her axe to her forehead. "You've been hiding your muscles from us."

Constance looked down at his coat. "It's the robes."

"That's not—"

Syka appeared, hunched with her daggers gripped in each hand. She sneaked forward and the rogue immediately bounced off the barrier.

Syka rubbed her nose. "Oof. Let me in."

"Of course, sorry." Divine released the hold on the magic. The dome receded.

"But maybe get it back up as soon as you can, sweetheart."

Divine looked where Saph pointed. The werewings were back on the snow in their humanoid form, walking straight for the wagon.

Saph frowned. "Why do they keep changing?"

Popping sounds came from Sage's pot.

"No, I will not turn around so you can get a better view." Divine's examined the patches of bright and dark on the snow.

"It's the light," Divine breathed. "The light of the moon changes their form. If it's easier to fight them in their shadow form, we should get them to the trees."

"Shadowbone," Syka muttered her favorite Crossroads George suit name. "No, I think light is better here. Then they can't fly out of reach."

"Then we take them to the light." Saph laid her axe on her shoulder. "We'll never get back to Ada with these things trying to haunt us."

"Barrier any time!" Syka shouted.

Constance launched one of his fighting sticks at the nearest walking werewing, whacking it in the nose. The creature snarled but continued forward, clacking its claws together.

Sage's pot sizzled loudly.

"I'm trying!" Divine grabbed Constance's arm. "My magic...it's not working."

"Everyone, compliment Divine." Constance patted Divine's hand before lifting it from his coat. "Think of something positive about her and mean it. Aloud or in your head. But remember"— he drew his face inches from Divine's—"if you rely on the belief of others, you'll never break free of the need for validation."

He was close enough she could feel the heat of his breath on her forehead, and it carried through her like warmth from a fire. He dropped her hand and stepped away, his eyes closing.

Giddiness tickled Divine inside every part of her and she stifled a laugh. She centered on Saph, an overwhelming need to kiss the tavern owner topping her thoughts, but she pushed past the desire. Focusing, Divine drew buckets from her well. She could do this. She pushed a river of satisfaction over the approaching werewings. The creatures hesitated in the shadow of a tree and became once again winged forms.

"Let's lure them to the light," Saph directed.

Syka and Constance moved to the left into a large patch of flat snow while Saph and Divine did the same further back.

Divine held up her hand. "Everyone just...keep doing what you were doing. Send me your...praise? Let me keep trying."

Closing her eyes, Divine breathed deeply. The giddiness resumed, though lesser. She clutched Sage's pot, the twine beneath her fingers a grounding texture.

The wings seemed to beat in a rhythm that said, *"Our home, our home,"* and Divine echoed, *"Yes, to home, to home,"* as she sent the feeling of belonging, of safety. The peace of trees creaking in the wind, the chirps of tree inhabitants, and the rhythmic drop of melting ice onto brush below.

When she opened her eyes, the two smaller werewings were in the sky flying back toward the woods. At the tree line they disappeared. She had lost track of the larger one during the shifting, but it must have already entered the forest.

Saph's hand squeezed hers. "Think they're gone? For good?"

"Maybe." Divine shrugged. "My magic is gelatin cubes in a cup. It's like it will work sometimes and then it won't, like I'm getting clogged or something."

"Well, good thing we're on our way to answers."

"You first." Divine smiled, holding her hand out and helping Saph climb into the wagon.

She looked toward the woods. Constance was telling them how many flatnuts they'd unearthed but Divine didn't catch the amount. Something felt off, but as Divine took in the mounds of rock and the snow she couldn't find anything. She pivoted to the wagon.

The snaps of wings beating like a whip crack. Werewing claws dug into Divine's shoulders and her feet left the ground as Saph reached for her, shouting her name. A shriek issued from Sage, and they climbed higher until the creature carried them over the trees. They hadn't flown far before the large werewing descended onto a tall cluster of trees.

The werewing sat her down in a nest of woven branches and layered in brown leaves. As she swiveled Sage to her front, Divine realized she wasn't in a tree canopy. Crumbling walls surrounded her on three sides, the tallest one behind her with woody vines. Snow sagged the middle of a canvas stretched over the space like a merchant stall. Inside the nest sat a werewing with its wings wrapped around itself.

The werewing looked up, red eyes watching Divine's abductor alight on the top of another wall, before locking on Divine.

Swallowing a lump, Divine squeezed her hands against Sage's pot and forced herself to take even breaths. She dipped into her well, gently swirling the imagined waters and pushed all thoughts beyond harmony and security far away. She let it seep into her bones. And then she listened.

Sage shivered, perhaps too stunned from their flight to speak. Squirrels darted over the forest floor in search of nuts. An owl slept. A cloud of worry hung over the nest.

Images flashed into her mind. Shouts. Her shouts. Traveling through the roots of the trees. Exiting through vines to mollusks gripping the walls of the ruins, the bark of trees. Shells that should have been closed through the winter opening to exhale their toxin. This place should have been safe for the werewing family until the trees began to turn green again. The older children and the parents would feel better in a few sunrises. But the baby...

The vision vanished. The mother werewing opened her wings. Pressed to her chest in her arms was a baby, its wings no bigger than Divine's hands. Its chest rose in shuddering breaths, too pronounced for such a small thing.

Divine blinked hard against tears. Her wild magic had caused this. Her inability to control her talisman, her connection. Her frustration with Saph unchecked had been a call to all nearby creatures. As if she had whispered "Awake" in each ear. She knew this, just as she knew what Sage was saying. Because she was finally listening to the werewing's song in the beats of the forest.

"I can help," Divine said softly, holding out her hands. She flicked her eyes to the perched werewing. "That's why you brought me here, isn't it?"

The mother shifted closer, cradling the young werewing as her wings shifted out for balance. She sniffed the top of the baby's head then stretched to hand the baby to Divine. Attempting to mimic the cradle hold, Divine looked down at the short snout and flat nose. She traced her fingertips across the soft fur on the baby's forehead. Her shoulders shuddered with a sob. Gritting her teeth, Divine chose to act. She would fix this.

Divine dove into her well, the water around her forming an outline and she *saw* inside the smal werewing. The heart. The lungs. The necrotic tissue lesions. Divine swirled her hands through the water, drawing out the poison—negating it with the water of her well—and she mended the wounds.

Cocooning the baby in protective water, Divine reached tendrils of her well to the others, siphoning the noxious air from their lungs and their blood. Then she swam deeper as she listened to the sounds of the forest. The vibrations of Divine's emotions had mimicked increased activity in animals and trees of the spring. She thought of a lullaby and emanated the serene energy, the slow pace. *Stay in your shelter. It is cold for a while yet.*

An image of faint light narrowing to a crack, then darkness. The shells had closed.

Divine blinked. She still held the tiny werewing delicately in her arms. The baby's breathing was even, restful. Divine handed her back.

The mother werewing nuzzled her scaled snout against the baby's horns, so tiny they were just nubs.

Shouts of Divine's name began to grow closer. She scrambled to the edge of the tower.

"I'm up here!"

Below, Divine saw the tower was among other ruins dotted throughout the woods. Some of the trees grew against collapsed walls and Divine thought she saw the frame of a door. And through it...

Her heart leapt.

"Saph!" She waved her arms. "Up here."

Remembering the werewings, Divine sat back in the nest. The father werewing stood with his wing wrapped around the mother, and the two adolescents had crept beneath the fabric canopy. One of them bent around their back to lick at the wounds Syka inflicted. Divine crawled closer, cradling Sage.

"May I heal you? I healed your sister, and I can help you."

Divine held her palm out and the young werewing snapped his head around, gnashing his teeth.

Sage grumbled a warning in his pot, but Divine ignored him. Behind her, the father growled and clicked and Divine understood. *He wants his son to trust me.* Sniffing, the young werewing lowered his head to Divine's palm, then rearranged his legs to face his injured back at Divine.

The slashes inflicted by Syka's blades oozed with green fluid. Holding her hands over the wounds, Divine's mind swam within her well, drawing buckets of healing energy that she stretched into threads. Back and forth she stitched her cool tendrils, pulling the skin together and bonding the torn flesh together once more. She nodded to the father werewing.

"I am very sorry this happened. I'll tell the others about the misunderstanding." She turned her attention to the nest's edge. "Will you let me return to my friends?"

Releasing his mate from his large wings, the father werewing approached and Divine let him lift her in his furred arms.

The werewing set her down at the base of the tower and ascended again.

"Are you alright?" Saph threw her arms around Divine, pulling her into a tight embrace. "Are you hurt?"

Divine squeezed back. "I'm fine. They just needed my help. I don't know if they knew that I had caused the polypacors to poison their air, or if my magic told them I could help when I calmed and sent them away. But this was my fault. They wouldn't have attacked if I hadn't disturbed the peace of the forest."

Smoothing the hair on the sides of Divine's head, Saph placed a kiss on her forehead. "That close, we could have disturbed them regardless."

Divine took a deep breath. "I'm able to communicate with creatures, I should have been more careful. I just don't know how. My magic failed when I needed to protect you all and I'm sorry."

"I'm still stuck on polypacors," Syka, sheathing her daggers.

"They're small." Divine made a circle with her thumb and forefinger. "They go dormant in the winter, and in the spring they slide open their plate mail like shell sections to...cleanse."

Syka wrinkled her nose. "That's gross."

Saph shot a disapproving look at Syka before focusing on Divine again. "What do you need now? How can I help?"

Saph's consideration gave Divine confidence. "I need to figure out my magic."

Saph adjusted her eyepatch. "Well, Goodly One, do you have some answers hidden under there, too?"

Constance stood with his chin raised as he watched the silvery woods, the white trunks seeming to glow in places as the moon's light broke through.

Divine sighed. "He's not going to tell me until we get to Arosia. Let's just get back to Ada."

"This place was called Ferrum," Constance expressed dramatically, as if the trees too were his audience. "You could call it Old Arosia."

"The past is a whisper of truth." Syka balanced her palms on her dagger hilts at her sides. "Even as it clings to ruins."

Constance rotated his torso and nodded at Syka. They seemed to share a moment before he faced the group.

"The old ways were crushed, and a new city was built. Ferrum faded from memory. But it is still here." He raised his arm to his sides. "This is what I think is happening to your magic. You severed your connection to your talisman, which released the limits the Goddess of Souls had. Your old magic is still there, but it's crumbling. It is the past. Your new talisman is tethered not to another deity, but to yourself. And as you learn your new magic, your old magic hides in the shadows. The pathways are still there, just...overgrown."

Divine stiffened. "That's why you brought me here. Not in search of flatnuts. To see these ruins? But why?"

"Have any of you heard of Ferrum?"

Sharing glances, the three women shook their heads.

"If there was a city here," Syka puzzled through the thought. "There would be records of it in the capital, right? We'll find them when we get to Arosia."

Constance tilted his head. "You will find no trace of the city in any Trelvanian records. They were...very thorough when they established the pantheon. I wanted you to recognize that there will be things I cannot show you proof of, but they are true all the same. People like the Goddess of Souls and the Goddess of Condemnation want this system to stay the way it is and will do anything to keep it that way. They are capable of more than just their magic affinity." Constance motioned to the forest.

"I like the deities less every day," Saph grumbled.

"It is why I took steps to hide my association with you, Divine. And to travel by a method no one could follow. If I am correct, the more prominent deities will want you on their side and if you do not...they will destroy you."

Divine's stomach tightened. "Then I need to learn how to control my magic immediately."

Constance bobbed his head, the flaps on his hat jostling. "For now, I think only using your creature affinity will help you learn and master its intricacies. Try to not use your Soulshield abilities."

"I thought you said anyone can access all magic if there wasn't a talisman binding them to a deity."

"You are correct. However, how many years did you have perfecting your Soulshield magic?"

"Ten." Divine groaned.

"You need to learn that much in a very short time."

"What if I break the connection to my new talisman? If I start over…"

Constance shook his head, looking up through the branches. The stars overheard were like frozen drops, waiting for the right moment to fall.

"If I am correct," a puff of fog accompanied his words, "any talisman you create will attach only to your well."

"Because of my age?"

Seeming to weigh his words, the Goodly One took two breaths before turning his blue-grey orbs on Divine. He bent his head in a way that felt pitying.

"Because you are becoming a Goddess."

Saph snorted.

"Say that again?" Syka asked at the end of a turn of pacing.

"You can understand creatures." Constance flattened his hands against each other. "Influence them. Have you ever heard of a deity of animancy or beastcalling or anything creature related?" Constance paused. "Because it doesn't exist. Yet."

Divine ran a hand through her hair. "What, Goddesses just suddenly become?"

"It's a matter of being born with the right trait." Constance lifted a hand in a shrug as Divine started to pace, chewing on her thumb. "Like how some people are born with brown eyes or are tall, or how some people can stay focused or are better socializing. When we locate records in Arosia, your heritage will likely show signs of manifesting magic not found in the temples."

"So you're telling us"—Saph placed her hand on her hip—"deities are just humans with good breeding?"

Constance folded his arms, his hands moving as if seeking the comfort of his missing robe sleeves. "No one is breeding anybody."

"This is—this is ludicrous!" Closing the distance, Divine pressed her forefinger into Constance's coat until she pressed the bone of his chest. "You promised to help me control my magic and now—now I'm supposed to believe that Madeline needed me because I'm a Goddess?" Divine laughed bitterly. "Syka's probably a Goddess and Saph's a Goddess." Pointing at Saph and Syka in turn to accent her words.

"Everyone's a..." the words froze in Divine's throat as she locked her gaze on Constance.

She couldn't say it. Either another person had lied to her, or she was being manipulated. And she could not bear the thought of either.

She opened her mouth to yell at him. Then the forest shifted sideways as Constance's hand gently wrapped around her wrist. In place of trees and night-shadowed snow, wisps of white floated through an endless pale blue that seemed painted with a coat of pearlescence. Her body was a reed block inside an accordion, vibrating so strong with the power around her that she thought her teeth would chatter. It smelled of sea and moss.

"What is this place?" Divine's words travelled no further than an arm in front of her before losing their sound.

"Where our feet are anchored, think of it as my well. For me, the well's aquifer isn't made of rock, it's open. From here we can see how it connects to all other wells. This is how I can feel the intent of others. How I can anticipate what may happen next."

"Are those wisps...magic users?"

"Magic users, wells, everything is connected to the same source. Magic the person is strong enough to use gathers in their well, so close they can touch it. It's easier, while other magic is further away. When tethered to a deity through their talisman, the well fills up with that kind of magic and closes off to the rest."

"What scent does your magic have?"

"Have you ever eaten those little sugar puffs that feel like you're eating clouds made of sugar and vanilla?"

"That sounds amazing. Mine's roses."

A wisp floated close enough to touch. Energy coursed through Divine's veins, and she fought the urge to soar. She knew she could if she just had the magic. If she could just grab it for herself.

Constance's hand touched her shoulder, stopping her from following the thin cloud.

"You see how access to another's magic can be...alluring. I can't use another's power, not like they could use mine. But I can feel it. And knowing what that power's potential is..." Constance shook his head. "I no longer teach any who become a Goodly One how to access this space. They could lend their own power if they choose, but to feel the source of all magic...to covet it. It is too dangerous."

Divine studied his face, the way his eyes crinkled at the corners as if holding back pain. Divine wanted to trust what he said, but it all seemed too convenient. Too specific to what Divine needed to hear, filling the missing details that would explain why her magic had been needed by Madeline.

"Yet, deities are humans."

"Humans that attract massive amounts of one type of magic, who can wield it better than anyone else could."

Divine looked beneath his feet. Not a single wisp but uncountable tendrils of milk through magical tea.

I've been here from the beginning. His words from their first meeting came back to her.

"Well, God of Virtue. You lied to me."

Constance lowered his head. "Just call me Constance. Everything I have ever said to you was the truth."

Divine huffed and clenched her hands. "I just berated Saph for the same thing. I've been lied to by the temples. Manipulated. Used. Madeline or the First Servants, it doesn't matter. And you expect me to just believe what you're saying? You're one of them."

"Blind faith, I believe, has put our world in this unbalanced state. No, I did not expect you to trust this revelation. I had hoped to wait for clues in Arosia but your abilities are progressing quicker than I expected. Now felt like an opportune moment."

Swirls of white rose and fell in a silent dance.

"I have never been one of them," Constance murmured. "And I have never lied to you."

Divine watched Constance as he stood still, his head bowed. Here in this place, he looked like how she had met him, his autumn-colored robe looped over his shoulder, his head uncovered. She had never sensed deceit from him, but at times his emotions felt like looking into a fogged window—only able to make out the basic shapes beyond. Why was everyone associated with the temples turning out to be cryptic drawings behind stained-glass windows?

"Imagine if I gave you half a cup, or played half a song." She circled her hands over each other, trying to find the words. "Not telling the whole truth doesn't allow me to make the right decisions. And it breaks our trust."

Constance nodded, seemingly unable to make eye contact, and instead watched the swirls of white in the distance.

"I let the Goddess of Souls use my magic well once, and the demon you fought was the result. She's craved that kind of power ever since. And the others. They get a boost from their believers and their servants, but that doesn't compare to direct access to a magic well. The boradain was an experiment. Infused with the power of Souls, Storms and mine. He was to be a well of power any of us could draw from. I was blind to think it would be for good."

"Why haven't they taken you then, and forced you to donate your well?"

Constance laughed, though his face reflected something strained in the way his brow knitted minutely. "They've tried. Even if they could, I'm just one. All of those talismans out there and the wells they're connected to..."

Divine's stomach twisted. "What do they want to do with that kind of power?"

"To finally get rid of their opposition."

"You've felt this here?" Divine motioned to the infinite blue.

He shrugged. "Enough to make a guess."

"If—I'm not saying I believe it—but *if* I'm a Goddess, what can I do in all of this? You've been here since the beginning."

Constance took her hand in his, raising it near his chest. "I believe you have all the right characteristics to make a difference. Your care for others. Your fight against injustices. Your capacity to love."

"Are you calling me virtuous, God of Virtue?" Divine asked, a crooked smile forming.

His hand tightened around her fingers, then slid until they were palm to palm. "I've been waiting for someone like you."

Mouth feeling suddenly dry, Divine forced a swallow. "I have a girlfriend."

Constance rolled his eyes. "I'm older than your grandfather."

"I'll be sure to tell Saph that the next time you hold my hand."

As if that was what he needed, Constance intertwined their fingers. "You're deflecting with humor. Can I say something serious?"

Divine nodded, her limbs suddenly feeling cold.

"Soon, you'll be presented with a choice. To shrug off your old magic and embrace your full power—become a Goddess. Or live the rest of your life trying to keep the new magic tamed. I hope it's the first. The few of us could use another on our side. A power the deities haven't seen has the potential to ripple across the landscape. Either way, I hope I can be your friend."

Friend. Wasn't she just wondering how many friendships she could have been missing, misreading the interactions? Here was Constance, clearly and plainly setting the sentiment before her. But could she trust him?

"Do you think you can stop hiding things from me?" she asked.

"As best as I am able."

Divine scowled, but then her features softened. It wasn't that long ago that she had kept Madeline being her ex a secret. Shame and embarrassment had kept her silent. And she hadn't told Saph about her father leaving her and her mother until Saph had asked about her family during the harvest festival. Anger had kept that locked. Divine had her reasons for when and why she opened up. While letting someone in was freeing, the choice to do so remained in her hands. Divine hoped she was trustworthy enough that people like Saph and Syka felt revealing their truths was not a dangerous venture.

"Then at least don't hide the things that directly impact me?"

"It will be so."

He kissed the back of her hand and the world shivered back into view.

Darkness and trees. The scent of clean snow and pines. The creaking of branches. Sage against her hip. Constance's hand on her wrist as Divine's finger pressed into his chest.

"Could you imagine?" Syka scoffed. "Maybe I'm the Goddess of Undead. Not being able to smell is really the worst."

Divine angled her head and frowned.

"What?" Syka crossed her arms. "Maybe I have magic. I just can't smell mine and then obviously that makes it so I never knew, and it's too late to make a talisman to lock it in."

"You can't smell?" Divine asked.

"You just proposed everyone is a Goddess, and *that's* what you focus on? It's why I could take all of the dirty jobs. Stench has no hold on me."

Had no time passed while she and Constance were inside his well? Divine refocused on the God of Virtue, who shrugged. She lowered her hand to her coat pocket. Her hand gripped the black object Listhinci had given her. At any moment she could sever her talisman and create a new one; see if Constance was right about her well. Her hand loosed its grip. *What if he's wrong and I can't connect to magic ever again?*

"You might not be a Goddess, but Constance...Syka, Saph, meet the God of Virtue."

Constance pressed his curled fingers together. "I prefer to not use that label. I neither want nor need anyone's worship."

"How does one figure out their godhood?" Saph asked, circling her finger in the air as Divine stepped back beside her.

"There's a test the Iguions can do. For me, it was realizing no one else could do what I could."

"And then you gave yourself a God label," Saph concluded.

Constance shook his head so hard Divine thought he'd fall over. "That was the others. When they established the temples."

"The rise of the temples, the fall of the Old Ways." Saph nodded, her eye focusing somewhere in the branches. "How easily they bowed to those with power."

"Not easy." Constance motioned to the nearest ruin, a wall of once well-placed rock leaning and crumbling.

"Oh." Syka brushed the pink section of hair from her face. "Destroy the mountain of existence and sunder the foothills of understanding."

"Well, you didn't send us to Solhavn." Saph crossed her arms and shifted her weight to her left hip. "So how do you plan to prove Divine is *divine?*"

"You wanted to understand why Madeline sought you." Constance pulled his hat down lower on his ears. "If I'm right, what she found will align. If I'm wrong, the information will still give you the closure you need on your involvement with the First Soul."

"Have we asked him what he gets from this?" Saph asked.

"Allies, he said." Divine tried her best disbelieving expression. "He apparently hasn't made many friends."

Saph scoffed. "I find that hard to believe. The man must be ancient."

"It has been a necessity." Constance cleared his throat and produced a small lantern from his sleeve. "Come on. Let's return to Ada."

Divine and Saph exchanged smiles as Constance led.

"We should be able to get into the city now, under the cover of night," Constance supplied. "We'll avoid the gate checks by transporting directly inside and find somewhere we can stay while we find what we seek."

The weight of everything descended in a blink. Shivers coursed through her body, jerking her arms and she hugged herself to stop the shaking. Divine was no longer certain she wanted to find the answers.

CHAPTER FOURTEEN

Meve and Memories

Divine rapped her knuckles on a plain white door with the number 310. One of three other doors in a familiar hallway of the habitspace building, and behind them dwelled servants from the temples of Arosia. Servants who, like Divine, hadn't been lucky enough to get one of the coveted rooms in the larger temples, and then others who served smaller less popular temples that didn't have living spaces of their own.

When the door in front of her finally opened, a woman in a cream gown with waist-length golden hair yawned. Her messy locks gave an appearance of coarse hair, and the top puffed into a heart shape. Meve blinked, then squealed.

"Divine! You didn't tell me you were coming back!" Meve began to speak in her rapid-fire delivery that Divine knew well. "I guess my message got to you. Though, to be here now you would have left before you got my message, which means...I need to yell at you *again* for disappearing on me. I mean, yell at you for the first time. Eep! But I'm so glad to see you."

Meve threw her arms around Divine's neck, bouncing, her nightgown rasping against Divine's coat.

"Can we come in?" Divine said in a hushed tone. "I don't want to wake anyone."

Meve seemed to notice Saph for the first time. "Oh. Oh! Of course."

She stepped back, allowing them inside. Along Meve's far window hung a string of green and pink lantern lights for Midwinter Nights. It made Divine miss the cozy feel of the tavern. Now back in Arosia, she felt like shadows kept reaching out to steal her away. But Meve's walls were hung with display shelves overflowing with colorful vases, cups, and containers of all sizes.

"Though no one is here to wake up. Just me. Jim and I ended things."

Divine closed the door behind her. "Sorry to hear that, Meve. You doing alright?"

"Oh, yeah. He wasn't the right fit for me."

"You have a nice place," Saph complimented, motioning to a large purple vase in the corner, housing a small palm tree variety.

Sage wobbled, trying to get a better look and Divine shifted him forward.

"Oh thanks! That one I got on a deep discount. The Conservatory was having a plant sale two years ago from their propagation. Divine could probably tell you more about how it works but the plants...reproduce? And their little baby plants need new homes since the building can only fit so many and they have this plant sale which pays for maintenance of the facility but if you wait long enough, they have left over ones that they still need to get rid of and you can practically get them for free." Meve clapped her hands which quickly transformed into a wringing motion. "But you probably meant the vase. I collect things you can put things in. I can show you if...if you're interested."

Meve approached a wall of shelves. Sage was very interested in the containers and Divine fought from shushing him. No one else was under a deluge of decacacti dialog.

Divine cleared her throat. "Meve, I could use your help. My friends and I need a place to stay for a few nights. And I hoped maybe you wouldn't mind?"

Meve tilted her head, her long hair swaying. "Friends? Plural? So more than your axe carrying friend here?"

After emerging from water troughs in a candy store closed for the evening, Divine and Saph had left the others to hide behind the crates and barrels in the alleyway while they exited. They were to leave separately and rejoin in the bottom foyer of the collection of single-person habitspaces Meve lived in.

"Girlfriend," Divine corrected. "This is Saph."

"Ooo. She's gorgeous. And those muscles. Why not at your place?"

"It's not let to someone else?"

"Nope. In fact, the temple just had it cleaned up. I assume in preparation for your arrival, now that I think about it. Otherwise, why would they be in there?" Meve laughed. "I should have realized."

Divine touched Saph's arm, who raised an eyebrow.

"Well...about that." Divine cleared her throat again. "Meve, we get along well, right?"

"Of course! You're the only one that doesn't grumble when we get paired together. You know, Shasja the other day rolled her eyes when I told her about the new cup I found at the All-Temples Exchange. It's so dainty and has a gold rim with a purple outside, but inside there's pink blossoms. So when you sip, you get to see a secret no one knows." Meve nearly sighed into a flower petal shape. "It's right over there. At least she's making it easier to know she hates me."

"I don't think anyone hates you. Some people just need to practice empathy and patience."

Meve beamed. "That's why you and me are such good Soulshields! Oh! Would you like a cookie? Hot chocolate? Or some tea?"

"What kind of tea?" Saph inquired and Divine shot her a look. Saph shrugged. "What? I'm in the tea business now."

"Desert Flower, I think? It has quite the soothing effect. Great for a sore throat. Are you sick by chance?"

Divine couldn't hide her smile. "Meve, we appreciate the offer. We'd love to sample your tea. If I caught you up on where I've been, can you make tea and listen?"

"Not if it's a good story. Which I'm sure yours is. I better just sit here. Oh I'm so excited!" Meve plopped down, tossing her locks over her shoulders and wiggled her legs. "Oh, do you want me to, er, hang up your plant?"

Cupping Sage in front of her, Divine sat across from Meve.

Meve squealed. "A decacacti! It's so cute. You know, they get such a bad name just because they have thorns to protect themselves. People think they have thorny dispositions."

The clay pot's soil crinkled.

"Sage thanks you and compliments your greenery."

Meve's eyebrows shot up.

"I have quite the tale. Can our other three companions join us?"

"Of course!"

Divine launched into telling the tale of the last six months as Saph retrieved the others from the first level. Though Constance had told her to only use her new magic, Divine couldn't help feeling for Meve's emotions. As a Soulshield, Meve could shield herself, but she was open, letting Divine feel her fluctuations of surprise and apprehension at all the right places. Divine trusted Meve with the full truth, though she left some details vague, like how long they had actually been traveling. The others had found places to sit in the small place as Divine brought the story to a close.

"I'll check my mother's things first for clues," Divine concluded. "But I don't feel safe staying there."

"I completely understand." Meve bolted up and maneuvered to the kitchenette. "Let me get you all some tea."

Like Divine's own residence in the same building, pipes delivered heat produced from the Fire Works beneath the temple of the Deity of Love and Fire. The ever-burning crystals were a mystery to many users, but it provided the city with light energy and heated items like the stove.

Her golden head bobbing around, Meve rummaged in her cabinets, pulling out cups as she continued speaking. "I didn't know your mom went to Solhavn. I've always wanted to go, but I think being out on the water would just be miserable. Endless ocean everywhere. You'd forget there was land and despair. I would anyway. What if you don't find anything from your mom?"

Divine's shoulders tightened. "Then I might need a second favor from you. Help us find information from our temple."

Meve's hands froze, spoon hovered over a cup while her other hand reached for her kettle. "Oh no. You know the First Servant of Souls doesn't like me around papers."

Meve had once organized the First Servant of Soul's desk, and in rearranging the various containers by size she knocked a plant over, spilling the soil and water all over a stack of important documents. Another time, she left books on the windowsill, and a mating pair of rainbow birds had used them as a washroom.

"No, I mean talk to some people. Maybe the older Soul Shapers. Someone has to have heard about Old Souls and the real story behind the feud between the Goddesses of Souls and Condemnation."

Boilspout clinking into place, Meve looked at the ceiling. "You know who's ancient and has great stories?"

"Ewan!" Meve and Divine said together.

"I was late for everything when he was instructing." Realizing that Meve had the same tendency to speak long, Divine hastily added, "I couldn't leave without knowing how the stories ended."

"I think he remade every morality lesson from those books to fit the situation he was showing us."

Meve rounded the corner of her kitchenette carrying two tea mugs with flowers floating in the glass edge. She sat them on a little table.

"Let them steep for a few minutes—they won't taste good yet. Ewan volunteered for nights during the faire so 'us young bodies' could avoid missing out."

Divine watched Meve as her fellow Soulshield grabbed other cups and distributed them. Syka took a cup and sniffed it hesitantly. Ada crunched a handful of nuts as she held her cup in her free hand. The teas permeated the room with the scent of a desert flower; floral combined with spiced coconut.

"Does he make in-person visits?" Divine asked. She reached for her mug but Saph waved her hand, mouthing, "*The tea is hot.*"

"I don't think he has lately, now that you ask. Maybe about the same time you left. That's odd, isn't it? But he's working this week and he wouldn't be able to anyway. But we could visit. There's hardly anyone else there, which you know. Sorry, don't know why I told you that."

"It's alright, Meve. Saph doesn't know much about temple life."

"Except that you probably shouldn't go, dear." Saph picked up her mug. "Like Constance said."

Removing the strap from her shoulder, Divine sat Sage on the table. He wiggled his side stems and Divine took off his mitten hat, careful of his thorns. The decacacti thought the warmth of the room was sufficient. Divine's mouth quirked up. *Sufficient.*

"If I gave you some questions to ask, do you think you could talk to Ewan for me?"

"Of course! Tonight even." Meve sipped from her cup. "I'm already awake."

Divine glanced at Saph. "We could enjoy the Midwinter Nights faire for a bit. That way you aren't stuck inside just waiting."

The tavern owner raised her mug. "Keep your hood up and avoid interacting with anyone you recognize. I can pin you against a wall and kiss you wildly anytime that happens. It'll be fun."

"After we check my mother's things. I don't want to delay in case whoever was in my room comes back."

"You know"—Meve gestured with her cup—"it was odd that—before I sent you that message—that guy said he was your brother. I remember thinking you would have told me if you had a brother. It must have been an Agent of Condemnation or something. Well, don't you worry. I'll ask Ewan your questions and you distract yourself at the faire. Goddesses know you need a chance to relax after all that's happened. Goddess protect me, werewings!"

Having a distraction from everything did sound nice. Trusting her friend to help take away some of the pressure, she'd be able to help Saph get more Night Coins for the special merchandise.

Constance began leafing through a book from one of Meve's shelves, and Ada peered into several vases with water and cut flowers. Divine raised her mug and took a sip. The mug had the same design as the double-walled glasses she had hoped to find in Iramont. The flowers were crocheted blossoms with large petals and bright colors.

"Saph," Divine said, scooting closer, "notice how the mug isn't burning your hand with the hot water?"

Saph clasped her other hand around the mug and her eyebrows shot up. "Well, what do you know."

"I meant to tell you about them in Iramont but things went a little...dunaru. And I don't think the makers are in the city."

"Oh!" Meve's bounce sloshed a splash of brown out of her mug and onto the floor. "There's a glass shop. You know the one, Divine. Near the brothel—"

"Interesting place for transparent materials," Saph said, blowing on the top of her mug.

Meve continued nonplussed. "I saw half a dozen in the window just yesterday."

"Oh, that's fantastic!" Explaining how the glass style worked, she conveyed her idea to use them in Steeped in Sapphire.

"Then let's get this mystery solved so we can go shopping for tea supplies. And explore what Arosia puts out for their faire." Saph inhaled deeply and Divine wondered if she could detect the woody citrus from the tea as well. "Tea first, then where's your home?"

* * *

A mix of emotions stirred within Divine as she surveyed her living space. She'd spent most of her adult life in this small habitspace. The last memories were of being with Madeline and her subsequent betrayal. Divine spun from the bed, unwilling to resurface any memories of their time together. She had Saph now.

Her accordion case sat in a corner and the plants that she used to tend to were gone. Perhaps the temple had removed their dried stalks. She was glad Sage didn't see the evidence of her dismal plant care. Meve was looking after him. Divine realized she could have asked Meve to look after her plants before chasing Madeline, if she'd realized their friendship earlier.

After meeting with Meve, Constance joined Divine and Saph but Ada and Syka stayed in Meve's single habitspace.

"I'll check for any water that could be used to scry," Constance volunteered, "and other items that could be used to let anyone know we are here."

His proposal broke Divine's ruminations. "My mother's things are in my closet. I'll get them."

When her mother passed, the house had quickly sold. Her father had stopped living there, and her mother had already sold possessions to 'donate' money to the temple for their healing services. Before the new homeowners arrived, Divine returned to her mother's garden and made her first talisman. She also took a few decorations and a box of things her mother would have written in. As if the words kept her alive.

Now, she flipped through papers and old letters, hunting for anything that would have set her mother on a course that left a trail for Madeline. Divine flipped through a book about gardens, when a folded piece of paper fell out of the place it had been saving for all these years.

Unfolding it, Divine read the lines from an advertisement cut out of a community bulletin note or a city periodical. It was next to an article raising skepticism over the treatment of human-adjacents and quotes from the author, who had been let into the city of Zax Solhavn.

"My mom saved this." Divine handed the clipping to Saph.

The tavern owner studied it, then read it out loud. "Regardless if you are admitted into the city of Iguions, the warm sands and waters of the Pink Shell Coast will work wonders on your constitution. Boats set sail weekly from Pariatan until first frost." Saph shook the paper. "Does this help?"

"No idea. I'll see if I can find anything else."

Divine sat the book to the side, her eye catching her accordion case. She brought the black box onto her bed and opened the snaps. Red as bright as her hair revealed, swirling with darker tones. The folded bellows were yellow, but when she expanded and contracted the instrument, the colors always reminded her of an autumn sunset. As she lifted it, several pieces of sheet music tumbled out like snowfall. Picking up the nearest one, Divine was transported back in time.

Her mother had just arrived from Solhavn. Divine was maybe twelve. Leena gave her a piece of music, a traditional song from the island of Solhavn. "Keep it safe," her mother had whispered. "You have the only copy like it in all of Trelvania." At the time, Divine had felt like she held a secret treasure and practiced the notes when no one was around. As time passed, she had come to think of the music as a gift from a mother who recognized how much her daughter enjoyed music. She had wanted Divine to feel special with a made-up story. Nothing magical about it. Divine hadn't played the piece in years, as the notes breathing from her accordion always sunk her emotions into guilt and despair over losing her mother.

Now, Divine turned the parchment over in her hands. She couldn't recall having heard the melody but by her own hand in all of those years since. She placed the piece carefully back in the case with the other sheets and latched the case shut. Wherever she ended up, her accordion was coming with her this time. She carried the case and sat it next to the door.

"Does this mean anything to you?"

Saph waved a leather-bound notebook embossed with roses and when Divine held out her hands, she tossed it over the bed.

"It's my mother's gardening notebook." Divine unwound the leather ties and opened to the middle. Her mother's handwriting filled the page, accented with floral drawings. "She would notate everything. The rain we'd receive, the growth for the month. Even the number of blooms from each rose bush."

"I can see where you get your plant tendencies."

Divine sniffed. "She loved that garden."

Soft hands rubbed her shoulders. Divine patted Saph's hand to signal she was fine and began flipping the pages. A shorter list caught her eye, and she thumbed the pages back.

Ennium. Attracted deadly insects.
Alyst. Hooweet pet.
Elyon. Accumulated cats?
Ask Devon.

Divine's heart started to race.

"What did you find?" Constance asked, suddenly at her side.

"I don't know." Divine angled the book for him to see. "I think Ennium is my great-great grandfather on my father's side. Alyst might be on my mother's side. I don't know why she has this list here."

Constance nodded, tapping his lips with a finger. "This is what we needed."

"Really?"

"There likely would have been signs several generations before you." He tapped the page. "Find out what your mother asked this Devon, and it may give us more confirmation. Do you know who he is?"

Divine's stomach turned. "He's my piece of shit father."

* * *

After providing Meve questions to ask Ewan, Divine felt like her bones were rattling, having to sit and wait for answers. Thus, Saph activated their earlier idea. They entered the night streets of Arosia dressed in their Midwinter best. Constance and Ada were resting, Syka explored, and Sage shivered with excitement at Divine's hip. He'd let her know in serious terms that he resented not being shown the faire in Iramont. They would look for tea supplies and let the faire distract them for a bit.

The Arosian faire-goers wore everything from celebratory hats to pretend wings; a decacacti wouldn't seem out of the ordinary. His mitten hat even seemed festive.

"I'm surprised you packed your dress, too," Divine said, pulling her hood up and trying to sink her earmuffed head back as far as it would go. The fur's warmth was welcomed, but the feeling was tinged with Divine's remorse for using it.

"I'm always ready to dazzle and dance. A big city like this, love, and there's bound to be somewhere you can go dressed up. You packed yours."

Divine shrunk. "I packed everything."

"You really thought I didn't want you to come back. Oh, come here darlin'." Saph offered her arm. "I'm not letting go of you that easily."

Divine slipped her arm into Saph's, her heart light, and they headed to the center of the Market District. A trio of children ran past, clutching globes swirling with snow.

"A start of a quest!" Saph declared looking across the street. "This way."

The shop Saph raced them to had musical instruments on the walls and shelves of music sheets. Divine smiled, her mood lifting.

"What's this about?" Saph thumbed at a sign in the window. It had a similar message to Flitch's Stitches in Iramont, though this one read 'Start Here'.

Divine squinted to read the smaller print. "It's a city scavenger hunt. Each participating venue has a piece and at the end the parts can be put together to make something and trade it for Night Coins."

"Let's do it." Saph grinned.

They spent the next hour gathering all the parts from the locations. The last piece of their hunt retrieved, Divine and Saph revisited the Market District center. It wasn't as cozy as Iramont's bazaar, but similar in set up. Purple and yellow lantern strands crisscrossed over the square and vendor stalls.

"Look at this." Saph held up a green mug in the shape of a boot. "I have got to get this for the Sapphire."

Divine leaned closer. "It's cute. You could put it on a wall shelf."

"And if anyone misbehaves, they have to drink from the boot for the next round. Consider it a warning."

"Their next boot is a boot out the door."

Saph booped Divine's nose. "Clever."

Divine peeked at the cost. Maybe she could get this for Saph if the Stacked Creations couldn't finish her order in time. *Twenty Night Coins!* The item was part of the special merchandise only available to faire participants in the cities. And a steep one.

Divine hooked her arm in Saph's, determination rising within her. "Then let's build our puzzle and collect our Night Coins. There's a boot to buy."

As they put the collected pieces together, Divine surveyed the area. They too, had bells that started the festival though no one was attempting to ring one. Divine clicked her last piece in place. A wooden clock with a buck's head, its gears on the outside.

Nearby, a table collected the timepieces in exchange for five Night Coins. Handing over hers, Divine pocketed her snowflake embossed coins as Saph exchanged her clock. Still not enough between them for the boot, even adding it to the identical coins from Saph's bell ringing win in Iramont.

"Should we find another game?" Saph asked, leisurely weaving them around others. "I see an eating contest, a—"

Divine's feet halted and she spun around, tightening her grip on Saph's arm.

"What is it?"

"There's a man at the hot drinks stand," Divine whispered. "I think he's an associate of Madeline."

Saph leaned her head close. "Are you sure?"

"He has the same glove. Singular. He only wore one and this guy just has one red-black glove."

"Alright." Saph rotated. "Then we go this way."

"Deities above," Divine sibilated. "Over there, I see someone from my temple. I shouldn't have come out here. This was stupid."

"Everything will be alright." Saph was already leading them through the crowd to the opposite side of the street.

Divine pulled the side of her hood against her face.

"Your alley awaits."

Divine blinked. It was Syka speaking beside them and the mouth of an alley. Her black coat and hair blended with the shadow from a lamppost against the wall.

"Following me again?" Divine pursed her lips. And ignored Sage's protests to go back.

"Just in the area. Meve's back already. Her meeting must have been quick."

"Eyes on us?" Saph asked.

Syka inspected the crowd, though Divine didn't know how she saw clearly from under her bangs.

"Sufficiently preoccupied."

Syka stepped back into the alley. There was a crash of glass and Syka...vanished.

"One of her potions," Saph tugged gently and Divine joined her in the alleyway.

Divine sighed, making her boot steps quiet as their group continued forward. "I have a feeling all you're going to see of my city is alleys."

"Whatever keeps us, and you, safe." Saph patted Divine's hand. "Shall we see what answers Meve has for us?"

Sage's pot crinkled. "No, Meve didn't have a fireplace, but it is warm in there from the Fire Works, remember?" The decacacti's pot slurped. Apparently, he preferred a real fire to the magical method. "It's the best I can do. And I'll take you out again wherever we go next."

Sage wasn't ecstatic but at least seemed content.

"I'll go ahead and make sure the exit's clear," Syka said, then jogged ahead.

A mix of dread and curiosity settled in Divine's stomach like a stone. "Hopefully Meve has some answers."

* * *

"He remembered your mother," Meve nodded. She'd tied her long hair back at the base of her neck, but the thick locks were still voluminous. "He seemed truly rueful that he and the others had been unable to heal her. Said it was an enigma they saw from time to time where they healed the symptoms but couldn't find the cause. He offered to bring out her record as he thought something might be there, but then recalled the First Servant of Souls had recently moved all of the older records to the Council's archives. He remembered that he suggested she look into...alternative methods."

Divine's brows shot up. A servant suggesting non-temple methods? Ewan was more rebellious than she thought.

"An apothecary. The store is still here. Potions and Prophecies."

"Sounds like my kind of place."

Divine ignored Syka. "That's near the back of the Essentials District. I've been past it a few times. Might be alright to visit during the day as it's far from the temples."

"And I'll be with you," Saph nodded.

"What about the founding of the pantheon?" Divine asked Meve. "The First Soul. Anything there?"

"Ewan said there used to be books with really old stories in the Soul's library, but they were moved to the Council archive when he was in his early twenties, maybe because they were asking all of the temples to create a central library. But he remembered reading about the Goddess of Souls and the Goddess of Condemnation working together—can you believe it? It had to be a morality lesson about making your enemy your friend unless, oh Goddesses of course! This is what you're looking for. Lost history."

In Meve's breath for air, Divine glanced at Constance.

He shrugged. "Do you want me to say anything?"

She shook her head. "I might think you influenced what we find."

"We definitely have to check out the archives." Syka laid on the floor, one leg propped on her knee. "This Ewan guy mentioned it at least twice, yeah?"

"It's not open to the public, though the building is. And that's only open during the day," Divine clarified.

"Not a problem. I can get in." Syka wiggled her fingers in the air. "I just need a distraction and someone with me to show me the right bookshelf."

It was probably when Meve was supposed to transport scrolls to the archives that she made her last predicament with paper, bumping a cart of scrolls onto the floor, mixing hers with them. The First Servant had sought future alternative tasks for Meve.

Meve wrang her hands. "I'm not good with paper."

Divine clasped Meve's shoulders. "I have faith in you. When people have faith in me it gives me strength."

"Possibly a Goddess," Syka coughed.

"I won't have to touch them, just show you? I'll do it." Meve bobbed her head. "What are friends for?"

CHAPTER FIFTEEN

Pirate Complaints and Following A Mother's Path

"I feel ridiculous," Divine said through clenched teeth.

She glanced down at her own pillowed breasts lifted by a pink corset. They weren't half as voluptuous as Saph's, which Divine would be pining over under normal circumstances. And except for freckles, Divine's were as white as the snow outside in the city center green. As white as some of the creatures on display in the building's entry. Another day, another adventure.

"I'm in awe that you never bump into anything." Divine adjusted the strap of her eyepatch disguise for likely the fifth time since joining the line for city complaints. The right side of her vision disappeared in blackness, and she couldn't see the other lines queued for their government post without turning her head.

Her line shifted forward. Divine transferred her coat to her other arm and peeked at her heeled boots. She stood in one of the larger rectangles made of the pattern of white blocks and grey strips in the polished floor.

"I've gotten very good at adjusting my perception over the years," Saph replied. "But I still bump things from time to time, especially when it's dark."

"Really? You always seem to navigate a dark bedroom fine."

"Sweetcakes, I'm bumping into you. Fiercely."

Divine's stomach knotted pleasantly at the thought. "Sweetcakes?"

"Not my best creation, I'll find another fun name to give you."

"Whatever passes the time. My feet are aching."

Divine thought of their walk to the center of the city. Separating the government building from the Holy District might have been a visual aid to imply leadership gathered under a single roof, but that was a sham. The Goddess of Souls temple was the largest in Arosia, just as it was in Iramont. But in the center of Arosia, the area around the government building was a gathering place for the people not tied to any of the smaller spaces in the city's districts.

"You still want to do this? We could go."

Divine wished Sage were with them. He'd tell her she wouldn't have hurt feet if she stood in a pot of moss, or to be thankful she didn't have to be carried everywhere like a satchel. But a woman with a potted decacacti was more likely to be recognized.

"Yes. I need to do something, even if it doesn't amount to much. I can't think of beings like Shroombal being left without help from people like us."

"You mean people who aren't seen as less-than."

"Exactly."

Divine thought of Shroombal's deflated fungi shoulders when they'd said the mistreatment was more common. She could still be the voice they needed while pretending to be an entertainer.

On their walk through the center green around the Council building, the mental din of creatures there inundated her senses. In the summer, the space served as a tranquil gathering place full of flowers; a bit of nature bottled up and released between the towering temples and merchant buildings. But for Midwinter Nights Faire, the grounds became something different.

This year, it had been turned into lodging for animals from Nelithor and the frozen lands in the Horns of Trelvania. There were snow sheep that looked like boulders with their blunt heads and short quad horns, and icetalons with their broad wings folded so that their cream and brown speckled feathers made them nearly disappear against sedges and rock. They lived in the forever cold near the Frostshard Sea, and were a perfect association to the Goddess of Frosted Wilderness. An assortment had been brought inside, ranging from rodents to birds and elk, of the tundra species. Divine had never seen them out of books.

When the line shifted again, Divine could see the narrow booth-like counter set up beneath their line's archway. They were almost there.

"I don't think I'm going to fool anyone," Divine whispered.

Saph made circles on the space between Divine's shoulder blades. "They'll fool themselves. Just make sure to lean forward and they'll forget your face."

When the preceding individual left, Saph moved in, planting one hand on the flat surface while the other propped on her opposite hip.

"We've got a serious grievance to lodge with this Holy Council."

Divine steeled herself against reacting to Saph's drawl, a perfect imitation of the more remote western towns. It was a bit like Shroombal. And she had blatantly used the wrong name.

"This *is* the desk of complaints. What can I take down as your issue?"

"We were visitin' Iramont, and human-adjacents were gettin' harassed by everybody. People refusin' to pay them for their services." Saph smacked her other hand down on the table, her breasts jostling. "It was ridiculous. What kind of chaos are you allowin' down there?"

The complaint-taker's voice rose in pitch, flicking her attention to Divine. "Is this true?"

Leaning forward further than necessary, both of her hands pressed into the boning at her stomach of her corset, Divine tried to copy Saph's accent adding a layer of sweetness.

"Truly. We're travelling entertainment, you see." Lying to the temples that lied to her felt justified, and she plowed forward with their prepared story. "We'd planned on joinin' up with performers we knew but they weren't allowed in the taverns. How are we supposed to dance without any music?"

"And to the top of Zenith I swear to you"—Saph added, lifting her hand high—"they weren't allowed in the Holy Districts."

"That's...it's very unfortunate." The worker scratched details on parchment with a pencil. "The Holicratic Ruling Council usually leaves the provinces to create their own rules. But all should be welcome in the cities, as it's important for commerce and the natural order of the temples. And certainly, the Holy District is a place for all. Without magic of their own, there's no better way for human-adjacents to feel closer to the deities. I'll escalate this for accelerated review."

It took everything with Divine to not shout what she really thought of these conclusions. Human-adjacents deserved respect. They were more than sources of business and coin. They didn't need to worship a God or Goddess to have worth. They needed fairness and basic decency.

"We appreciate you." Saph flicked her hand toward the worker. "We don't want to have to tell our acquaintances to avoid that city."

She paused writing. "Just how many associates do you have?"

Divine stiffened. This was the moment. She tried to clear her thoughts and find the rhythm of the creatures in the building's foyer.

"Have you got the time? There's Berrette from Mistwater..."

Divine barely registered the made-up names of associates Saph began to rattle off.

She could feel the animals in their cages she and Saph had passed earlier. Decorations for the festival; some that lived in the frozen reaches of Nelithor and the larger Horn of Trelvania, and some that exuded sunlight and warmth. Day and winter uniting in the symbolism of the time of year, as bundled city-dwellers rejoiced at the path to a return of spring. Divine loathed the tiny cages that stiffened backs and wings and paws.

Come. Break free.

Divine sent the thought to every creature's mind she could touch.

You are strong. Knock your cage.

Faint brushes against her magic told her she had been perceived.

Hurry.

She tried to send an image of the hall she stood in, with its multiple lines sectioning the long room into topical regions under decorative arches.

And then she waited.

"Jexster and his fisherman in Pariatan," Saph said, ticking another finger out so that her thumb and index fingers were extended on each hand.

The worker held up a hand. "Alright, I think that's enough."

Before Saph could protest to buy more time, a cacophony of shouts and bangs flooded the space. Divine spun.

People scattered as bodies like long foxes and beady-eyed rodents bounded across the polished floor. Animals ducked under feet as wings carried others high into the skylights. Employees rushed from far corners of the room in an attempt to wrangle the creatures as citizens awkwardly danced with their neighbors trying to flee. A lopsided grin formed on Divine.

I did it.

The complaint worker rose, glancing from the line to the rest of the hall.

"Please, make your way to the side doors," a voice rose above the noise. "The Council building will temporarily close for...maintenance."

The worker stepped around the booth and gently turned Saph and Divine by their shoulders toward the outer wall. Divine glanced back, catching movement at the furthest door into the archives; a hunched-over Meve wringing her hands, following a figure in black that seemed like a shadow from the lights on the wall. Divine silently wished Syka and Meve good luck.

"Time for tea leaf shopping," Saph said, slipping her arm into her coat. "And then the apothecary, or your dad's place."

"Definitely apothecary." Divine's hands paused, buttoning her coat over her squished bosom. "Do you think we can get better prices if we stay dressed as pirates?"

"I'd keep you dressed like this because it's giving me steeped-in-pleasure, but we should at least change your boots to your real ones."

"Alright, let's swing by the brothel. We can check out that glass store. Then we can try the Pepperwall Warehouse and see if there's any bulk tea for sale."

"Nice of them to let you borrow some clothes. You know, corsets really look good on you."

Divine blushed. "Thank you, but I think I'll leave them to you. Being so easily noticed really flares my magic."

"Not the only thing you flare, darlin'."

Unable to suppress a giggle, Divine cleared her throat. "They know what I did for Madeline. Several of them saw me save her from that man's assault. Though they don't know the aftermath and that it was just a ruse for me to meet Madeline. To them, what we do is our business and they won't tell anyone."

"Sounds like great allies to have. Well, it's settled. We'll stay pirates and hide in plain sight. Lead on, captain of my attraction."

Returning the borrowed ones, Divine changed into her more comfortable pair of boots, but stuffed her outfit into her bag. She liked the anonymity the guise of a traveling entertainer gave her, and how Saph's eye traced her curves. Next door in the glass shop, Saph purchased two cups like Meve's to try back at the Steeped in Sapphire, then hurried to search for brewable leaves at the warehouse before their final destination.

* * *

Saph and Divine travelled snowy streets and alleys navigating to the location of Potions and Prophecies as they chatted about their warehouse experience.

"What a ridiculous price they were charging for tea grown in Iramont's province," Divine said. It had taken gripping Sage's pot tightly to not tell the merchants within the Pepperwall Warehouse what Divine thought of it all as Saph haggled at prices.

"It was harvested before the black spot, so the red leaf is rare right now. Shrewd business move. I think it's arrogant and a load of dunaru dung. That yellow leaf one was interesting."

"The Fox Tail?"

"Yeah. Didn't that guy say the plant twists itself and the leaves fall off and *that's* when they know it's ready to steep? People just watch and wait. Too bad that one cost even more."

Sage's pot crackled, an image forming in Divine's mind that she immediately wanted to erase.

Divine tilted her head, looking at Saph from the corner of her eye. "Fox Tail is sentient. You'd be drinking its dandruff."

"Aren't all herbs and leaves just plant body parts?"

Sage squeaked and Divine crinkled her nose. "Is that really you or Syka wearing a Saph suit?"

"Honey, she couldn't pull off these hips."

Divine grinned. "I think the Arosian black leaf you picked up will be great."

"Better than nothing. We can keep making the Foggy Iramont at least. Maybe crush the flatnuts we dug up with Constance to add variety." Saph pointed. "This the place?" Painted with bottles and vials surrounded by mushrooms and lavender sprigs, the sign of Potions and Prophecies had a central mortar and pestle, though the mortar looked like a teacup. Had Divine's mother sought draughts and herbs before finally going to Solhavn?

They stepped inside and immediately Divine's senses were accosted. Herbs and flowers and perhaps even tree bark swirled in a breathable quagmire. Saph and Divine skirted a round table inconveniently placed in a direct line to the shop's counter. The shop was warm and humid, and Sage asked for his hat to be removed.

"Is anyone here?" Divine called.

There was nothing but a stool behind the counter ladened with display racks of small vials. The seat was a white circle with a slightly convex surface and from beneath it a voice seemed to seep out.

"Be with you in a moment."

Divine leaned over but could not find the source of the sound.

Suddenly, the circle popped up and tilted back. A stout stem and black orbs for eyes showed beneath the wide top. Like Shroombal had been shrunk, squashed, and robbed of their color. The Thospor climbed onto something that raised them to eye-level.

"Tinctures for staying up late? Balms for frozen fingers? Hmm?"

"Oh, no. I, uh, had hoped to ask you about my mother," Divine stammered. "I wondered if you remembered what she...needed. It would have been about ten years ago and—"

The Thospor harrumphed, jumping down. They raised a thick arm. "Rule number one. Bream never reveals clients' doings. Rule number two. Nothing is for free."

"I have money—" Saph began, but the Thospor, Bream, waddled around the counter, their white cap like a floating disc.

"You humans. Think I have a memory of a Spore-thrower. Lucky for you, I have something better."

Divine and Saph exchanged a look as Bream scooped items noisily into their arms from nearby shelves. They deposited the pieces in a clatter onto the table.

"Sit," Bream demanded. "Honey or sugar?"

"Pardon?" Divine scrunched her nose.

"For your tea." The rest of what Bream said was lost in mutterings and hmm-like sounds.

"Uh, either is fine?"

Bream tilted their cap back, clearly exasperated. They disappeared into the back.

"I think Bream is grumpier than you," Divine whispered to Sage on the table. "A teacup?" Divine searched and found what Sage saw. There were two cups in the middle of bottles, a mortar and pestle, and a wooden box.

Saph tried to make idle conversation, but Divine found her nerves prevented any real participation on her side. Several minutes later, the white Thospor emerged and poured steaming water into the teacup. They opened bottles, splashing a bit of the contents into the cups, and pinched herbs from the box, throwing them into the water. Soon, the cups were swirling with loose ingredients, and the water began to turn darker. Bream added a small spoonful of honey to the cups.

"Five friggons each," Bream ordered.

Divine paid and Bream pushed one of the cups toward her and the other to Saph.

"Drink this. Try not to swallow the pieces."

Divine's stomach soured. "Why not?"

"You'll destroy the message."

Glancing at Saph, the other woman smirked.

"This is intriguing," Saph commented, then sipped her cup. "Not bad. Little bitter."

Tapping the side of her nose with her piercing, Saph locked her eyes on Divine. Divine covered her laugh with a sip from her own cup. Even Sage knew she meant Bream.

The pair sipped in silence until they reached the bottom of their cups, the leaves and pieces clinging to the bottom with a thin puddle of tea Divine didn't dare try to sip.

"Push them back." Bream's thick hands opened and closed.

Cups retrieved, Bream tilted Saph's cup this way and that before pressing their hand into the remnants.

"Sorry about your tea supply, Saph. There's blends from Syphondor you might like. Try the shops in the Market District others avoid."

Bream pushed the cup to the side. Divine couldn't remember telling Bream their names.

"You got all of that from the tea particles?" Saph asked

"That's not the message the leaves had for you. I got that from Shroombal."

Saph leaned forward, folding her arms on the table. "You've talked to Shroombal?"

"I can smell the soil on you. You come from there. We are all connected, us Thospori. We share...memories. Yours was a strong one."

"What did the tea say, then?" Saph asked.

"Be wary of gambling. Capture the flame before the music stops."

"That's it?"

Bream shrugged, their white cap bouncing. "Sometimes the leaves are simple."

"Simply confusing," Saph muttered.

"Your mother," Bream said, turning toward Divine and examining her cup before plunging their hand inside. "Humid jungle and salt spray. Sand and song tickled scales. A mother's search for survival. For her child. Knowledge in the music."

Divine blinked back tears. "Is that my message?"

"It's both of yours. Your mother received a very similar reading. I remember her. You smell similarly. She came into my shop seeking healing. But nothing in my shop could heal her. The Iguions, however... The sea, the music. It points to what you seek. And what she sought. Though her leaves formed more of a healing image and yours bends to knowledge."

Divine scrutinized the cup as Bream set it aside. The Thospor stood, gathering the items from the table.

Saph leaned close. "What do you make of that?"

"We already know my mother went to Solhavn. This must be why. She couldn't get healed by the temples or by potions, so she sailed. But I don't see how this connects to me being...you know."

"Bream, dear," Saph called as the Thospor put things back. "Can you tell us anything else about your message?"

"I have read what the leaves say. That is all."

Divine patted Saph's arm. "It's alright." Standing, Divine picked up Sage. "Thank you, Bream. Your reading led my mother to healing, for a time. It was the best she'd felt in a while."

"Glad to help," Bream said from somewhere behind the counter.

As they exited the shop. Divine pulled Sage's hat back on as he crinkled.

She glanced at his stems, the little fabric scarf waving in the wind. "I, too, wish we were going to sandy beaches, Sage."

* * *

Divine seethed. It was stupid to come here. Stupid to knock on his door and let her palms sweat over him. Stupid to ask about her mother and her list of names. She'd taken off the eyepatch on the way, but he still hadn't recognized her. But she needed to know.

"I'll tell you what I told that archivist," her father said. "We don't talk about my family."

Devon tossed a handful of nuts into his mouth. Memories of sharing roasted nuts with her father at various faires, her hands nestled into her mother and father's, rammed against her later opinion of him. Despite herself, disappointment filled her when she had to tell him she was his daughter standing at his door, and his subsequent shrug.

Devon continued his answer between munching. "Some weird rumors started generations ago, and we just haven't escaped them. My great-uncle Elyon was the town spook. Everyone said he stole cats and made them live forever. They all avoided his house. And my great-grandad Ennium they said was cursed, insects always following him around. He died from some insect bite, ironically. But I got out of that town. No one knew my last name in Arosia."

And her mother met him here in the city, finding a cottage not far away to raise a family and flowers. They were happy once. Everyone holding hands on the walk to the city. Rides on his shoulders to see over crowds or pick fruit from a tree.

The names. Her father had said the same ones on her mother's list.

"After going to Solhavn, Leena started asking all of these questions about my family. She was always sticking her pruning shears into my business."

"You got along then," Divine interrupted. "I remember coming home from the temple because Mom felt better after her trip. The arguing stopped." *For a while.*

"Then I found out she'd seen an apothecary—some human-adjacent—and that's why she went vacationing. Gods, Leena went weird at the end."

Divine crossed her arms, her frown narrowing her eyes to slits. *How would you know? You weren't around.* He'd kept his whole other daughter a secret until her mother was too ill to take care of Divine. Divine had never met her, and, as she'd told Saph on their fall journey, her sentiments were unlikely to change.

"Did you ever even love her?" Divine blurted. It wasn't why she was here, but the words burst out of her anyway.

Devon's expression wavered, softening. "I did once. We were both independent people but together, we could do anything. She had the most beautiful voice. Do you remember her singing? And she loved to dance. That's how we met. She was dancing and her skirt was spinning and I— I was mesmerized and walked right into her." His smile faded. "But then she got obsessed with human-adjacents and started talking about old magic. It was all blasphemous. The temples...the Goddess of Condemnation would punish us for following these Old Ways."

"And then you just left us."

"When she died, you were already at the Temple of Souls. You didn't need me."

"I needed a father!" Divine shouted. "As Mom got sicker, you were hardly ever home. She *had* to put me in the temple because you. Weren't. There!"

Saph touched the grip of her axe behind her back. "Clearly, you're a fickle leaf if your love changes because of someone's ability to take care of themselves. Divine, darling, do you need anything else from this man?"

Her emotions whirled and Divine struggled to keep it all inside. *Don't think of any creatures. Don't think.* She focused on her breathing, letting herself sink into her magic well and float.

"Let's go."

Divine hesitated. "Wait, you mentioned an archivist? What did she look like?"

"Brown hair with an undercut. Oh, and a bird tattoo. A red bird. No, a blue bird."

"A rainbow bird?"

Devon snapped his fingers. "That's the one."

Divine's breath caught. "When was she here?"

"A year, maybe a year and a half ago? Said they were reconciling family records at the Archives or something. You know, she asked me about you. I don't remember why we were talking about animals, but you loved to care for all of the critters around our home."

"Yeah..." Divine retreated toward the door.

"You—you can come back sometime." Her father's voice almost pleaded. "We could catch up."

"I'll think about it."

Outside in the twilit street, Divine's breath immediately fogged as she huffed out her frustration, moving away from her father's house.

"Well, we know the apothecary," Divine said, thinking of Bream's white cap.

She halted as Saph took Divine's hands, a green eye searching Divine's face. "Forget the mystery for a moment. Are you alright, beautiful?"

"I don't know what I thought I'd get from him. An apology? Picking up where we left off at ten or twelve years old? 'Hey Dad, want to go to the faire?'." Divine shook her head. "Mom didn't get any of that. But I'm alright."

"Whether you want to forget him, or break his nose, I'm with you."

Divine's magic burst with florals. Breathing in the comforting scent, her muscles lost their tension and she felt confident. Sage rustled, offering a good thorning if needed.

"Thank you." She tapped Sage's hat. "And you. I'm alright, really. Now we know Madeline was here asking the same questions. My mother went to Solhavn and must have learned something that made her interested in our family histories. It's all leading to the Archives."

"Maybe Meve and Syka found something. Want to go to your friend's place?"

Divine nodded. "I don't know that I feel up for any more walking."

She squeaked as suddenly Divine's legs were scooped up. She wrapped her arms around Saph's neck, tucking Sage safely in her lap as the woman strode forward.

"I didn't mean—"

"Perhaps I just want to hold you close and show you how strong I am."

"I can think of warmer ways you can do that."

Saph hummed in Divine's ear. "Too bad there's a four-person audience there."

"I thought you didn't mind people watching. 'The world needs more pleasure?'"

"That it does. But sometimes I don't want to share. The things I want to do to you…"

Divine nipped Saph's ear and snuggled into her neck.

"Thank you," Divine whispered. "For coming with me. You give me strength."

"You are strong. Sometimes you just need to steep a little for all the flavors to come out."

When they returned to Meve's, only Constance and Ada were there. Despite Saph's confidence in Syka's abilities, Divine worried for her two friends. She fell into a fitful sleep, with dreams of talking trees on fire.

CHAPTER SIXTEEN

A Conservatory Was In The Cards

To distract themselves in the morning, Saph and Divine pursued Bream's suggestion for finding tea. Divine led them to the Market District, the sky a blanket of grey.

"Almost every province and continent has its own sub district," Divine recounted. "But each has its similarities. They exist to trade goods, yes, but also stories. Small restaurants and street vendors will have food that's local to them. Everyone wants you to share in the best from their home. In exchange for coins."

"Wonder which shop Bream thinks 'others avoid'? Otto mentioned he'd heard of a tea from Syphondor. Having tasted Meve's desert flower, I'm intrigued."

"You better not be tasting her 'desert flower'." Divine stuck out her tongue. "The section is right this way. The east continent has many shops represented there. I think that's all Bream meant."

"Iramont doesn't get much from Syphondor. If I can bring back something no one's heard of, it might rekindle their interest even though the festival is over. Entice their thirst for all things hot."

Divine rolled her eyes. "You're not leaning into what Viktor said, are you?"

"Hot teas for all of your hot needs." Saph winked.

"That's a terrible slogan." Divine teased.

A bell clanged as Saph and Divine entered the shop. While decorated, it lacked any trace of Midwinter Nights. Like stepping into another land, or a different time of year, it was bright and full of warm colors, sectioned displays, and crates.

Lidless cartons showed their dried meat and fruit, nuts, and seeds. What looked like rugs made of reeds hung behind the shopkeeper, a smiling man in a long-sleeved indigo shirt.

Several domed cages hung at either corner with birds the colors of sunrise within.

"Welcome to Mateo's Sundries." The man had rose colored tattoos that swirled along his cheeks and neck. If he followed the traditions of his home country, the inked markings travelled over his arms and chest, though his shirt hid them. "Can I interest you in a poultry stick?"

Divine's throat constricted. The bird in the nearest cage wished *let me out* and Divine struggled to keep from staring. Had the orange and red winged bird thought the words, or had Divine interpreted their intent?

"Uh. No thank you." Divine peeled her eyes away from the long down-curved beak as the bird sipped from a trumpet-shaped flower. "We were wondering what teas you have."

"In bulk," Saph added.

The man tutted, tapping his lip. "We don't get many requests for bulk. Single users mainly. Ahh you have a decacacti! I haven't seen such a fine example in all my time here."

Divine dropped her hand protectively onto Sage's pot at her hip. The string sling continued to prove useful in carrying the sentient succulent around.

"He was a gift." Divine beamed at Saph, bumping her with her shoulder.

"Such interesting creatures, don't you think?" Mateo spun around. "You know, I should start carrying them in my shop." When he faced them again, he held a trio of insects by their long antennae. "Come closer, hmm?"

Sage *meeped*, bending his prickly stems. Divine understood the ask and lifted Sage onto the counter. His pot crackled as Mateo placed the insects beneath the fabric into Sage's soil.

"Sounds like the soil is settling," Mateo pointed. "You might need to water it."

Saph hid her laugh with a cough. "We'll make sure to check it. But about those teas."

"Mmm, yes. I might be willing to part with some of my supply. Do you have a store yourself?"

"I do! Just opened one in the south."

Divine drifted, looking at the other items in the store as the two shop owners conversed. A case of soap wedges caught her eye, and she lifted a pink one, the grittiness of the texture scratching the tip of her nose.

"Ahh yes. I heard about the black spot. Too bad. Too bad. No wonder you are here needing teas." The man disappeared behind the counter, returning with three canisters. "I find sniffing gives a good idea of the taste."

Divine sniffed the soap in her hand and noted floral and citrus but heavy with the scent of wax. She put the cleanser back.

"That almost smells spicy. Divine, smell this one."

Shifting closer, Divine leaned over the canister and took a long breath. She pivoted to cough into her elbow. The scent made her feel like she had inhaled a piece of cracked pepper.

"That would certainly burn a few throats," Divine croaked, her words triggering another cough.

Sage tapped her elbow in brief consolation.

"No, no," Mateo corrected. "Fire cactus root has just a little bite. Like a well-seasoned stew."

The shop owner peered at Sage as the decacacti crackled loudly. "I say, you may need a new pot."

Divine leaned over Sage and whispered, "They wouldn't eat your kind."

Saph grimaced. "I don't think anyone is going to want to drink stew."

Mateo waved his arms, bumping a canister into a teetering spin before it settled safely.

"It does not taste like stew. The tea has a strong...outdoor flavor and a smokiness from the tafa leaves being dried by fire. The taste is similar to the local brews of alcohol. Though, combined with the fire cactus root's bite."

"Alright, I'm feeling persuaded." Saph pressed her hand to the small of Divine's back. "We can work with the fire in the name, too. 'Warm up with a cup of fire.'"

"Dragon's Breath?" Divine offered.

Saph pulled her closer, so their hips touched. "I love it. And we can appeal to some of our usual patrons who drink the Arosian beers I offer." Saph leaned closer to Mateo. "Let's say I needed to make ten cups a day for three months. How much would that be?"

"My, my, that's…" Mateo's mouth opened and closed as his chin rolled to the ceiling, like he was mentally measuring the scoops.

"Shouldn't we just take a little back home?" Thoughts of nibbled sacks made Divine squirm. "What if it doesn't sell and you've spent all of that money?"

Or I ruin it again.

"Mateo, are they having wagered Crossroads George games during Midwinter Nights?"

"Yes, yes. But I don't participate. I'm too poor a player to risk it."

Saph clapped her hands together. "Then I'll just win a few matches and get the funds back."

"I can offer you a ten percent discount from my single-use buyers."

"Ten? It would take you all season to sell that much. What could you get if you had half of your sales right now? Fifteen percent."

The shopkeeper wrung his hands. "You make a good argument. It is a deal."

Saph grinned. "I'll take half of the three-month supply in this desert flower tea, and the spicy one. There's a need for delicate and sweet options to compliment the fire. Right, Divine?"

Divine looked at Saph through her eyelashes, conjuring as best of a seductive look as she could muster in front of an audience. She couldn't help but read innuendos in Saph's statement.

"Are there tea shops in Syphondor?" Divine asked as Mateo scooped the tea blends from a large cloth sack into two smaller ones.

"Oh yes. And there are tea halls."

"Is that like a storehouse?" Saph asked.

"It's a place where the community comes together for tea. Friends gather, grandson takes his grandfather, business deals are made, marriage proposals...and many other things."

"Do they serve food?" Saph asked.

"Oh no, just tea." Mateo laughed. "Then it would be called a Tea and Food Hall."

Divine wondered what a tea hall would look like, imagining it an oasis in the desert for wanderers with colorful fabrics draped for walls. It seemed like Saph's breakfast and tea idea was fairly unique. Divine hoped they could make it popular in Iramont.

"Why do you think there are no tea halls or tea shops in Arosia?" Divine asked.

Mateo put his scoop away and tied the new bag. "Hmm. When Syphondor began trading with Arosia, the city here had already been built. Businesses go here, food goes there. There really wasn't a place to put one, so I've heard. Taverns, yes. Syphondor tea is a supply like nuts. No one grew tea leaves around Arosia in the early days. Eventually mixes from all over became available in the stores. And in the Arosia Province now there are growers and there are tea drinkers—but not like my home. One day I'll see what they have west of your mountain. Here you go."

Saph grasped the bags and handed the man his coins. "Thanks, Mateo. I appreciate you parting with some of your supply. If you get to Iramont, come find me at the Steeped in Sapphire."

"Happy sipping!" he called as Divine and Saph made their way to the door.

But dread and desperation flitted through Divine's body. She paused and turned from the door, Sage faintly squeaking at her side.

"How much for the birds?" she asked.

"These? Nothing, nothing. Not for sale. These ones have a few more cycles of laying eggs and then they will become poultry sticks."

Sage squelched and Divine snatched Saph's free hand, squeezing urgently.

"*If* they were for sale," Saph added. "How much?"

"I'm sorry, my friends. Too valuable."

Rage rattled around Divine's head into a thunderous roar. Such beautiful birds held back from living how they wanted. If Saph said anything else Divine didn't hear it. She blew out a breath and opened the door, hearing the cages rattle in sync with her racing heart.

* * *

The pair walked along the streets for a place that would host a game of cards. Saph insisted on having some Arosian earnings to boast about to Sylus and the others when they returned to Iramont. Too disappointed in leaving the birds behind, Divine halfheartedly accompanied the search.

"What about what Bream said?" Divine asked as they checked out the buildings.

"About gambling?" Saph scoffed. "Bet they tell everyone that during the festival. Lots of people lose lots of money."

They located a games shop, a sign on the door advertising Crossroads George games as well as offering decks and special cards designed for the festival. Divine popped next door to a restaurant, grabbing drinks and snacks with her ever dwindling coins .

When she reappeared, Saph had settled in at a table. A hot cocoa in hand, Divine sipped the creamy rich liquid and watched. Slowly her spirits raised.

Knowing now how Saph viewed their relationship, Divine marveled at Saph's command of the table and the attention of her audience without jealousy. It helped her confidence when Saph declared Divine her lucky charm and kissed her before every play. The action also seemed to confuse the players; one moment Saph was flirting with them and the next flirting with Divine. Several players made poor card decisions and stormed away. Saph added new coins to her pockets.

"Mm, these are good," Saph said through a mouthful of pastry that dropped crumbs like fallen leaves onto her plate. "Bustleberry jam, how I've missed you. Sweet and tart. These would go great with tea. Next summer."

Saph held the half-eaten triangle out and Divine leaned closer, taking a bite. The warm pastry was both soft and crunchy and the jam made her mouth pucker. She would prefer it a bit sweeter, but admitted it was very good and the apposition of the different flavors was a bit like harmonizing music.

"Do you know how to make them?" Divine asked.

"I can learn. Can't be that hard to whip it up and bake it. I bet Sylus knows."

"You could pair it with eggs." As soon as the suggestion left her mouth, Divine regretted it. Normally it wouldn't have bothered her, but she thought of the birds in Mateo's, stuck in a cage to lay eggs for people to eat but they wanted to be free. "On second thought, I think the pastry is fine by itself."

"Exactly! Bite, sip. It'll be a festival of flavors in your mouth."

In the middle of their third game, Divine's magic flared; burning wood and overripe citrus. A worker pointed toward their table. Figures stood with deep maroon armor and long black cloaks. Agents of Condemnation. Divine whirled a shield around herself and Saph to prevent mind muddling. Agents at this shop?

Divine leaned closer, as if nibbling on Saph's neck. "We've got to go. Agents are here."

"Lovelies, it has been fun, but I must withdraw from this round. I'm afraid this one"—Saph snapped her teeth playfully at Divine— "has tempted me and I must take her to bed."

The table chuckled and Saph took Divine's hand, leading them to the back of the store.

"Don't look back," Saph instructed. "I noticed an alley door."

Through it, Saph commanded they run. They slipped and slid on the frozen patches that had partially melted and refroze as soon as the towering buildings hid the marginal sunlight. The alley seemed dark for the hour.

Agitation flicked through the air before she heard them.

"That's her!" the voice cracked against the close walls.

Divine risked a glance over her shoulder. Two figures sprinted after them with three others behind them.

"Where do we go?" Divine's voice squeaked.

"Where there's people. What's the busiest place here?"

As she tried to get her memory to focus, a bolt of lighting smashed into the stone above their heads, raining dust and pebbles. An Anvil was with them? Hadn't Madeline said she was working with an Anvil? Saph tugged Divine and they veered into a connecting alleyway.

"We just want to talk," one of their pursuers called.

"Like condemnation they do," Saph groused.

They wanted to take her. What Constance had warned her of was coming true. Her heart raced even faster, and she knew she had to act. The lack of control of the situation, of her current life, needed to be rectified.

She redirected her fear, encouraging every creature nearby to break their hiding and flee, to come to the alley. A few rats and mice and other rodents entered the passage from cracks and grates and slimy wigglers of green and black slithered over the stone. But it wasn't enough to make a difference. The city was too clean. If only there was a flood of creatures from every corner of Alistraysia.

She had reshaped Saph's bones from a distance, called dunarus from who knows where, and summoned flutterwings in her ecstasy. Maybe she had more power inside her than she'd ever known was there.

Divine imagined the sunrise birds from Mateo's Sundries bursting from their cages, wings a blur. She felt them struggle against the bars, rippling her well. Then they appeared in the air ahead, flapping their wings haphazardly before orienting themselves and soaring over Divine's head.

"Was that you?" Saph asked and Divine sensed her admiration.

She let the feeling flood her well. "And I'm not finished. Think good things of me."

"Always. Can they be dirty good thoughts?"

She smiled, her stomach leaped as Sage hummed, then she flipped through pages of creatures in her memory; roachoids of Solhavn with their boot-sized carapace bodies, slender sword-backed jackals with narrow muzzles and sharp teeth. She willed them to come.

A line of brown lengths topped with antennas created a miniature river down the center of the alley. A wulf appeared mid-bound just shy of the far end connecting street. All parted around Divine and Saph on their journey toward those who chased the women. She pleaded with them, rather than demand, to protect the alley from intruders.

Shouts made Divine look back, catching sight of birds diving at her pursuers' heads and carapaces climbing legs, while snouts snapped and growled.

The light at the connecting street flickered as people passed by. They were almost there. Divine glanced back at their followers. One figure stopped to swipe at the creatures on his pants.

Divine's breath caught. Grey eyes that swirled like the storm. The man Madeline had worked with, who once pretended to assault her so that Divine would take notice of her. Did he have powers from the God of Storms? He raised a red and black glove that extended up his forearm like a gauntlet.

She ran harder, thinking of dunaru quills and then she sensed they were there, popping out of holes that didn't exist, shooting their spines into boots as feet got too close.

Bursting onto the connecting street, Divine spun, trying to orient herself by the multistoried colorful buildings. The nearby Market District was likely empty with the merchants coming out at night for the festival. The Holy District was too far away and other Agents of Condemnation possibly waited.

"What day is it?" Divine asked.

"Uh, day six of the faire, I think."

"It's gift-giving day! This way." Divine picked up her pace. "The artisans always give gifts in the square on the sixth day. It gets packed with people hoping to take home a unique treasure."

When they reached the edge of the square, Divine couldn't see its sculpture of Alistraysia for the thick crowd of people. She plunged in, offering apologies as she pushed through, leading Saph deeper into the crowd. Rotating Sage to her front so that she could create a protective barrier with her arms around the decacacti, Divine didn't pause to see if the platform was set up beneath the square's wide-based conifer or if jewelry, swords, or dresses were being given away this time to the lucky few.

"They'll expect us to go to the nearest side street," Saph said behind Divine. "Keep going to the furthest main avenue."

The emotions of the crowd swelled, over and over like waves on a shore. It reminded Divine of a day she spent with her mother at Deities Bay, catching crustaceans in tide pools and building sand tunnels and towers, and how every moment brought a surge of joy and laughter.

A woman dropped a bundle wrapped in iridescent paper and Divine scooped it up, handing it back to its owner. She couldn't hear the woman's thanks, but it crawled up her neck like kisses from Saph. Nearby, a boy was jostled between much larger adults bouncing between them. Tapping one of the men on the shoulder, Divine asked them if they would lift the boy to see the event. As the boy climbed on the shoulders of one of the men, his elation tingled Divine's head delightfully. Continuing through the crowd, Divine found small ways to help others and in return, her well grew with their appreciation.

When the sculpture, a large disc of colored wires that always seemed more of an eye than a world, came into view, a crack of thunder accompanied a flash of lightning across the open sky, barely missing the top of the tree.

"Snow lightning?" several denizens gasped nearby.

Divine ducked, lowering her head below those of the crowd, and grasped Saph's arm tightly.

"It's them," Divine whispered.

Feigning looking for a lost ring, they continued, hunching through those gathered. With the tall evergreen tree on their right, Divine led them left to the next main street.

"Over here!" Divine tugged Saph toward a structure with a domed roof made of glass. "They'll never guess this place."

Glass panels lined the front with a foggy sheen. Throwing open the large iron door etched with vines, they rushed inside.

The sounds of the city faded into silence broken only by a faint dripping from somewhere unseen. Unlike any other building, palm trees stretched high into the domed ceiling, wide bromeliads reached their succulent green fronds, and large colorful blossoms at the pathways blocking any deeper view.

"What is this place?" Saph asked, her head tilted as she followed a looping vine through the treetops.

Divine inhaled through her nose. If the moment before rain on a summer seaside garden had a scent, this was it. In the weighty air, vibrant florals mixed with fruity sweetness, reminiscent of sipping fruit juice while a breeze blew in off the ocean.

"A conservatory. There're plants from many of the islands. I think Solhavn, Dragons Roost Island, and the Lonely Island. There might be plants from the Tail of Trelvania, too."

"That explains why I suddenly need to take off my coat." Saph tugged at her neckline. "It's like the Dalga Hot Springs in here."

"There was a fire years ago and they replaced much of the local foliage. I never got to ask my mom what she thought of the changes. If it reminded her of her time with the Iguions."

"Do you come here often?" Saph asked.

"Yes. In the winter, the gardens of the Holy District are dormant. Here, it's like a breath of summer that shakes out the cold from your bones."

"I'm feeling rejuvenated already." Saph removed her coat and presented her elbow. "Will you be my tour guide?"

Divine surveyed the door and the glass panels on either side. Though opaque and hazy with condensation, there didn't seem to be any figures nearby. Maybe they'd escaped after all. She caught Saph's playful grin. How could she say no to that? She slipped off her coat and took Saph's arm.

Rather than the route immediately forward, she led Saph to the right on a path that circled the edge of the building. She knew glass windows were there, but the plants concealed the structure, allowing immersion in the beauty and serenity. Arm in arm, they followed the curve of the path as it twisted in and out around large growths and several pools, until they came to one with a small outcropping that mimicked a waterfall. Multiple paths connected to the semicircle space. At a nearby bench, they sat down.

"Maybe this is what Bream meant by, 'be wary of gambling'," Saph breathed.

"What do you mean?"

"If I hadn't played cards, maybe they wouldn't have found you."

"I've been all over the city, in daylight and dark. If anything, it's my own fault. Don't blame yourself."

"Still, I want to protect you."

Divine snuggled close. Flutterwings of all shapes and sizes flitted to flowers, like the inflorescent cluster of bright red low near the path, and a tall stalk of vibrant blue. Sage hummed contentedly. Divine laid her head on Saph's shoulder and they watched, the gentle crash of the waterfall and their breaths the music of the room. Divine's eyelids became heavy.

"They're at the center!" a voice shouted from the pool.

Divine shot up, but the image in the waterfall's base vanished before she could identify the scryer. Warmth drained from her, despite the heat of the building, her face and hands feeling like she was rolling in snow.

She couldn't see them, but she felt their zeal and animosity. They craved retribution for the alleyway.

"We've got to get out of here," Divine whispered. "This way."

She stepped toward a connecting path and froze. The man with the swirling eyes stepped forward and as Divine and Saph retreated to the pool, a figure emerged from each path surrounding them.

Saph spun her axe from her back, presenting it like a barrier.

"Here now," Madeline's accomplice said. "We just want to know which side you're on."

Divine shifted behind Saph, readying her protection magic. "I don't know what you're talking about."

"The deities' side, or the renegades'?"

"I don't—"

The man stepped aside and someone who had been behind him thrust a shape forward. She landed on her knees, black and a streak of pink spilling over her face.

"Syka?" Divine stepped forward, but Saph's arm shot out, stopping her.

The man nudged Syka with his boot. "We caught her stealing our talismans."

"Just stealing what was stolen." Syka blew her hair out of her face. "Didn't think you needed so many."

The man raised his arm as if to backhand Syka and the world seemed to slow down. Whether her own or combining with those around her, rage and dread burst through Divine's mental barriers. Like a mother werewing seeking the source of her baby's malefactor, Divine curled her fingers like claws and snarled.

"Stay back," Saph warned as a woman on a nearby path took a step closer.

Divine raised a magical barrier around herself and Saph, the action sending waves fighting for dominance as they clashed against each other within her well.

"Renegades like this one want to upend the balance of the world," the man continued, pointing to Syka. "There are those with power, the deities, and there are those who want to give it to the undeserving. The human-adjacents can never be born with magic. No, they have to steal it."

Syka whistled a short bird-like chirp, shifting onto her knees. "And what are you doing with the stolen magic, I wonder?"

The man ignored Syka. "So I'll ask again. Which side are you on?"

Everyone wanted Divine to be something. A servant, a healer, an unlocker of demon prisons. A Goddess. Her focus fell on Saph, who shifted a foot forward, and then Syka, seemingly unbothered by it all. The people Divine had surrounded herself with in Iramont never asked her to be anything but herself. And they were in this chaos because of her.

Divine clenched her hands. "I'm on my side."

"Now!" Saph shouted.

Syka swiped out with her legs, sweeping the man off his feet, and she rolled backward. Meanwhile, Saph darted forward and grabbed Syka's forearm, lifting the rogue to her feet. The pair dashed back to Divine, who extended her shield to accommodate.

Breathing deeply, Divine mentally bounced on the edge of her well and then dove in. She barely registered Syka rushing forward, stabbing with her daggers or Saph spinning her axe against their foes. Divine swam deep. Designing the images she wanted to create, she gathered an endless supply of buckets full of her magical water. She dropped magical energy on the nearest woman foe, weighing her down. Then she tore open a wave, swirling a tunnel that stretched from the Conservatory to a ruined tower.

A horned head turned. It launched into the tunnel and appeared above the waterfall. The werewing shrieked and dove, catching the man in her claws and dropped him next to the woman struggling to move. Divine asked the werewing to snatch the last adversary, vibrating her plea across a thin strand of water drops that seemed to connect them.

As if she had been underwater and surfaced, Divine gasped. Her connection broke, and the strand disappeared from her vision. The werewing snagged the last agent by the back of his coat and dropped him near the others. Divine didn't know who commanded it or if they moved by instinct, but Saph, Syke, and Divine hurried to the other side of the pool.

Sage's pot cascaded a series of sizzles, buzzes, and crackles.

"What do you mean 'hold you out'? I'm not letting them take you." Divine tilted her head as she listened. "Yes, I trust you. Like this?"

In answer, all ten stems rotated their spine sides away from Divine and toward the far side of the pool. There was a rapid sequence of pattering as thorns burst from Sage and shot toward their enemies. Necks and cheeks beaded tiny dots of blood, and within Divine's next breath her enemies crumpled like melted snow.

Divine leaned on a knee, laughing in delirium.

"Sage, you thorny little succulent." Saph grinned. "You've been holding out on us."

The decacacti squeaked and burbled.

"He says no one asked." Divine lifted his pot in front of her face. "You're very helpful for a grumpy decacacti. Well done, Sage."

Syka approached the figures, nudging one of the bodies with her boot. "Are they dead?"

"He says they're very tired," Divine said, joining Syka. "His thorns help him consume live insects by paralyzing them."

Saph made a hum of curiosity. "Good thing we never got spined."

Divine shrugged. "He says humans are too big to get paralyzed by a single thorn."

"And he knows this how?" asked Syka.

Lids fluttering shut, the man Divine had recognized as Ehmin managed to speak. "She'll be back. Madeline will be back. And you'll get what's coming to you."

Sage made a *bppht* sound as Divine stepped over the man.

"How did you know I was in the city? Why do you want me?"

The man grinned smugly. "Been having nice dreams?"

"Are you behind my nightmares?"

Ehmin snickered. "Madeline really did know how you think. You just had to solve the mystery of the First Soul. Have an agent enhance your memory of that day over and over in your sleep, and you had to come running back to Arosia."

So he had been there in the glade of Willow Way. How else would anyone know?

"Why me?"

The man mumbled, slurring his words. "Didn't predict you could summon creatures...take your magic like the First Soul."

His eyes finally closed and with him went the answers. Did he and the others know that the deities were just humans? If they did, why were they helping steal talismans for the Goddess of Condemnation?

Saph dropped her axe onto her back. "We should get out of here before more of these poorly dressed jerks show up."

Divine used her foot to push down Ehmin's glove. Lightning scars wove up his forearm. For a moment, Divine pitied him and wondered if his injury had been self-inflicted during his early days of mastering his magic. But he wouldn't have the same compassion for her.

"Wait." Divine's voice came out as a whisper. "The werewing."

As if called, the creature let go of her perch on the domed ceiling and soared down.

Pressing her hands together, Divine bowed her head. "Thank you. For giving me the aid I needed."

Trying to convey to the werewing to stay still, Divine recreated the tunnel, like a wave bending over itself in a rush of magical water that only she could see. With a mental nudge, the werewing flew through and disappeared. The water crashed into itself, released from Divine's hold, and settled into her well.

Divine's mouth began to salivate unpleasantly, and her stomach rolled. She rushed to the ferns and low bushes and heaved. The acid burnt her throat. In an instant, Saph steadied her as Divine tottered, everything spinning.

Syka whooped. "That. Was. Legendary!"

Approval tickled Divine's chest and some of the sourness in her belly vanished.

"Here, put your arm around my neck." Saph's strong arm gripped Divine around her waist.

Divine chuckled. "I think with you two around, I'll be alright. Just keep contemplating how awesome I am."

Saph kissed Divine's temple. "I'll tell you how awesome you are. We never would have outrun all of them if you hadn't used your new beastcraft. You called all of those creatures?"

"I did." Divine hiccupped. "But I'm thinking I should have listened to Constance and not mixed my magics. I feel rotten."

"Can you direct us back to Meve's?"

Though her head protested with a vice-like grip, Divine nodded.

"There you are." The three women spun toward the sound of Ada's voice. The hydromancer continued, her words tinted with annoyance. "Constance had me checking every sink, toilet, and pitcher in the city to find you."

In the pool, Ada and Constance leaned near. Divine could just make out Meve bouncing behind them to get into the view. Divine's heart jumped. Meve was safe.

"Did you know we were in trouble?" Divine asked.

"I could...feel the extent you were using your well and surmised. We've filled Meve's bathtub with water. Step through and we'll catch up in the safety of your friend's home."

"You won't catch me here when they wake up," Syka said, then jumped into the pool.

Saph caught Divine's wrist as she stepped to follow. She brought her lips to Divine's ear, her breath warm and alluring.

"Someone tipped these people off through scrying." Saph whispered. "And Ada easily finds us?"

"Constance's well connects him to other's wells." Divine whispered back. "I don't know how it works, but maybe he could sense where we were and that's all."

"Maybe. Let's just be cautious."

Divine gave Saph a quick peck on the cheek.

"Leap into adventure." Divine echoed from their first pool transportation months ago, and hopped into the pool.

CHAPTER SEVENTEEN

Knowledge in the Music

"Sit down everyone," Constance gestured, ushering Divine to a chair. "We have a lot to catch up on and then I want to get us out of the city." He bent closer, lowering his voice. "Are you feeling up to this now?"

Divine nibbled on a bit of spinetooth plant, making her mouth feel cleaner, and nodded, looking to Saph. She grabbed the tavern owner's hand, pulling her down next to her.

"We found a lot of documents." Meve shook her hands in the air delightedly.

"Brought some back." Syka reached into her pants and pulled out several rolled-up pieces of parchment and folded sheets. "Desire, acquire."

No one moved to touch them.

"How did you get out without being caught?" Ada asked, an eyebrow raised.

"Wasn't too hard." Syka sat back, propping her boots up next to documents. "Only lost a sock."

Saph crossed her arms. "But you did get caught, *Professional Thief*. Luckily, they were after Divine and me or you would have been on your own. What happened?"

Despite Saph's incredulous tone to start, she finished with the care in her voice that Divine knew well.

Syka dropped her head back and opened her mouth dramatically. "I was shadowing you two and got distracted by a mockingcrate."

A smirk tugged the corner of Saph's mouth.

"In my defense it was a barrel at the time. I wanted more coins." Syka folded her arms across her chest. "Don't. Say. A. Word."

Saph held up her hands.

"What did Ehmin mean that you took talismans?" The thought had been itching at Divine's mind. "The leader."

Syka's eyes darted to Saph then back to Divine.

"I trust Divine and I think you do too." Saph lifted her chin toward Constance and Ada. "These two I'm not sure of."

Ada tutted. "Smart woman. I wouldn't trust me either."

"I'm part of a movement, of sorts. We all are. Edward, Sylus, Listhinci. Saph, though she just lets us use the tavern and keeps our secret. Please don't be mad she didn't tell you—it was to protect us. Viktor is oblivious and a perfect cover. Who would hang around that bigot and not think like he does?"

They hadn't trusted her enough to tell her before. Anything they could be doing would certainly land them in the clutches of the Condemnation Agents. But couldn't Saph have trusted her? Divine swallowed her frustration. She had only just talked to Saph about being more open.

"You steal talismans? Why?" Divine leaned on her knees.

"She does what now?" Meve squeaked. "When was this?"

"To give to the Iguions. They're doing research. You saw Liz's machine? The talismans are either freely given or already stolen. We don't steal from their true owners." Syka leaned toward Meve, moving a long lock of Meve's golden hair behind her shoulder. "It was when you were reading. I dashed away for a bit. Don't stress, I would have given the slip to anyone."

Frustration gathered behind Divine's ears. "Is that the actual reason you came?"

"I came because you asked. Bonus that it was the capital and maybe I could find information for our cause. Double bonus, they kept talismans behind a sequence of only two locked doors. Bad move on their part."

Divine pinched the bridge of her nose. "Anyone else have secrets to reveal?"

"I was going to tell you." Syka tucked her pink strands behind her ear—something Divine had never seen her do. "I tried to hint at least. That day we shopped and I walked you to the Hydro Spondence. We've just tried to be careful. We are but a thin string, and all it takes is one wrong card play and the thread is cut."

Syka lowered her boots to the floor and handed a sheet to Divine. It appeared to be torn from something larger.

"I think this answers your First Soul question."

Unfolding it, the page contained an illustration that depicted the Goddess of Souls, the God of Storms, and the God of Virtue around a boradain. Their powers flowed into the creature. Divine glanced at Constance. The drawing looked like him. The scene aligned with what Madeline had said, and what Divine had surmised after speaking with Iramont's First Servant of Souls. Not the story the temple told everyone; that the Goddess of Souls rescued a man from eternal punishment, someone the Goddess thought still had good in him.

Divine squinted at the page. Another person with dark curls stood behind the three, but the face was smudged.

"If I may steer the conversation back to what you uncovered about Divine," Constance said, pressing his hands together.

Meve straightened, eyes flashing with excitement. "First, we followed the records Ewan mentioned and found your mother's! There was a reference on it being part of some Old Souls...collection? We found other records, other people marked like this. Divine, they had whole family lines gathered together like they are tracing family trees and—they all showed abilities not part of a temple. People who didn't Confirm as a servant and who didn't have talismans."

"That's where I found my clue for the talisman trail," Syka threw in. "Whoever is organizing this information made a reference to talisman research. They must be looking into them, just like the Iguions are."

Syka handed another sheet to Divine, then resumed.

"If they are locating these people, there's at least two they won't ever find, as you're holding them."

Divine stood. "None of this proves that I'm a Goddess. Just that there are people who have different magical abilities than what the temples have. And the temples are tracking them. Based on what Ehmin said, that concerns me. But Saph's family believes that magic is everywhere and I'm starting to think the Old Ways aren't wrong."

"The proof is in your blood." Constance said softly. "Which the Iguions could find."

"And now we're back to Solhavn." Divine plopped back down. Saph rubbed the top of Divine's knee and Divine continued. "We met a Thospor who sent my mom to Solhavn for healing. There had to be something my mom learned there that made her ask questions about my father's family, and then she visited the archives. The same questions that Madeline asked my father before she found me. But what did she find..."

Divine's thoughts drifted as the others listened to more of what Meve and Syka had to say. There was something Bream had said. *Something about sand and scales and...*

Constance cleared his throat.

The Goodly One had kneeled beside her. "You've been testing the boundaries of your magic, rather successfully. I congratulate you. Are you summoning the creatures, like a Harvester summons vegetables? Or binding your will to them like the Soulshields do to control emotions?"

"A Soulshield influences emotions, they don't control them."

"Mm. I see."

There always seemed to be something Constance wasn't saying. Divine felt judged.

She huffed. "All of it at once, I think. The werewing was one from the Ferrum forest ruins. I wonder how far I can pull..."

"Do you believe me now? That you can become a Goddess?"

Divine rubbed her forehead. "Maybe? I don't really want to believe it, but sometimes you can't ignore the music that keeps playing. Wait. Bream said there was 'Knowledge in the music'..."

Dashing to her accordion case, Divine flipped it open. She removed the piece of music her mother had given her from Solhavn.

"Bream gave my mother a similar prediction. They said the sea and the music pointed to what we sought."

Divine examined the music. *"Keep it safe," her mother had whispered. "You have the—"*

"I have the only copy like it in all Trelvania," Divine quoted her mother. "I've never played this piece all the way through. There's words but they are in Iguionish."

She picked up her instrument and after prepping herself and the accordion, she launched into transporting the notes from the page into an audible story. As the last note vibrated from the bellows, the words on the page shimmered. They coalesced, swirled, and rearranged.

"It's in common!" Divine breathed and set her accordion aside. She read it to the others.

> "We are the secret keepers.
> The record keepers.
> Thorenvessh.
> When truth was wiped, we remembered.
> Thorenvessh.
> By the Old Ways, all will be revealed.
> By your blood, truth can be rewritten.
> Thorenvessh.
> When your power becomes,
> seek Thorenvessh.
> Sanctuary for Divine born of Leena.
> Thorenvessh."

The words swirled back into Iguionish and Divine blinked at the music. Meve began hurried conjectures of the magic being from Orators or Creators, but Divine focused on handwriting that had appeared in the corner.

Divine, my dearest daughter. The pantheon is a lie. Gods and Goddesses have strong magic, but that is all. And you may have the trait. When I am gone, I still want to protect you. There are friends all around, if you know where to look for them. Find the helpers and stay safe, my little one. Keep what I have told you secret. This music will tell the Iguions. I know you will use your power for good. I love you always.

"What in all of Alistraysia is a Thorenvessh?" Syka broke into Divine's silent reading.

Divine shook her head, unable to look away from the music. "I don't know. A name maybe."

Her mother had left her words unread for all of these years. She knew she would die and tried to help anyway.

"The Old Ways, your magic, and your name were in that." Saph rose, arriving by Divine's side and resting a hand between Divine's shoulder blades. "What do you make of it?"

"The Iguions know something. Though I think Constance was right all along. My mother—" Divine fought back a sob, biting her bottom lip. "She learned something in Solhavn that told her the pantheon is just powerful humans. And I have the trait. She wrote it there."

Saph continued to rub circles on Divine's back. "What do you want to do?"

Divine blew out a breath. Constance, Syka, Ada and Meve watched expectantly. Sage popped an island suggestion. She wanted to go back a few days to hunting decorations and being excited for Midwinter Nights. But that couldn't happen.

"What do you need? How can we help?" Saph added.

"We should leave Arosia. Servants like Ehmin are after me. He's an Anvil, so at least the God of Storms and the Goddess of Souls' temples. They know I'm here. I don't want them to come after Meve, or any of you." Divine considered Ada. "Can they travel through water?"

Constance's words echoed in her mind. *She doesn't teach anyone anymore.*

Ada crossed her arms. "I am the only one who knows how."

"Oh Divine!" Meve jumped out of her seat and threw her arms around Divine's neck. "I wish you didn't have to go, but I understand. Your secret is safe with me and if they ask, you went north to Nelithor. Will you be coming back? I mean, I guess you wouldn't want to come back until they stop chasing you. Let me know if there's anything I can do to help."

"Thanks, Meve. You're a great friend. I have a lot to figure out. But we'll stay in touch, no matter what. I'm really sorry I left without telling you before."

Constance rose, motioning Ada toward the bathtub—to prep for the travel, Divine guessed. "We can keep working on controlling your magic. Then you can decide if you want to go to Solhavn to—"

Divine held up her hands. "I don't want to decide anything right now. I'll figure it out. Eventually. But for now, I want a warm fire and a hot cup of tea and"—she met Saph's eye—"to enjoy life's pleasures."

"As you wish." Constance bowed his head. "Before we left, the God of Storms predicted severe weather coming near Iramont soon. It would prevent travelers in, or out. I can see what the latest news is, and how to use it to our advantage."

"Hey Virtue God Guy," Syka said, poking Constance in the ribs. "The lady said she didn't want your meddling right now."

"I wasn't—I understand."

As usual, Divine couldn't precisely read his emotions. She nodded her thanks to Syka as Constance moved to another task, and focused on using her well to calm herself, even though the magic aggravated her nausea. Meve bounced toward different directions, the eagerness to help palatable in the air.

Saph took Divine's hand and kissed her knuckles. "My girlfriend is a Goddess. In and out of bed. She also might have some really powerful magic."

Divine kissed Saph firmly, only pulling back when her whole body tingled.

"Do you think anything can be normal again?" Divine asked, staring into Saph's green eye.

"Nothing has been normal since I met you. And that's good. Normal is overrated."

"Think we can try for a few normal days as a distraction?"

Saph moved her lips against Divine's. "I can provide many distractions."

"What about secrets?"

"Is this about Syka's actions here?" Saph asked, touching their noses together.

"Why didn't you tell me she was after talismans?"

"I didn't know." Saph huffed. "I knew of her work, their work, but I'm not included on any plans."

"Honestly?"

"Really. Truly. I support them, but the less I know the better it is for them. If you ever have anything you want to know, just ask me. If it's my secret, it's also yours."

"You trust me?"

"With every part of me."

"Every part of me wants every part of you."

Then Saph kissed Divine fully. Their hands were in each other's hair when something crackled, though it felt like the clearing of a throat in her magic. Divine opened an eye only to narrow it at Sage.

"I'll carry your bag," Saph offered.

Divine scooped up Sage and placed him cross-body. He looked different without his thorns and seemed tired. That would explain why he hadn't added his thoughts to the conversation earlier.

"Let's find a warm mantle for you," she whispered, grabbing her accordion case. Sage hummed approvingly.

When it was time to leave, everyone gathered at Meve's bathtub that shimmered with an image of Ada's place. The curly-haired woman had a candy bubble in her mouth but held it to the side of her face as she spoke.

"I'll take us to Weathered Crossroads, then send you wherever you want to go."

Divine wanted at least to get the others back to Iramont. If the person causing her nightmares was still there, she could deal with the restless sleep. But if more of Ehmin and Madeline's associates came, agents or Anvils, or—

"I know that look," Saph said quietly, interrupted Divine's thoughts. "Trying to solve everything on your own?"

"What if Ehmin's people come for me? I don't want any of you to get hurt."

"I've got friends in the guild. Remember Nable from the bell ringing? She's a fantastic guard. There's Syka, who can blend with the shadows. If it's alright with you, I'll ask my guild friends to help us figure this out."

Divine nodded.

"I bet all of the people at the Edge, and the Kellas and Iguions you've helped, they'd all find ways to make you safe. To Zenith, I bet even Otto would find a way to stack his crates so they fell on our enemies."

Divine laughed, then sniffed against the tears forming in the corner of her eyes. "You're right, we'll figure it out. Let's just get to Weathered Crossroads first so I don't feel like Ehmin's about to walk through the door."

"Maybe you can show me how to use this bathtub properly sometime." Syka winked at Meve, who blushed. "This is my new favorite method of travel," the rogue announced then jumped into the water.

"Go ahead." Divine motioned for Saph to follow Syka. "I'll be right there."

When Saph vanished through the water, like she'd been pulled through the drain, Divine approached Constance.

"I do want to keep training. Just give me a day or two. I'm not frustrated with you, I'm frustrated, and overwhelmed, with everything."

"If I had told you who I was earlier, maybe this whole trip would have been unnecessary."

"And miss the werewings and meeting the Goddess of Standing Water?"

Ada pulled the candy bubble out of her mouth with a loud pop.

Divine smirked. "It's why you're the only one who can use scrying for travel, isn't it?"

"Perceptive."

"Thank you again, my friend." Divine gave Meve a tight hug. "We'll see each other soon."

Divine turned again to Ada. "I won't tell anyone unless you want me to. But I hope when you do pick a side, you choose ours. And visit the Elder you had created once in a while. We call him Leafy, and he's alone. But he still remembers you."

Taking a deep breath, Divine raised her leg and stepped into the tub.

CHAPTER EIGHTEEN

Coming Home

The Iguions in the steam blinked, their yellow and orange eyes becoming momentarily clearer as their translucent membrane lowered, then settled into place. Divine and her friends stepped out of the hot water recess of Iramont's bath house at the Edge. Sage hummed delightfully in the humid air and straightened all ten stems. It would take time for his thorns to grow back, but his green color looked the boldest Divine had seen since setting out.

After a rest, Ada had asked them to pick a place that wouldn't be frozen and wouldn't raise any questions. The Edge seemed the best option.

"Sorry to disturb you." Constance bowed his head to the handful of green and tan scaled occupants in the steam room. The silvery underside of their scales disappeared as Divine sensed their initial alarm subside. "If anyone is in need of a meal or necessities, the temple of the God of Virtue will be at the Edge the day after the festival's end."

"The day after tomorrow?" one of the Iguions asked, in a voice laced with an undertone of susurration.

"Ah, I've quite lost track of the days."

"We'd appreciate it if you didn't tell anyone about this." Divine motioned with her accordion case, her two-handed grip barely swinging the box out over the water. "The Council would have questions and well..."

Several Iguions nodded, their jowls puffing as they breathed deeply, highlighting their large, shiny, shield-like scales. Divine and her friends moved to the front and conferred at the door.

They agreed that exiting separately was the wisest course. Syka departed first, which left Constance with Saph and Divine.

"I'll come find you at your temple when I'm ready," Divine said. "And I expect a proper tour this time. What do your Goodly Ones do all day? And how have they not figured you out yet?"

Constance grinned, his pensiveness from earlier in the evening breaking. "I look forward to satisfying your curiosity. We can work on controlling what the admiration of others does to you, and I'll connect with some of my contacts to root out who's been causing your nightmares. As I promised at Ada's, I'll deliver Saph's message to the guild straight away. Then I'll see if anyone from Arosia ever arrived and get the latest winter storm activity. I do hope you get some rest and clarity."

Once enough time had passed after Constance's departure, Saph held open the door and Divine stepped through. The cold immediately stung her face, but the Midwinter lights further in the city filled her with a different type of warmth than the bath house. Their twinkle was just beginning to show as the sun's last light faded.

Carrying their things, Divine and Saph strolled leisurely toward the Essentials District. People filled the streets, taking part in the various offerings of Midwinter Nights Faire. The city was a mix of joy and contentment. It was familiar.

It felt like coming home.

At the Sultry Sapphire, Saph pushed the door in. Fire roasted logs touched with alcohol laid heavy in the air, as did the scent of fresh stew. Half as full as usual, the tavern had a larger crowd than she expected for the last full night of events. The final night saw many of the vendors close up early.

"Heyo! The boss is back!" Sylus called from behind the bar.

Several patrons called out Saph's name—and Divine's, to her surprise. The atmosphere of emotions nearly cleared any haze left on her soul from Arosia. Edward leaned on the counter between serving, saying something to Sylus who smirked and touched Edward's hand briefly.

Divine sat Sage on the mantle, feeling an absence where his pot had been hanging against her. She couldn't believe she had thought about leaving him in Iramont. The previously thorny decacacti had become a constant companion, and a secret weapon.

"If you want to rest, I completely understand. These last few days have been a lot. But if you want a distraction now, we could enjoy the faire. And if you want to meet my parents, we could go tomorrow evening. I'd love to introduce them to my girlfriend."

Divine grabbed Saph's hand. "Let's do it. Oh! I almost forgot. I have to see if something's ready before the place closes. Do I have time before we go?"

"Of course."

"Do you need to tell your parents about tomorrow?"

"Nah. They always make too much food anyway. They'll be glad you're there to eat it."

"As long as they won't think this was my idea. I don't want to impose."

Saph chuckled. "Look at you, already worried you'll disappoint them. Relax. They'll love you. There's no way they won't."

Divine leaned into Saph's kiss against her temple. "Do they not approve of your tavern still?"

"I mean, I haven't checked in much this year to know, but it's usually the case. They're alright, but can be a rock stuck in my shoe sometimes. Need help with your errand?"

"You stay here," Divine said, rebuttoning her coat. "I'll be back soon. It's a surprise."

Saph's green eye lit up. "I love surprises."

"I know you do."

Divine hurried across town and arrived at the Stacked Creations a few minutes before closing. To her delight, they had finished her order. A tube tucked under her arm, Divine returned to the Sultry Sapphire with a bounce in her steps.

"Close your eye," Divine commanded, shuffling out of her coat and letting it drop to the floor.

"You missed the peg."

"No time. I can't wait to show you your gift. Sit at the bar and close your eye."

Leaving a pile of light strands she had been removing, Saph covered her eye with a hand and Divine slipped behind the mostly vacant bar. Popping the end off the tube, Divine removed the materials and set to work. She pounded a small hook into the wall with the bottom of a tankard.

"Should I be worried that you're destroying my tavern?"

"I probably should have sent you upstairs." Divine groaned. "Almost there."

Reaching on tiptoes, she hammered a second hook on the other side of the sapphire board that was the bar's centerpiece.

"I like this view," Saph said behind her.

Divine whirled, nearly crashing into one of the wall shelves. "No peeking! I mean it."

Some patrons had exited while she was gone, but Divine found she didn't care if the whole tavern saw them flirt. As she pulled the final piece out, a transparent material rolled up like a scroll, Divine noted the new tea canisters on the highest shelf and the two new glass cups. Some of the décor had been moved by Saph to rearrange the space, but having the tea there looked safe. As long as Divine didn't summon a bird with an appetite for desert flowers. She shook her head, trying to stop the thought before it could manifest, and focused on hanging the ends of the roll on their new hooks.

"Alright, it's ready."

Divine stood to the side, giving Saph a clear view of the wooden sign. She waited a moment for Saph's eye to scan the area then released her grip on the waxy material's edge.

"Merry Midwinter Nights!"

The paper unraveled, covering the sapphire design with a translucent layer that was visible one moment then melded seamlessly with the wood. Just like Divine had seen the material do with a map or Solhavn inside Stacked Creations. The design made the teal sapphire float in a cup of brown liquid with tea leaves and rose petals. Creators Devaux and

Tania had been flawless. The ingredients swayed gently and steam rose from the lip in white swirls like it was real.

When Saph's parted-lip stare continued into silence, Divine wrung her hands.

"It goes back up." She hastily spun the rod, retracting the image. "I just thought you could switch the look whenever you served tea. But I could—"

A swell of lightheadedness made Divine stumble to the side as the scent of heady roses filled her nose. Admiration sizzled through the air and Divine wanted to drink it. Saph climbed onto the lacquered counter and spun on her backside to Divine's side of the bar.

"Darling." Saph opened her arms and Divine stepped into the gap made by her legs. "It's amazing. You designed it?"

Divine grinned. "I told them what I wanted it to look like. It's just like I imagined."

"It's very thoughtful. I love it. Even more so because I know how much time I spend on the tavern bothers you, but you still support me."

"I can feel a bit jealous." Divine's cheeks warmed. "But I recognize its importance to you. I'm now considering it more as a mutual friend rather than a rival."

"I can't really do this with a tavern."

With Saph sitting on the bar, Divine had to tilt her head up to meet Saph's bend. Their lips connected in a soft kiss. Divine shivered, loving the feeling of being squeezed by Saph's legs, and flicked her tongue over Saph's lips.

"While I don't think many will mind the show," Sylus cut in, wiping a mug, "I've seen this path and know where it ends. You might want to climb the stairs before you start other types of climbing."

Sylus winked and Saph responded by catching Divine's top lip between her teeth.

"Shall we?" Saph's voice was sultry.

"I have been starved for you."

"Sharing a space with three others and a cactus really limits time for heating the senses." Clasping Divine's hand,

Saph rushed to the stairs and the pair hurried into the upper hall.

The door to their room was barely shut before Saph pressed Divine against the back of the door. Mouths connected, walking as their hands stroked arms and hips, Divine steered Saph to a dresser.

"I liked how we were before," Divine rumbled.

As if reading her mind, Saph hopped up and let Divine press her body between her legs. Caressing the tops of Saph's thighs with her hands, she trailed her fingers around Saph's waistband. She turned her mouth to Saph's left thigh, planting slow kisses along the inside.

"Do we have time for a side quest?" Divine asked,

Saph drew in a shaky breath. "What did you have in mind? I do need help getting into an outfit for the faire."

Divine's mouth had reached where Saph's leg connected to her body and she blew a hot breath between her legs before kissing the fabric keeping her from Saph's pleasure spots.

Saph's legs tightened around Divine and she groaned with want.

Divine kissed the length of Saph's corset from navel to breasts. "I think you need help out of this."

"Will you wear your new dress tomorrow? You really looked like a Goddess of sex in it."

Divine laughed as she traced the swell of Saph's breast with the tip of her finger. "Is that the impression you want me to give your parents?"

"Zenith, yes. I want them to know that you make me euphoric, and not just when I'm wet with desire."

Divine's breath caught in her throat. "I do?"

"I've received jewelry and flowers and clothing, but no one has thought to gift me something for the place where I spend all my energy and time. And do you think any of my previous lovers would have sat around crafting teas to sell? Absolutely not. You see me, Divine. Not the flirt, but the woman who has dreams."

Saph cupped Divine's cheeks and Divine palmed Saph's neck, bringing their foreheads together.

"There are moments I never would have had without you." Divine whispered, her lips nearly brushing Saph's. "You bring out parts of me that hid before."

"They've always been within you," Saph said, taking Divine's hands.

"I know it's just—you know I have trouble trusting sometimes. And no matter how unlikely it is I fear losing...the wonderful things that come into my life."

"If you lose them, I'll help you find them. Or find new things." Saph brushed her lips on Divine's palm. "I want to keep making discoveries about you. About us."

"Me too." Divine squeezed Saph's hands then tugged Saph from the dresser. "Starting with faire fun. There's a boot to buy, remember?"

Saph tilted her head. "No side quest?"

"Call it...dessert." Divine tapped Saph's nose on her bauble. "I want to savor you, not rush to get out the door."

"I'm really not opposed to being guzzled."

Divine smirked. "We could do both."

"Let me communicate my utter obsession of you with my body."

They hurriedly removed their clothes and relocated to the bed, Saph's strong arms holding her over Divine. Saph trailed kisses down Divine's stomach.

"When my eyes meet yours," Divine whispered, "every heartbeat hums your name."

Saph's hand teased Divine between her legs and stopped. "Did you compose poetry for me?"

Divine chuckled. "You are the first light of the morning, chasing shadows away."

Saph groaned hungrily. "Don't you stop."

"If the stars could speak, would they tell tales of you and me?"

Divine became lost in the pleasure Saph gave. They rolled and traded urgent strokes, climbing faster through slick warmth until the room exploded with ecstasy.

Staring at the ceiling and the new autumn colored flutterwings circling on spear-shaped wings, Divine caught her breath. She rolled over to stare at Saph.

"You're the best prize." Divine rubbed her hand over Saph's stomach. "But I'd really like to get you that boot. Shall we play a few games?"

Saph rolled over and kissed Divine gently. "Just enough to get our coins. And then I want to come right back here and do this again."

"A perfect night."

CHAPTER NINETEEN

Family, Friends, and Fireworms

Saph's foot traced the inside of Divine's calf and Divine knew her face had turned as red as her hair. She fanned herself, feigning the spice of the food.

The table was a veritable sunset; bowls of creamy orange soup filled with legumes and diced carrots, with other ingredients that gave it a sharp kick, a dish of chunked sweet potatoes roasted with sugar and cinnamon, salad made of thin slices of pink and yellow and red radishes topped with slices of oranges from somewhere tropical.

"Everything is delicious, Mrs. Venamar. Thank you again for allowing me to take part in your family tradition on this final evening of Midwinter Nights"—Divine gave a discerning look at Saph across the table—"without notice."

"So polite. Not like..." Saph's father's voice paused as he searched his wife's round face for the answer. "Whatever that girl's name was. The one with the knife obsession. Had something sullen to say about everything."

Inwardly Divine groaned. *Syka?* Saph had last brought Syka to meet her parents?

Saph put a bright orange, perhaps carrot, muffin down. "Chloe. She was a knife thrower. An entertainer, and you know that. But she always found the negative in everything. Life's too short for that."

"Dear, you really should come by more often." Mrs. Venamar said. Her skin was more bronze than Saph's, but she had the same curvy build. "Your father can't tend to the garden as much on account of his knees and the beds are in such disarray. Between my stretch classes and the party planning, I just don't have the time. Iramont really has grown since you were little. But so many people means more parties for me to plan." Mrs. Venamar laughed, touching her husband's arm.

Divine glanced out of the window. A candle burned on the sill, reflecting in the dark pane. She couldn't see the small side garden but assumed it was like other houses in this area of the eastern Living District. Unlike the multi-family habitspaces, these were houses like Divine had grown up in.

"I could help," Divine offered. "I'm not bad with plants."

"She's underselling herself. She is magical with plants." Saph winked.

"That's very kind." Mr. Venamar ducked his head.

"This new venture must be keeping you away," Mrs. Venamar continued. "We heard about your tea shop. It's good to see you doing something that the undesirables of the city won't be interested in." Mrs. Venamar bit into a slice of red cake with pink frosting, turning to Divine. "I assume we have you to thank?"

Divine choked on a spoonful of soup and seized her glass, taking a gulp of wintry pink.

"Saph already had the idea before we met. I just helped taste her." Divine's mouth fell open. "Taste them. With her." She buried her betraying lips into her glass for another drink of the sweet and tangy liquid.

Saph's foot brushed the inside of her thigh and for the fourth time that evening Divine regretted wearing the tight leggings and side-split dress that plunged a heart shape over her breasts. She tried to focus on Mrs. Venamar.

"Divine does far more than that. She helps out at the tavern and once we get Steeped in Sapphire ready, she'll serve the tea. And she helps the human-adjacents."

"See, darling," Mr. Venamar soothed. "Saph found someone who does more than lay naked in her bed."

"Well anyway, we're glad to have you here." Mrs. Venamar shot her husband a side glare. "I know our traditions aren't exactly the dazzle and dance that the temples maintain."

Divine folded her hands into her lap. "I actually hoped to learn more about your beliefs. I have a couple of friends who have mentioned the Old Ways."

Mr. Venamar's eyebrow arched.

"Oh, really?" He glanced at Saph with a small tilt of his head. A momentary flicker of unease brushed Divine's magic. "We don't meet very many who openly talk about the Old Ways."

"I wouldn't call it open," Divine corrected him. "We were very much in a safe space."

"Ah, yes there's always the risk that the Condemnation Agents hear and decide it's enough to be charged with a crime."

Divine held up her hand, palm out. "I don't want to trouble you. Perhaps another time, if you feel comfortable?"

"How long are you staying in Iramont?" Mrs. Venamar asked.

"I was thinking...indefinitely." Divine caught Saph straightening in her chair. "Though I should probably find a residence and have the rest of my things transported from Arosia."

"I know we've done things a little out of order. Living together and then declaring we're girlfriends." Saph reached across the table and took Divine's hand, rubbing her thumb over Divine's thumb. "Darling, what's mine is yours. And I don't think I could take not waking up to your beautiful face every day. I will make room for all of your things."

Divine beamed. "I should have just asked. I don't want to go to sleep without you there to hold me."

"Did you place flowers under your pillow during Midsummer?" Mrs. Venamar asked, a twinkle in her eye.

"Mom, please."

"What's that?" Curiosity made Divine lean closer to Saph's mother.

"It's an Old Ways tradition. If you place flowers under your pillow during Midsummer, you'll dream of your future partner. If you do it every night, well, you might summon them." Mrs. Venamar swung to Saph. "I think it worked."

Saph rolled her eye, but she wore a wide smile.

"You are welcome back any time, Divine." Mr. Venamar reached past his wife to touch Divine's hand. "I can tell you care for each other. And you are different than the others. A good different."

The topic changed to the festival and the winning ice sculpture, and Mrs. Venamar revealed her hand in some of the city garlands. Divine shared about visiting the cart of the married couple from Norfel the night before, and it's delicious soft pretzels and hot apple cider. The evening passed with joy and full stomachs before Divine and Saph returned to the Sultry Sapphire to put away Midwinter decorations.

* * *

People gathered all along the dim street, lit at intervals by a bonfire-like glow, though smokeless as no bonfires were lit. Even the lamps gave off no light in anticipation of what would come next, their crystals draped by black covers. Divine could feel the crowd's anticipation, and she bounced on her feet, rubbing her gloved hands together.

The Midwinter Nights Faire bells tolled, ringing crisply through the city as if the snow resonated with the sound. The tone heralding the end to the festival. Murmurs increased into an excited roar as people shifted and dots of light began to fill the street, rising through the buildings.

Divine, Saph, and Sylus congregated just beyond the overhang that held the glowing cut sapphire sign of the tavern. Piled at their feet, the strands of lights from the Sultry Sapphire glowed a tarrow tea shade, the purple and yellow lanterns so close their colors blended. Saph pulled part of the strand's cord and the tops of each lantern opened. Fireworms quivered their tiny wings, rising out of their incubators of the last week to bob their fuzzy bodies here and there, before finding their map in the sky.

Divine held Sage up to see over the heads of the crowd, his sling hung over her neck. His blue and orange scarf fluttered, and his pot crinkled and popped delightedly.

Saph shifted closer, wrapping her arms around Divine's waist from behind, the coat crunching and turning concave with the touch. Divine leaned her head against Saph's. The city street was a corridor of sparkles, dancing to the night's music.

"Each one a happy memory," Saph said gently, her chin tilted to watch the fireworms fly higher. "Joining the stars in a tapestry of light and love. The soul and the heart of the world from the beginning to forever."

"It's beautiful," Divine breathed, her smile nearly reaching her ears. "No matter how many years I watch it, my stomach still gets all giddy."

Soft gold dots hovered over the city, blending into the canopy of stars, twinkling with their own heartbeat and rhythm, going lighter then brighter. Divine looked back to catch Saph's reaction and found her gazing instead at Divine.

"But nothing is as beautiful as you," Saph whispered.

Reaching up, Divine placed the palm of her glove against Saph's cheek.

"Then we are knotted, as I think nothing is like you."

She pressed her lips against Saph's, delighting in the other woman's response, both arms squeezing Divine's stomach, pulling her close.

"Are you going to miss Arosia?" Saph asked quietly.

"I'll miss parts of it. It's my history." She paused, searching Saph's face for a reaction beyond the slight vibration of worry Divine felt through her well. "But the city reminds me of the old me, following the temple blindly. Pressing against their rules only to never break through. Living with regret and holding back. It reminds me of my mother. Madeline and all of that mess. Iramont connects me to the new me. But I promised Meve that I'd keep in touch."

"Does that mean you two are done with adventures for a while?" Sylus shifted closer.

"Never." Saph grinned tapping the side of her nose.

Divine detected Sylus's surprise and stretched to place her hand on his shoulder. "We've got some things to catch you up on, but we don't plan to leave the Iramont province for a while."

Sylus's shoulders relaxed. "Well, regardless I think we should hire on another. Business might be picking up. People were really interested in Steeped in Sapphire. And you know..." Sylus scratched the back of his head. "Edward wasn't bad."

Divine squeezed Saph's arm. "That's great! We have some lovely new teas to try."

"You just want to spend more time with Edward," Saph ribbed.

"I do not." Sylus crossed his arms. "I'm just saying he's a hard worker."

Saph smirked. "Interesting word choice."

Sylus frowned before his composure broke and he chuckled, shaking his head and turning his back on Saph to watch the flying fireworms.

The wind picked up, eliciting a shiver from Divine, and she adjusted her earmuffs to maximize their coverage.

"If we hire someone, but Steeped in Sapphire does well, could we save to travel to Solhavn?" Divine queried, continuing a conversation they'd started while packing up decorations.

"We will definitely find a way to make that happen. If that's what you want to do."

"I still don't know. But maybe. I think knowing for certain might be the closure I need, as well as finding out what my mother learned." Sage's pot vibrated. "Sage wouldn't say no to warm sand."

"Take me with you."

Divine jumped. "Syka! Condemnation, where did you come from?"

How often was this woman around and Divine just didn't know it?

"Always in the shadows." Syka stepped beside them, observing the sky. "While the world looks to the light."

Saph rolled her eyes before winking at Divine. "Tired of the winter fun already?"

"I don't think my fingers have warmed since the werewing incident. Can Ada send us?"

Divine shook her head. "Too far."

"Well, if you find a way to get south during the winter, I'll donate most of my stash toward the cause."

Saph whistled. "We should play Crossroads George outside to get you betting recklessly like this."

"You wouldn't resort to torture. Go, get back to smooching your girlfriend. The rest of us are here for the sights."

As Syka shifted near Sylus, Saph rotated Divine to face her.

"Thanks for meeting my parents tonight. I know they can be judgy, but they mean well."

"They mean a lot to you."

"They raised me." Saph shrugged. "They were there when people treated me differently. They tried to help—overcorrecting with the whole hide-my-hands thing—but I've heard some really bad childhood stories at the bar. I think I'm lucky."

"It's been a while since I've sat down for a family meal."

Suddenly Syka's arm draped around Divine's shoulder. "Hey, you're part of our family now. Every time you eat with us, you eat with family."

Saph pinched the coat fabric of Syka's arm between her fingers like it was a dirty rag. "Do you mind? I'm having a moment with my Goddess."

Holding up her hands, Syka backed away, but Divine identified the familiar tickle of someone's attention linger, a breeze that carried the scent of rose.

The regard of friends, the love of family. Romantic devotion. It all seemed to touch her magic well like warnings of danger had done before. Those came less now, replaced by people who *respected* her. It was an addicting trade.

"She's right." Saph tilted her head. "There's a lot of people who care for you here."

Syka's comment had warmed Divine. "It is nice."

But she wondered how long it would take her to trust that people weren't hiding things from her or trying to use her. Maybe it would be something she would have to work through for the rest of her days; recognizing her snags she could counter them.

Saph brushed the back of her hand against Divine's cheek. "How do you really feel, darling?"

Syka laughed with Sylus, punching him on the shoulder. The sign of the Sultry Sapphire squeaked overhead as it swung softly with a breeze that carried hints of melted chocolate and spiced apples from nearby cups. Fireworms had collected in a radiant cloud high above as they formed a flock that would share warmth into spring. Watching the lights made by the winter-hardened insects as people released their decorations was a tradition she never wanted to end.

Divine soaked in Saph, brushing a lock of hair off of Saph's eyepatch. "I feel like I'm home."

Saph pulled her close, planting a grinning kiss on Divine's lips. The world shifted; marionettes dancing without their strings, able to swirl as fast as they wanted without someone manipulating them. A hooweet flapped in her chest, longing to soar.

At the sound of beating wings, Divine glanced at the ground at the brown and beige plumes pumping on the summoned flightless bird.

"Whoops," Divine laughed into Saph's neck.

A lumbering shape moved through the crowd, people parting to let a wide teal hat move past as it rocked side to side with each step. The Thospor looked like a grandfather figure with their walking staff tapping the ground and their body seeming to glow in the darkness.

Shroombal stopped in front of them.

"How do you stay warm?" Divine asked, noting their appearance still lacked clothing. Divine pulled her hood up, layering her winter warmth.

The white puffs that served as Shroombal's shoulders shrugged. "A tolerance to the elements, I s'pose." They tapped their staff on their chest. "Thick skin. And lots of food."

Saph gripped Shroombal's puff of a shoulder. "I'm glad you came. I was about to invite everyone in to eat our leftover Midwinter food."

"Everyone?" Divine asked, surveying the crowd. While some residents had wandered off either to homes or to businesses still open for the night, the crowd was still formidable. Had she imagined it or were there orange robes behind a couple down the street?

"Just our Sultry family. I do need them to leave eventually." Saph winked with her uncovered eye.

Divine let her hand drift lower on Saph's back to rest on her backside. "Good. I have some private devouring I'd like to do."

"Oh." Shroombal withdrew a small box from somewhere within his stalk. "Bream mentioned your tea hunt. I have a Thorspor delicacy for you to try. The last I have from Thosporium. Consider it a Midwinter gift."

"I didn't think you celebrated." Saph took the box. "It's not mycelia bark, is it? The last time you gave me some I heard colors and tasted sounds."

"You had too much. Just sprinkle it. You humans and your sensitive stomachs."

Saph chuckled. "We'll save it for personal special occasions."

Shroombal bent their cap closer, their deep voice quieting. "I put a mark for anyone lookin' like agents headed this way. They're to be directed to the new road through Blueridge Forest while the main road is under repairs."

"There's no new construction...oh." Saph tapped the side of her nose. "Nicely done."

"A mark is a task, right?" Divine asked.

"In the mercenary guild," Saph added.

"And Bream will watch for any movement from the temples of Arosia. We'll know if any new visitors are planned."

"I knew I kept you around for a reason."

Shroombal chuckled warmly at Saph's jibe.

Hands intertwining, Saph and Divine progressed toward the Sultry Sapphire. Saph called for Edward across the street where he stood with his sisters. Favorably, Viktor was nowhere to be seen. Divine motioned for Syka and Sylus to follow them.

The couple Divine had spied moved, revealing a figure in sunset-colored robes. Constance's hands were folded into his sleeves, and he lowered his head for a breath before meeting her gaze. As if asking for permission. She waved him over.

"I did not want to come if I was not welcome," the Goodly One supplied when he reached Divine.

"We're friends, aren't we?"

"I know you do not appreciate my secrets."

Divine touched his shoulder. "You've given me your word to be forthcoming now. You're helping me with my magic. And we've battled werewings and mysteries together. I think that qualifies for friendship."

Constance's face lit up with his smile.

"But if you manipulate her or betray her"—Saph pointed to the axe on her back—"I have a blade that I will shove up your—"

He raised a hand. "There will be no need to, uh, shove anything anywhere. The virtues I've passed to my followers are true. Treating others with kindness is the greatest power of all. Divine has my help as long as she needs it."

"You are welcome whether or not I need your assistance." Divine tugged on the fabric of his elbow. "Friendship is not dependent on providing a service."

Constance squeezed his hands together. "I have good information to share. There were Soulshapers on their way to Iramont, but they got stuck in a snowstorm and turned back to Weathered Crossroads. We barely missed them. But Ada's having messages delivered around the town that will have people saying just enough to make them think you did pass through on your way to Arosia. They should return to their home from there."

Divine looked at him from the side of her eye. "A convenient snow."

"I do know individuals with certain skills."

"That's what you did before we left Iramont, wasn't it? And I thought you didn't have friends."

"Connections are not the same. But yes, I had a feeling we would need a barrier to prevent standard travel, and they owed me a favor."

"Then we have some time to breathe. Let's start tomorrow though on my...skills."

"As you will it."

Inside, Divine added logs to the fire and sat Sage on the mantel before heading behind the bar to brew tea. A new boot-shaped mug gleamed with the lights against its green glaze painted with a festive faire scene. Sylus and Saph heated leftovers from the Venamars, and pastries and mince pies in the kitchen while the others helped push tables together and arrange chairs. Shroombal seemed to converse with Sage before helping Constance remove the non-foliage decorations from the walls.

Soon the fire warmed the tavern, and everyone gathered around a table piled with colorful nourishment and cups of steaming tea at each chair. Laughter and smiles filled the room until Divine thought she could touch the joy in the air. Flutterwings flitted between the rafters, glassy wings alighting on the dangling vines like hopes shared for the coming spring; wishes perched on the rim of a teacup, ready to fall into sunlight.

The Pantheon

Deities as mentioned in Tea Tale

Turbulent Deities: Impacts a life physically

Goddess of Souls: Cares for souls of the living, saves from condemnation, guides into afterlife & rebirth.
Servants' Powers: "Soulshields," "Soulshapers," and "Soulsages" influence emotions, protect, heal and mend.

Goddess of Condemnation: Maintains laws and order, enacts punishment for the wicked.
Servants' Powers: "Agents" wreak mind muddling, illusions, can inflict mental or physical pain.

Goddess of Frosted Wilderness: Snow, frost, and ice as well as winter landscapes like mountains and tundra, and winter games are her domain.
Servants' Powers: "Flurries" can summon snow and freeze liquid. They take pride in inventing winter wear and games.

God of Storms: God of inclement weather and negative emotions.
Servants' Powers: "Anvils" Can summon lightning, rain, and storms.

Deity of Love and Fire: Non-gendered deity of flame and romance, heat and sexuality.
Servants' Powers: "Passionates" can summon fire and are responsible for technologies like the fireworks that heats some cities.

Goddess of Words: Goddess of science, speech, and writing. More educational than art.
Servants' Powers: "Orators" take a vow of silence, otherwise their words bring things into being.

Goddess of Stone and Sand: Goddess of mineral location and construction, barriers.
Servants' Powers: "Sandshapers" can summon stone, detect minerals, and mold sand into shapes like glass.

Tranquil Deities: Doesn't directly impact or influence a life

God of Virtue: God of good deeds, caring for others, passivists.
Servants' Powers: "Goodly Ones" can be a magic well for others, can feel intent.

God of Day and Deceit: Channeler of light energy, god of tricks.
Servants' Powers: "Tricksters" can enhance signs, crystals, etc. to emit light. Often their focus is nefarious actions.

Goddess of Fields: Goddess of autumn and crops, bountiful yields.
Servants' Powers: "Harvesters" summon fruit, veggies, wheat and other various crops from a location they've been.

Goddess of Standing Waters: Domain over calm waters like lakes, ponds, puddles. Ability to scry or see locations through water.
Servants' Powers: "Hydromancers" can use water to view locations, send messages, and thus they facilitate world communication.

Deity of Night and Art: Non-gendered deity of darkness, art and creativity.
Servants' Powers: "Creators" focus on the arts, adding to the enrichment of lives, and can capture moving pictures in paintings.

Steeped in Sapphire Tea Recipes

Foggy Iramont

"It's a bold, black tea that's smooth with a hint of sweet and citrus," Divine quoted. "It smells great. And it's made with milk, so, uh, it's foggy." The cup smelled lovely, the lavender like summer's first bloom, and she took a sip. Richer and more bitter than the tarrow root, the Arosian black leaf filled up her mouth in an enjoyable way."

For one cup of tea:

Ingredients

- 1 c water
- 1.5 tsp Arosian black tea leaf* (Tea with bergamot or citrus peel like Earl Grey)
- ½ tsp vanilla extract
- ¼ tsp dried lavender
- ¼ c milk or milk alt like vanilla almond milk
- 1-2 tsp sugar or to taste

Instructions

1. Combine dry ingredients into steeping ball or strainer.
2. Steep in boiling water for 3-5 mins and strain.
3. Steam or heat milk and froth with milk frother.
4. Into the hot tea add the sugar and vanilla extract and stir.
5. Pour in the warm milk and spoon the milk foam on top.
6. Serve immediately and enjoy!

Presentation

Top the milk with lavender flowers.

Tips

For less steps, replace dry ingredients with a blend such as "Lady Lavender" from The Tea Spot or "Earl Grey Creme" from The Spice and Tea Exchange.

Divine-i-tea

Blowing gently across the mug's top, Divine watched Saph over the frothy brim. The heat burnt the tip of her tongue but felt like a warm elixir, soothing as it washed down her throat. The vanilla was strong with a gentle earthy bitterness and a hint of something spicy or minty that she couldn't quite define. She took another sip. It was sweet. And she loved it.

For one cup of tea

Ingredients

- 1 c water
- 1 tbsp Tarrow Root* (Sarsaparilla root bark)
- 3/4 tsp licorice root
- 1–2 wintergreen leaves (or a pinch if dried)
- 3/4 tsp crushed or chopped ginger
- 3/4 tsp birch bark
- 1/2 tsp vanilla extract
- 1-2 tsp brown sugar or to taste

Instructions

1. Combine dry ingredients into steeping ball or strainer.
2. Steep in boiling water for 5–7 minutes and strain.
3. Stir in vanilla extract and sugar.
4. Serve immediately hot or over ice and enjoy!

Presentation

Get it foamy if you can and top it with an edible white flower to look like a snowflake.

Tips

This drink is inspired by root beer and cream soda. For less steps, replace dry ingredients with a blend such as Root Beer tea from Stash Tea, or Nelsons Really Root Beer.

Snowshroom Spice

"There's hints of chocolate and cinnamon, with other spices that's sure to warm you after a cold walk. It's sweetened with honey and almost smells like fresh baked pumpkin pie."

For one cup of tea

Ingredients
- 1.5 tsp snowshroom powder* (Mushroom powder, or make with a chai tea blend. See Tips below.)
- 3/4 tsp cocoa powder or chopped chocolate
- 1/10 tsp ground turmeric
- 1/10 tsp ground cardamom
- 1/10 tsp ginger
- a pinch of clove
- 2 small cinnamon sticks (ground or in chips)
- 1 Tbsp honey

Instructions
1. Combine dry ingredients into steeping ball or strainer.
2. Steep in boiling water for 5 mins and strain.
3. Add the cocoa or chocolate, stir until combined.
4. Add a dollop of honey and stir.
5. Serve immediately and enjoy!

Presentation
If adding milk foam, top with a sprinkle of cinnamon.

Tips
For a simpler set up, choose your favorite chai tea blend, steep, and add cocoa or chocolate and honey. Or, choose Mushroom Cacao Chai Tea from The Republic of Tea for an herbal blend, or Chocolate Chai Supreme from Harney and Sons for a black tea alternative.

*Denotes in-world fantasy ingredients with a real-life equivalent listed.

ACKNOWLEDGEMENTS

At some point when I was younger, I walked past a local bookshop window and said, "That'll be me one day." And then I lost the idea, or forgot it, or it was torn out of me, and it took years before I realized having books with my name on it was indeed possible. And I'm not stopping! This journey has had so many people who have cared enough to see that dream reawakened and continue to be a reality.

First, to the team at Space Wizard who do incredible work behind the scenes. Thank you for continuing to bring tales of Saph and Divine to the shelves of our lovely readers. William Tracy, you understand the characters and the world, and your insight and ideas have made this my favorite story I've written so far. Serene Chia, oh my goodness you did it again! Bringing the world and characters to life in a beautiful cozy scene for the book cover. Every author should be as lucky.

To my husband, the real-life source behind romantic lines like, "Just your smile" when I ask you if you need anything. Our adventures together began because of RPGs, and it was fitting that the first game we completed together, *Chrono Trigger*, was a big inspiration in this book. Thank you for cheering for me unceasingly and supporting my writing quests. I love having all of you be with all of me.

To my beta readers and street team, thank you for your suggestions and spreading the news of these books. To Diane Billas, Danielle Bess, and my other author friends for always asking how the writing is going and listening to my ideas or as I deliberated bits of the story. And to the 2025 Small Press Debut group for being there through the launch of *Tavern Tale* and the ups and downs in its wake. Having you all behind me was the greatest support I could have ever hoped for, and the best distraction from the endless dirge of marketing.

I have to give a special thank you to my writing and critique partner, Jonathan Fuller, for always being a friend first and a creative second. You were there to inspire me during writer worries and self-doubts, and encouraging the ideas when they were flowing. Without you, I likely wouldn't have the names for Constance and Longsuffering, nor the chapter title "Foggy and Flir-tea."

I'm sure there are others I've forgotten, or pieces I've failed to mention but please know this thank you is for you even if I didn't mention you by name.

Lastly to you, readers, for loving Saph and Divine and going on another quest with me. I can't wait to tell you the next tale.

ABOUT THE AUTHOR

Kristina W. Kelly is an author of poetry, short stories, and novels including the *Tales of Trelvania* series (inspired by RPGs), the sci-fi and fantasy poetry collection *Imaginari*, and a coauthored epic fantasy and sci-fi fusing series the *Etherea Cycle*. Kristina is published in online poetry magazines and anthologies, and has received multiple honorable mentions and semi-finalist from the Writers of the Future contest.

Since childhood, writing stories on her mother's typewriter or trying to catalog her own books like a library, Kristina has been in love with storytelling. Her undergraduate pursuits focused on Psychology, Music, and Computer Science. With trumpet as her main instrument and a connection to nature, Kristina often works music and visual landscapes into her writings. She takes photography, plays video games, and tends to her flower garden. She loves going on new adventures in the great wide somewhere (sometimes just by picking up a new book). Kristina resides in Indiana with her husband and sons. Visit her at kristinaseyes.com

Please take a moment to review this book at your favorite retailer's website, Goodreads, or simply tell your friends!